STR8 BOLT

J. T. Whitman

PublishAmerica
Baltimore

ISBN: 1-4241-3782-9
PUBLISHED BY PUBLISHAMERICA, LLLP
www.publishamerica.com
Baltimore

Printed in the United States of America

Acknowledgements

Cover design by Robert Boyd

ONE

Eisenhower Tunnel, Colorado – Wyatt Coleman
Fall 1999

Wyatt Coleman was driving an eighteen wheeler from Los Angeles to Denver, as he had done hundreds of times before, and narrowly escaped the direct hit from a lightning bolt as he exited the Eisenhower tunnel on the eastbound side of the I-70 freeway in Colorado. The weather that day had been crappy with lightning and heavy rain showers. He contemplated whether or not to continue but decided he needed to keep going if he was going to collect his bonus for an early delivery in Denver. An hour after starting that long climb up the mountain out of Glenwood Springs he wished he hadn't.

Within seconds, another bolt, so massive in size and what looked like a giant column of white light, cracked just to the left of his truck.

"What the," he gasped.

It was so bright and loud Wyatt had instinctively raised his left arm to shield his eyes. The energy emitted from that lightning bolt was so powerful it felt as though he had been broad sided by some other vehicle at high speed and was thrown from the cab. Having been in a couple of accidents before Wyatt was all too familiar with it and could not forget the feeling of everything moving in slow motion just before impact then suddenly coming back to full speed. He almost lost his life many yeas ago when he went through the windshield in a head on collision.

But still, this was somehow different. There was no pain and no slow motion feeling before the impact or what he thought was an impact. He was not really sure what had happened. He felt a little dazed and confused. As he slowly became aware of a feeling of weightlessness and flying through the air he now for some strange reason was experiencing the slow motion like feeling. It seemed endless, floating through the air then slowly changing to a falling sensation. It was surreal.

Wyatt Coleman was a healthy man in his late thirties with dark hair and slightly olive skin. He was six feet tall, 190 pounds, and had a naturally good build. He had been married and divorced twice with no children. He was a handsome man and never had any difficulty attracting women. In fact it was his looks that caused the problems in his marriages. He had always been a little quiet and reserved, and woman would often flirt with him, with or without his wives being present. He did nothing to encourage or initiate it. He would simply respond with a shy like smile and that infuriated his wives. They accused him of having affairs even though he had always been faithful. He gave them no reason to doubt his fidelity.

After his last divorce, 5 years ago, Wyatt lost his job as a manager for a government contractor and could not or did not want to find another job. He had had it with marriage. With alimony payments backing up he needed some time alone and wanted to just get away. He saw an ad for a trucking school and decided this would give him the time, solitude, and money he needed. He liked the alone time on the road and enjoyed the freedom of driving in the country without pressures or hassles from family and wives, ex or otherwise. They got their money each month automatically from his bank and he got seclusion. It suited him.

Now here he was flying through the air in slow motion, alone in his thoughts as visions of his life began to flash through his mind at an unbelievable speed. He saw everything very clearly from growing up in Southern California, playing 'Kick-the-Can' in the streets with the neighbor kids, surfing at the beach, playing pranks with old friends, playing football, making love to old girlfriends both serious and not, attending college, serving his time in the military, seeing the good and bad times with his family, experimenting with different career choices, reliving the loss of loved ones especially the death of his father, to why he again decided to take up truck driving. He saw his entire life right up to this lightning bolt strike.

Suddenly, with no warning at all, WHOMP, his body hit something hard, knocking the wind out of him and snapping him out of this dreamlike state. What ever it was he hit sent pain shooting through his body as he began bouncing and rolling out of control in a downward motion. The icy cold bite of the wind and ground began to rip through his skin and tear at his flesh activating all of his senses.

"Why can't I see? Why is it so dark," Wyatt suddenly thought when just moments before he was inside the Eisenhower tunnel, approaching the exit and reaching down to turn his lights off even though there was still plenty of daylight left outside. It was only late afternoon. The clouds and rain were dense but he thought it would be safer to just leave them on.

Unable to see anything now he continued to tumble. He tried to force his eyes open, thinking they must be closed or covered with something but he could not. *"Why was it dark,"* again he wondered. He likened the darkness to that of the desert in the middle of the night when there was no moon. Strangely, there didn't seem to be anymore lightning flashing and there was no wetness from the rain either.

The tumbling and bouncing began to slow down and he could feel the cold wet snow sticking to his body but how could that be. It was early October and usually too early for the snow to be on the ground in any significant amounts.

As he slammed into the ground again he heard and felt a loud snap in his right shoulder which immediately sent pain reeling through his upper body. He screamed and continued to do so as he bounced again and again smashing his shoulder into the ground with each roll. The pain was too much. He was losing consciousness. His last thoughts were that of dying. Then, in the cold damp darkness, he was stopped abruptly when his head struck a solid object and rendered him unconscious.

TC Laboratories, California – Dr. Rajiv Ramakrishnan PhD.
Spring 2005

The light was intense. Raj squinted and raised his hand to shield his eyes. He tried to stay focused on the leather ball in the glass chamber but his normal reaction was to look away even through the protective glasses he was wearing were dark enough to keep his eyes safe.

"Maybe we need to increase the power more and shorten the time Raj. Make it flash more like a lightning bolt should," screamed Tim MacCorrmack over the whining noise of the generator.

"I do not know Tim," Raj yelled back. "I am not sure that will do it. The ball is showing signs of burning again, but it is not as bad as before. Besides, there is still too much of an arc in the bolt. We need to get that resolved before we increase the power." Raj pulled the breaker to shut down the generator. He walked toward Tim, "Do me a favor and go back through the data and see what time variables and power variations we have used that were closer to this last test. Let us get back together and talk about what changes we can make then try another test tomorrow."

Tim nodded and headed for the door then stopped to yell back, "Are we done for today? I wanted to get home early. Laci has something planned for tonight and I thought I'd try to get home before sunset for a change." Laci was Tim's new bride and she was enjoying her new role of wife by trying to prepare romantic diners at home with a new recipe she discovered in a magazine or on the Internet. In more cases than not, her experiments were not as tasty as they appeared to be in the article but Tim, loving her as much as he did, couldn't care less. He loved the idea of coming home to someone who couldn't wait for him to get there.

Laci Jean Springer-MacCorrmack was a very rare woman in the twenty first century. Her views on marriage and relationships do not conform to the modern woman of today. Coming from a broken home where her parents divorced when she was eight years old could have ruined any chance of her ever finding happiness in a relationship with a man if it had not been for her grandmother. Laci spent a lot of time with her grandmother. They developed a very strong bond because of the selfishness of her parents trying to use her as a weapon against each other. She would always tell Laci to watch and learn from her parent's actions and behavior.

After her parents big fights Laci, feeling like the rope in a Tug-of-War, would have long discussions with her grandmother analyzing what her parents were doing to each other and why they were doing it. After each talk her grandmother would say, "Treat your man like a king Sweetie and he will treat you like a queen giving you complete control of your kingdom. But when you stop treating him like a king you will no longer be queen. It's just like in chess the Queen has all of the power as long as the king is protected. When the king is lost the kingdom falls." Laci understood this to mean mutual respect for each other will keep her home a happy place. When she met Tim it was obvious to her he was a man who lived his life just that way. She understood why Tim worked so hard. He wanted to provide both of them with a good and comfortable life, and he loved his work. She respected him for that and tried to encourage him.

Laci had her own career and Tim supported her too. She was an elementary school teacher when she and Tim first met but she was now working as a substitute because they were trying to start a family. They have been married almost a year and were financially sound. They felt secure with each other and decided they were ready. She loved Tim very much and knew in her heart they would be together the rest of their lives.

Walking toward the chamber to remove the scorched ball as the generators finished winding down Raj yelled back, "Yes, I believe we are done Tim. Go ahead and have a nice evening with your wife. You can get that data in the morning."

"OK Raj. Need anything else before I head out?"

"No, go ahead. We will pick it up again in the morning."

"OK Raj, see ya tomorrow."

"Say hello to Laci for me!"

"You got it Doc," Tim replied as he raced out the lab door.

"What am I missing," Raj though to himself as he removed the ball and stared at it as if it might give him some clue.

The lab door slammed shut causing Raj to look back, startled, then smiled and thought, *"Great kid."*

Timothy Luis MacCorrmack had joined Dr. Rajiv Ramakrishnan about 6 years ago as a Lab Assistant. Tim was the top physics student in his class at Cal Poly Pomona and demonstrated exceptional talents when it came to physics experimentation. Raj too was a graduate from Cal Poly Pomona about thirty five years earlier and always recruited talented graduates, like Tim, to work with him on his research. Tim had been with Raj longer than any previous student and would probably stay for many years to come.

After promoting him to Assistant Director, Tim was more than willing to put in extra hours to show Raj he was worthy of the promotion. Raj admired Tim's dedication and made it a point to send him home early when ever possible to prevent burn out and to keep Laci from feeling neglected.

Raj at an early age, showed a great desire to study science as well. Growing up in a small village, called Chenpur outside of Ahmedabad, India, he became fascinated with science fiction novels by authors like H.G. Wells who wrote 'Time Machine', Isaac Asimov, Ray Bradbury, Mark Clifton, Jack Finney, and many others reading every chance he got. When he played with the other kids he was always the scientist and would do mock experiments on them.

At thirteen he built his first time machine out of junk he had collected from all over the village. He called it the TESS (Time-travel Explorations for Senior Scientists), named after an English girl he liked in middle school. In his mind he could travel all throughout the past seeing dinosaurs, great wars, famous and infamous leaders, and compare his notes with renowned scientists and other time travelers. He was so very proud of his invention and thought one day he really might get to travel back in time.

His family was financially established enough to send Raj to some of the better schools. He excelled in his science studies. He won many science awards and was a member of several science clubs.

In high school one of his teachers put him in touch with a science student in the United States and they wrote each other constantly. They both had a passion for science and shared their ideas for several years. The two science pen pals never met but Raj's friend helped get him a scholarship to Cal Poly Pomona after he had completed two years at the Mani Nagar Science College in Ahmedabad. The end of that school year would be the beginning of a new time in his life that would lead him in the direction of fulfilling his dream.

Chenpur, India – Rajiv Ramakrishnan
Summer 1969

"Are you all packed for your trip," asked Shahni, Raj's mother.

"Yes mother," the twenty year old Raj replied as he packed the final items in his suitcase and looked around the room to see if he had forgotten anything.

"Do you have your plane ticket?"

"Yes mother," he repeated again as he leaned down to close his suitcase and fastened a strap around it to secure it.

"Do you have…"

"Mom," he interrupted. "I have everything." He affectionately grabbed her arms and looked into her sad face, "Don't worry, OK? If I forget anything or need anything I will get it when I get there. So stop fussing."

She pulled away from him saying, "I don't want you to go. I'm not ready for you to go."

"You've known I was going for month's now," he reminded her as he pulled her back and hugged her. "This is what I have dreamed about for years, mom. I'll be back next summer and I will write every day. It will go by fast. You will see. You will hardly know I am gone."

Half laughing and crying she pulled away from him then asserted, "Oh please. There isn't a day that doesn't goes by without you causing some kind of turmoil. The absence of all that commotion is going to leave a huge hole in my daily life. You can't go! I won't allow it!"

Raj tenderly hugged his mother and declared, "Mom, I love you and besides, you have Mahesh, Nitin, Kali, and Vijaya to raise hell and fill that hole."

Looking surprised because she never heard him say hell before she looked up and saw him smiling. She protested, "Raji, don't use that kind of language with me and it won't be the same!"

"Yes it will! Now that Mahesh will be the oldest he is going to be even more of a pain and since I will not be here to watch over him, you will have your hands full with him. So you won't have time to miss me."

"I will miss you my son and I can handle Mahesh. He's a lot easier to handle than you are."

He gave his mother a disbelieving look. There was a long pause. Looking at his mothers face he realized how much he would miss her. A lump began to well up in his throat and he looked away then said as he went through the motions of securing his already secured strap, "Thanks mom. Tell Mahesh not to get too comfortable on my side of the bed."

Raj turned and gave her a loving smile then started to gather his bags. He stopped to look at his mother one last time.

"What are you doing? Are you leaving now," his mom asked knowing very well he was.

"I am leaving in a few minutes to catch the bus into Ahmedabad so I can take the evening train to Delhi. Hopefully, I can get a sleep compartment then enjoy seeing the countryside tomorrow." He picked up the last bag and gave his mom a sad but excited look.

"Don't go, Raji," she pleaded with him almost crying.

He started to walk out of his room, "Mom! I already said goodbye to dad. I love you both." Raj turned back, leaned over to kiss his mother quickly then went out the door, and headed toward the bus stop in town.

Blythe, California – Jennifer Tomas
Summer 1992

Thrusting her thumb in an upward motion then holding her index finger and thumb about 2 inches apart, Jennifer Tomas signaled the boat driver to speed up a little bit. The spray from her ski, cutting through the cool water of the Colorado River, felt good on her skin. At 10:30 that morning the temperature had reached 113 degrees. Now, just a little after 3:00 pm, it was already pushing 120 degrees. The thunderclouds behind her were beginning to form cool air pockets as another summer storm moved in fast.

Yesterday, about this same time, there was a spectacular lightning storm just across the river on the Arizona side. The rain was always welcome because it helped to relieve the unending heat of August and it looked as though it was going to help break the heat again today.

The boat driver picked up the speed a little more and Jennifer began another set of slalom cuts on the glassy water. She could see up ahead the wind was blowing across the river and starting to form small white caps on the water.

Jennifer was a gorgeous twenty nine year old blonde tomboy. She began skiing in her early teens with one of her boyfriends and instantly fell in love with the sport or was it the idea of going away for the weekend and partying with her friends at 'The River'. Anyway, Jennifer's parents bought her the best equipment and she went skiing every other weekend. She was spoiled and usually got her way in all situations. Over the last 15 years she became an exceptional skier and it showed.

As she was cutting across the wake of the boat she saw a flash of lightning behind her. The dark clouds were gaining on her so she signaled the driver to go faster hoping to outrun the storm back to their base camp.

Again, another flash of lightning and now the rain was falling as the storm caught up to her. The droplets stung her skin as she sped through the water but she was determined to get back to camp before stopping.

Jennifer threw her thumb over her head signaling the driver to throttle up all the way. Just as the boat started to accelerate a flash of lightning so bright and powerful struck behind and to the right of her ripping the ski rope handle from her hands and knocked her off of her ski.

Settling into the water after several summersaults the water suddenly felt icy cold. Jennifer popped her head up from under the water and the cold made her gasp for air. "Holy shit," she yelled. She quickly looked around trying to regain her senses. She noticed the surface of the water was as flat as a mirror in all directions. There was no sign of a boat wake anywhere. There was no wind either. The only disturbance in the water was from the turbulences she caused when she hit the water after falling. The icy cold water bit through her skin and she began to shiver. Thinking she must have blacked out from the fall she looked again for signs of the boat further up river and saw nothing. She turned then looked quickly down river and again no boat.

"Where the fuck are those guys," she mumbled to herself scanning the water around her. With no sign of them anywhere she screamed, "Heeeeeeeyyyyyyy you assholes! Where are you?" She heard the echo of her voice bounce back from the canyon walls on the Arizona side of the river.

She loved this part of the river just floating with the current in a boat or some sort of flotation device. It looked like a miniature Grand Canyon on one side with sandstone walls shooting up from the desert floor in strict contrast to the California side of the river where it was flat farmland. It was usually calm and serene when there were no boats. She loved listening to the echo of the flowing water bouncing off the canyon walls as she floated by.

But, she didn't hear the water now. She needed to do something fast. She was beginning to shiver uncontrollably and the current was moving her further down river so she started to swim toward the California shore. Swimming helped to slow down her shivering. As she approached the rocky shore she carefully timed her approach toward one of the larger rocks and grabbed on. The current dragged her legs and pulled them around the rock. It was all she could do to muster up the strength to pull her self free of the icy current and on to the rock.

"I'm going to kill those guys," she grumbled in a low labored breathing tone.

She crawled up higher to a flat rock and laid down to catch her breath. She looked up at the sky then sat up suddenly. *"Where did the clouds go? Where's the lightning and rain,"* she thought almost verbalizing it as the realization hit her.

She stood up and scanned the skies. There was nothing. Not even a hint there had been clouds just moments before. "Blue skies in all directions but why is it so damn cold," she mumbled through her clenched and chattering teeth. It felt to her like it was in the low 60's. *"Thank God the sun is warm,"* she mused. She turned her back toward it trying to take in as much warmth as possible.

She folded her arms across her chest to also help warm her self then felt her bare breasts in her hands. Looking down and lifting her fingers slowly she cried out, "Oh great! I lost my fucking top. What else could happen?" She answered her own question as she looked down again and saw her bottoms were gone as well. "Oh my God," she giggled. She squatted to hide herself then realized it was useless. She started to laugh hysterically at her predicament.

As the laughter wore off she stood up and knowing very well she wouldn't see anything, Jennifer again looked down river to see if she could see her bathing suit floating. "Nope," she acknowledged. "I didn't think so."

"Now what," she asked herself. "I guess I'd better start walking back to camp and hope to God no one sees me."

Jennifer climbed to the top of the rock embankment where she knew there would be a dirt road which ran along both sides of the river. With a quick look in both directions to make sure no one was there, she headed north toward the campgrounds. Being fairly familiar with "The River," as everyone called it, she knew she was about five miles away from camp.

* * * * * * * * *

Jennifer had been walking for about forty minutes now. She was feeling thankful but at the same time bothered because of the lack of boats on the river. The usual dirt bikes and ATV's racing around were absent as well. As a matter of fact she hadn't seen anyone the entire time she'd been walking. She continued walking and began to really concentrate on what was going on. It was eerie and somewhat scary.

"Where is everybody," she uttered in a concerned low voice. She remembered a Twilight Zone episode where everyone disappeared except one person. She felt like that person.

She stopped at the edge of the bluff and looked in both directions of the river once again to see if she could see anyone. "There are no boats or Jet Ski's everywhere. They were everywhere before that damn storm hit and now zilch. No storm, no boats, nothing. What the fuck is going on," she asked herself again in a nervous voice. She continued on with her walk toward the camp.

A few minutes further into the walk she realized she finally got that stupid song out of her head. It had just popped in her mind shortly after she started walking. *"We gotta get out of this place. If it's the last thing we ever do."* She set a pace and as she got into the walk she began humming it. It helped her to not think about being cold. It struck her as funny how the rhythmic beat of her footsteps just brought it out. Her situation probably subconsciously brought it to mind as well. It sounded good and was funny at first. After a while though, she got sick of it and couldn't get it out of her head. It just stayed with her every time she would start walking again.

Suddenly she stopped, "Oh Shit!" She turned back and looked far down the river standing on her tip toes. "SHIT, SHIT, SHIT! Noooo! I don't believe it! I left my fucking ski in the water! HOLLY SHIT! What else can go wrong," she screamed angrily. She loved that ski. After years of trying different ones she finally found this one three years ago. It made skiing effortless. The manufacturer went out of business last year so there was no way to buy another one. "SHIT!"

Pouting now, she whined to herself as she continued walking, "That was my favorite ski. I loved that ski. Why didn't I grab it? Why couldn't I have lost

14

one of my crappy skies? Nooooo, I had to try and out run that damn storm? Now look at me. And those shit heads, why did they leave me out there like that? Why didn't they come back for me?" She stopped and clenched her fists. "God Damn it," she screamed looking at the calm water. She continued on, "My ski is probably in fucking Mexico by now. I'm going to kill those assholes when I get back."

Jennifer reached up to feel the old faded men's tank top she had found earlier and noticed it was almost dry now. She had taken it down to the rivers edge and attempted to wash the dirt, grime and stickers from it. She had seen it wadded-up under a large tumbleweed and decided it was going to be better than nothing at all. It had several sizeable holes and tears in it but for the most part it covered all of the essential parts of her naked body and served its purpose.

* * * * * * * * * *

Finally, after almost 3 hours of walking, she saw the campground up ahead. Her feet hurt. She was dirty, tired, and cold. All she could think about was going straight to the showers and bask in the hot water. She would kill those guys later.

As she got closer it suddenly became apparent the park was nearly empty. All she saw were two old sixties style trailers, in excellent shape, one at each end of the park. She saw two people sitting by the trailer on the right closest to the river. She approached cautiously and startled the older couple. They were sitting and drinking what looked like hot coffee.

"Oh my goodness sweetheart, what are you doing walking around like that? You're going to catch your death dressed like that! Lou, run in the house and get a blanket," directed Marvelle after spotting Jennifer. She stood up from her chair and gestured to the man sitting with her to hurry. She turned back toward Jennifer, "Honey, are you OK? Here, sit down."

Jennifer sat in the chair the man had been in and wrapped her arms around her waist as if trying to warm her self.

Looking at Jennifer, Marvelle asked her if she wanted something warm to drink but didn't give her a chance to answer and yelled to Lou in the trailer, "Lou, bring out another cup with you."

Lou was just about to step out the door then turned back to grab another cup. Upon exiting the door he gave the blanket to Marvelle then headed for the coffee pot. Marvelle wrapped the blanket around Jennifer's shoulders and rubbed her arms vigorously trying to warm her.

15

"Where did everyone go," asked Jennifer staring out at the rest of the campground looking confused.

Glancing in the same direction Marvelle said, "Who sweetheart? There's no one else here except Elmer and Angeline parked over there by the store. Most of the other Snowbirds left a few days ago."

Jennifer looked up at Marvelle and mumbled, "Snowbirds," knowing damn well what Snowbirds were. They were those old people who took up all of the good camping spots and usually started showing up in November then would stay the winter months until April. *Why is she talking about Snowbirds in August,*" she scrutinized.

"Yes sweetheart, most of 'em head back home around the first part of April."

"Head back home around April," Jennifer exclaimed. She was getting irritated, "April was four months ago. You're a little late aren't you?"

"No honey! It's still April," Marvelle responded then turned toward Lou. "Lou, run over to the store and ask Walter to call the Paramedics. I think this girl's hurt or in shock."

"No, no. I'm fine, L_Lou. Don't do that. Really! I'm OK," Jennifer assured them.

"Are you sure honey, cause you don't look or sound OK. You're talking a little crazy."

"Really, I'm fine. I'm just cold," insisted Jennifer as she reached for the coffee in Lou's hand. *You're the one who's crazy lady,*" she thought.

Several minutes went by then Jennifer queried the two of them, "So, you don't remember a white Ford truck with a boat camped out over there?" She pointed at the large tree which for some reason now didn't have any leaves on it. She looked around the entire park and noticed none of the trees had leaves.

She took another sip of the coffee, a little shaky now, wondering why she hadn't noticed until now there were no leaves on the trees. *What the hell is going on,*" she questioned herself as she looked around the park again. Having been here hundreds of times over the last several years, Jennifer knew that the trees usually started to bloom in April/May and would lose their leaves in October/November. Marvelle had said it was April. But Jennifer knew damn well it was August. *How could this be,*" she wondered.

Not wanting to sound like a lunatic or make the couple any more suspicious, Jennifer decided to just go along with whatever the couple was saying to assure them she was OK and figure out later what was going on.

After a short time, Jennifer had warmed up and convinced the couple she was all right. She explained to them that she had bumped her head on a tree while walking but was OK now. She told Marvelle she was supposed to meet her friends in town and that they were probably getting worried so she needed to take off. Marvelle asked how she was going to get there and Jennifer told her she had her car parked out on the road. Marvelle leaned in and out of the motor home quickly, slipped Jennifer a twenty-dollar bill, and bid her good luck knowing very well Jennifer was probably not being totally truthful.

With the baggy sweats and light blue tennis shoes Marvelle gave her, Jennifer gave the couple a reassuring wave indicating she would be fine then headed out the front gate toward Blythe.

Vail Hospital, Colorado – Wyatt Coleman
Winter 1970

"When can I talk to him, Doc," asked young Officer Dan Buckley.

"I don't know. He's been unconscious for three days and I don't think he's going to be in any shape to answer your questions when he comes out of it," advised Dr. Paula Leventhal as she checked the monitors.

Officer Buckley moved up to the foot of the bed, "Come on Doc. We need to find out what this guy was doing on the pass, down that hill, in the middle of winter, buck naked. Can't you wake him up?"

"No! He's better off sleeping for now. He had severe head trauma and hypothermia when they brought him in and I don't want him waking up just yet. I want to do a few more tests on him," she answered sternly then walked around Dan to look at the IV. "Why the rush," she asked. "He's not going anywhere for at least a few days."

"He's not going anywhere at all until I find out what happened and why he was up there. He'd be dead right now if those kids hadn't spun off the road at that same location and gotten stuck," Dan explained. He moved to the opposite side of the bed and continued, "Luckily for John Doe here, one of those kids started exploring the area. While they were waiting for the tow truck to come to pull them out, one of the girls just happened to look over the hill and saw him leaning against a tree half covered in snow. Another hour and it would have been too dark to see anything. Probably wouldn't have discovered him until June."

Do you have any idea how long he was there," Paula asked.

"We have no idea. It's for damn sure he would not have survived the night. This could have been a possible homicide. So, that's why I want to talk to him."

Paula scribbled on the chart then put it in the holder by the door. "OK!

17

You'll be the first person I notify. He's not going anywhere and you've waited this long. Another day won't make any difference. I'll call you when he wakes, OK," she offered.

Dan walked toward the door and started to walk by as he looked down at her hoping she would notice. "OK, I guess I have no choice. So, how's he doing otherwise?"

She pulled the chart out of the holder again and flipped through a few pages then itemized his injuries and explained, "He's got a concussion, a few broken bones, multiple bruises, and several lacerations. Looks like someone beat the hell out of this guy and left him to die."

Looking down at the chart and flirting just a little he asked, "Why do you say someone beat the hell out of him?"

Stepping away and into the hallway she replied, "Judging from the wounds and breaks he was struck several times by some kind of solid object like a bat or club or tool and he was hit by someone with a lot of strength. The head wound was more than likely caused by the tree he hit."

Realizing Paula was trying to keep their conversation strictly business Dan moved away then out into the hallway with her now assuming a professional stance and asked, "Couldn't he have sustained those same injuries if he had been thrown down the hill?"

"I don't know. I wouldn't think so Dan. The snow would have slowed him down enough to keep him from striking trees and rocks hard enough to do the kind of damage he sustained. But, if he was thrown from a speeding vehicle doing 50 – 60 miles per hour then I'd say yes it's possible"

"From the evidence at the scene there were no tire tracks or signs of anyone else being there. There was no evidence a struggle of any kind had occurred there either. If someone had beaten him up it was not at the scene. The first trace of evidence we could find was him hitting the snow about twenty feet down the hill. Then for the next seventy feet it looks like a small avalanche went through there. We're trying to piece together something that shows how he went over that hill. Your idea about being thrown from a speeding vehicle makes more sense. My first thought was he was ejected from a vehicle but we didn't find a vehicle or anything to support that."

"Maybe he was beaten somewhere close by and forced into another car then tossed over the hill as they rolled by the edge. That might explain the distance from the top to where he first hit the snow," Paula stated closing the chart then sat on the bench outside of the patient's room.

"I don't know. Like I said there were no tire tracks to support that theory."

"All I know Dan, what ever was used to inflict those wounds was used with a lot of force."

Dan started to head down the hall towards the exit then insinuated, "I guess we'll have to wait and ask Mr. Doe when he wakes up."

"There is one thing that struck me as weird," Paula contemplated.

Dan stopped then turned back toward her. "What's that Doc?"

"He has a tattoo."

"He has a tattoo? You've never seen a tattoo before? What's so weird about that?"

"Well, how many people do you know have a Marine Corp tattoo from Camp Pendleton with the dates 1977 – 1981?"

Dan walked up to her and asked, "Say again."

"Let me show you."

They walked back into the room then Paula pulled the sheets down and rolled the patient to his right side revealing the back of his shoulder and the Marine Corp emblem with the name of the base and the dates.

Dan studied the tattoo, "Hmmm. That is weird. I'll get one of the police photographers to come by later and take pictures. I'll have him finger printed too while my guy is here. We'll run him through our system and see what comes up. I'll send them to the FBI and the DoD too. They can start searching to see if they can track him down through military records while we're waiting for sleeping beauty here to wake up."

Paula gave Dan an annoyed look then rolled the patient back over and covered him up. They both left the room and she insisted, "Tell your guy to see me first before he goes in there to take the pictures or do anything. He is still my patient and has a right to some privacy."

"Nobody's going to bother him without checking with you first Paula," Dan responded with a smart ass tone.

"OK," she responded fighting a smile. "I'll call you as soon as he's awake."

Dan nodded then left the floor and headed back to his patrol car.

* * * * * * * * * *

When the doctor had rolled Wyatt onto his side it woke him up enough to hear the conversation between the two people in his room. Groggy and confused he decided to not move or say anything.

When they walked out of the room he opened his eyes to see where he was.

He recognized the monitors above him as hospital equipment but they looked old. Careful not to set off any alarms or alert the nurse, he surveyed the room. He could see two people outside his room talking. He assumed they were the two people that had just left. One was a police officer and the other a young lady who looked like she might be a doctor because of the stethoscope around her neck and the chart in her hand.

As he moved he winced in pain. He saw that his arm was in and there was a cast on his right leg. Several of his fingers were wrapped in splints as well. He shifted his body to help relieve the pain.

"*Why were they so interested in my tattoo,*" he thought. "*You'd think they'd never seen a Marine Corp emblem before.*" Wyatt had served four years in the Marines. After leaving boot camp at Camp Pendleton he did two tours overseas. He had gotten to see a part of the world in which he had no idea existed. It was a good experience. He was proud to have served his country but that was a long time ago.

Trying to get his bearings he remembered the accident. He flashed back on being ejected from his truck and bouncing on the ground. "*Well, that would explain the broken bones and bandages,*" he acknowledged. Still a little groggy, his mind wondered, "*What ever hit me must have totaled my rig. God, I hope no one else got hurt. There goes my insurance.*" Many other thoughts raced through his head as the medication in the IV kicked in and he trailed off to sleep again.

* * * * * * * * * *

Deciding to drive back to the scene Officer Dan Buckley radioed the dispatcher to send out a photographer to the hospital. He had explained what he wanted pictures of and made sure specific instructions were given to contact Dr. Levanthal upon arriving at the hospital. He instructed the dispatcher to make sure they bring a finger print kit with them as well. After signing off he continued to drive toward the scene and began to reflect back on his first meeting with Dr. Paula Levanthal.

Dan had been a State Trooper for less than a year when he met Paula for the first time. He had been on the graveyard watch and was dispatched to an accident involving a head on collision. The victim, a young woman visiting from France, appeared to have hit some black ice and slid her vehicle into on-coming traffic. She was in real bad shape so Dan followed the ambulance to the emergency room at Vail. There he would meet with the doctor on call and discuss the victims injuries and prognosis.

He arrived at the hospital a few minutes after the ambulance and saw her working on the patient. She was so striking. No make-up, hospital scrubs, and long red hair pulled back into a ponytail, she just took his breath away. He just stood there for a moment and watched her take charge, ordering people around trying to save this young lady's life.

Dan moved closer and waited for a chance to ask if the victim was going to make it. Paula looked up while barking out orders and stopped, just for a moment, when she saw Dan. She then continued giving orders then told him she would talk to him when she finished stabilizing her patient and completed her evaluation.

It was almost an hour later when she found Dan talking to an ambulance driver. Dan noticed her looking his way and walked over to her. She proceeded to give him a list of the injuries. Dan lightheartedly interrupted, "Whoa, slow down Doc. Take a deep breath."

She was tired and didn't see the humor in his attempt at being cute then continued with her debriefing. Dan could see she was in no mood for levity so he took out his pen and jotted down some notes then asked where the victim was now. She told him the patient was in surgery.

Paula let out an exhausted sigh and asked if there was anything else he needed. He said no, but he added she looked like she could use a cup of coffee. She let out a fatigued laugh then headed back to the emergency room giving a casual wave over her shoulder as if to say there's no time right now. Then she disappeared through the hospital doors.

It was not a good first meeting but it was enough for Dan. Over the next year he tried to find any excuse to go to the hospital. He visited and talked to her many times and each time they got to know each other a little bit more. There was an obvious attraction developing but there wasn't any free time to pursue it further.

Almost down through the Loveland Pass now Dan could see the construction of the tunnel. He thought to himself how much time would be saved when the Straight Creek Tunnel was finished. That would be in a couple more years though. There was some talk about renaming it to the Eisenhower Memorial Tunnel when both sides were completed. He didn't understand the thinking behind that when Senator Edwin Johnson had been mostly responsible for getting the support to build it. It was time he got his mind back on the case. "*Something's missing*," he mused as he pulled the patrol car to the side of the road where John Doe was found.

He got out of his patrol car and walked over to the edge of the hill looking for anything that may have been missed. With the unusually warm weather the last couple of days the snow had melted considerably, and with all of the emergency people who helped move snow away from the immediate area where John Doe had been laying, the ground was completely exposed. So if there were anything there it should be uncovered.

After a long look around he started his climb down the hill and followed the apparent path John Doe made to the tree where they found him lying. There were still depressions in the remaining snow where he had bounced down the hill. "Nothing! No clothes, no paper, no nothing," he mumbled to himself as he kicked at the ground. He walked toward the tree and squatted down to take a closer look at the ground around the tree but there was only wet dirt.

Just as he started to head back up the hill a small shiny object caught his eye. It was laying in some pine needles just past the tree. He reached down to pick it up. It was the top part of what looked like a gold ring with a Marine Corp insignia on it. Closer examination showed it was scored and had been melted in some places. It looked old and worn but he could make out 'Camp Pendleton' with the partial dates '1977-8' on the bottom. The last digit looked like it was melted off. "Why would a ring have 1977 to eighty something on it in 1970," he whispered somewhat perplexed. "I need to talk to this John Doe as soon as possible."

Los Angeles, California – Rajiv Ramakrishnan
Summer 1969

The train ride across India was all and more than Raj had ever expected. He witnessed sights he had only read about or had seen pictures of, most of which were black and white. He was in total awe throughout the entire train ride. He stayed a couple of days in Delhi then caught his plane to Los Angeles with stops in Taipai, Guam, and Hawaii. He was allowed to clear customs in Hawaii giving him several hours to go into Honolulu and look around before catching his flight to Los Angeles.

At the terminal, in Los Angeles, Mr. and Mrs. Weston were waiting at the gate holding up a sign with Raj's name on it. Raj signaled to them and they ran over to him.

"Welcome to America Rajiv," Mrs. Weston announced excitedly and gave him a hug.

"Welcome Rajiv," Mr. Weston repeated shaking Raj's hand.

"Please call me Raj."

"OK, Raj. Shall we go get your bags," asked Mr. Weston pointing in the direction the other passengers were heading.

Walking to the baggage claim area Mrs. Weston asked how the flight was but never gave him a chance to answer. She just kept talking and very fast too about everything and nothing. Raj was having a hard time understanding her but just smiled and nodded. The only thing he really understood was that the college was close to their home and that he had five days to learn his way around before starting his classes which he already was aware of.

"Do you see your bags Raj," asked Mr. Weston standing on his tiptoes looking at the luggage going around on the conveyer belt as if he would spot them first.

"Yes. There is one of my bags over there."

The others were not too far behind it. After they collected all of them they each carried a bag and headed for the parking lot where the Weston's had their light blue Chevy station wagon parked. They loaded the bags in the back and headed to Raj's new home for the next year in a new community called Diamond Bar.

The drive took about an hour. Mrs. Weston was talking most of the trip. Mr. Weston interrupted her a few times and asked Raj a couple of questions, which he got to answer.

"*They seem like very nice people,*" he thought. "*Just a little too talkative.*"

The house was a little larger than Raj's home in India. It was two levels, light green, and stood by itself. The other homes were at least forty feet on either side of it. In Chenpur, houses were almost on top of one another. He could feel the openness of it and liked the feeling immediately.

As they pulled up to the house a large door opened and they drove the car inside. "*Imagine having a garage and with an automatic door too. They must be wealthy,*" he supposed. He was very impressed by this. But as he looked at the other houses they all had garages too. He wondered if they were all automatic as well. They got out of the car and walked around the front. Mr. Weston opened the double doors and they walked inside.

There was a large staircase directly in front of them. To the right a formal room with what looked like expensive furniture. Through that room toward the back of the house Raj could see a large dining table with a chandelier hanging over the center of it.

To the left of the staircase was a long hallway with a door about half way down on the left. They walked down the hallway and Mrs. Weston pointed to the door and revealed, "This will be your room Raj." She opened the door and there was a large bed in the center of the room.

"How many people will be sleeping in this room with me," Raj asked.

Mr. and Mrs. Weston laughed loudly and Mrs. Weston said, "Oh my goodness dear. This is your room. You have it all to yourself. No one else is going to be in here with you. The kids have their own rooms upstairs. I just thought you might like it down here away from all of the commotion when the kids wake up in the morning."

Raj was beside himself. *"This large bed just for me,"* he thought smiling. At home, in Chenpur, he shared a bed with his two brothers. He was starting to like it here already.

They left his room and continued down the hallway and there at the end of it was a sizeable room with a large table, sofa, chair, and television. To the right was a long counter that separated this room from the kitchen. Mr. Weston walked to the back of the room to a large window that slid from side to side. He stepped out to the back of the house and motioned for Raj to join him.

The view was spectacular. The house was set on the top of a hill that over looked a valley filled with other houses and rolling hills in the background. Mr. Weston called to Raj from the right and when Raj looked Mr. Weston was standing next to a large swimming pool.

"The pool is heated so you can go swimming anytime you like," Mr. Weston informed him as he walked toward the other end of the pool. "The diving board has a crack in it so don't use it until I get it fixed."

"Diving Board," Raj questioned himself. He had never seen one before but knew what it was for.

"That's pretty much the Grand Tour Raj. I'll show you the upstairs later or one of the kids may drag you up to their room before I get a chance to take you up. They will be here later. They are at my sister's house right now. Either way, this is your home now. Make yourself comfortable. OK," expressed Mr. Weston

"OK Mr. Weston."

"John! Please call me John. And you can call my wife Carol. OK?"

"OK, John."

"You're probably feeling real dirty after your trip. There are towels and other toiletries in your bathroom."

"My Bathroom," Raj asked looking very surprised.

"Yes, just inside your room to the right. Dinner will be ready in about two hours so you'll have some time to rest or look around before we eat."

They walked back inside the house. Raj excused himself and headed for his room. He walked around the room then sat on the edge of the bed taking in the vast space that was all his. He liked the idea of no one else to share it with.

Mr. Weston knocked on the door and placed Raj's bags on the floor next to the bed. "We'll see you in a couple of hours, OK," he interrupted.

"Yes. OK."

"Just make your self at home," he repeated then excused himself closing the door.

It took Raj a few minutes to figure out the shower. Having never taken one before, only baths, he enjoyed the experience. He dressed in a new set of clothes and lay on the bed to relax then fell asleep.

* * * * * * * * * *

The knock at the door seemed to come immediately after he had closed his eyes. Two hours had passed and he felt renewed.

"Are you ready for some dinner dear," asked Mrs. Weston – Carol.

"Yes," he replied now realizing he was starving.

"The kids are really excited to meet you. Come and join us as soon as you are ready," she called out as she headed back toward the kitchen.

Raj jumped up and followed behind her then heard the children talking loudly as he approached the large room. When he stepped into the room the noise quieted.

"Everyone, this is Raj. Raj, these are my children," she stated putting her arms around the tallest child. She continued, "This is Jimmy, my oldest son. Our family and friends call him, J'Dub. He's ten. He'll be eleven next month." She moved to the next child, "This is Ellen. She's seven. We've always called her Boo Boo but she hates that. She's asked us to call her Ellen now but she'll always be my little Boo Boo." She moved over to the last child, "And finally, this is Tommy. He's five and a handful. He'll definitely wear you out if you let him. Of course you know John. Everyone, say hi to Raj," she concluded then sat down.

The three children yelled enthusiastically their hellos. They all sat down to dinner and Raj enjoyed the banter back and forth between the children. They all took turns asking him questions about India and his trip. Everyone talking at the same time reminded him of dinners at home. The food was a little strange to him at first but tasted very good. Raj was going to like it here in America.

Blythe, California – Jennifer Tomas
Spring 1968

Jennifer climbed down from the International Harvester tractor parked at the corner of 7ᵗʰ Avenue and Main Street in downtown Blythe. She thanked the kind farmer who offered her a lift after she had walked about three miles north on Highway 95. Across the street was a supermarket so she decided to go inside, grab a snack, and find a phone booth so she could call someone. *"But who, "* she wondered. She hadn't thought about whom she should call for help. *"Perhaps, my father, "* she guessed. He was always coming to her rescue.

"Jeeze, this is an old store, " she suddenly realized. She had never been in this store before. In fact, she didn't remember ever seeing it here in Blythe. She had always gone to the Ralphs, which was an Alpha Beta several years before, on the other side of town. Looking at the cashier as she walked in Jennifer did a double take. "Haven't you people heard of scanners, duh," she mumbled sarcastically. She walked through an empty cashier station then got in line. She grabbed a few items off the end cap and waited for the cashier to ring up her powdered doughnuts, peanuts, and Coke.

Devouring the doughnuts she found a phone booth next to the newspaper stands. She laughed saying, "Oh my God! Rotary dial phones? I didn't think they made these things anymore." She picked up the phone and started to dial her parent's home. The operator came on and asked her what number she was dialing.

"I dialed 949-555-3646," she told the operator. "I want to put it on my credit card," she demanded.

"Credit card? You mean Phone card, right," the operator asked.

"No, my credit card," Jennifer retorted then began to tell her the number again.

"Excuse me ma'am. The phone number you are asking me to dial is not a valid number," interrupted the operator beginning to get annoyed.

"Yes it is. It's my parent's number and they've had it for at least ten years. Try it again," Jennifer demanded in a snotty tone.

"Ma'am, there is no such area code as 949. Are you sure you have the right number?"

"Look you dumb bitch. Just dial the damn number." At that the operator hung up on her. Pissed off now Jennifer started to dial the number again then noticed the newspaper in the dispenser next to her.

"Viet Nam War," she questioned then bent down to look at the front page. The date read April 17, 1968. "What the hell is going on here," she asked aloud. She looked around the store and some people were starting to look at her. She walked over to the cashier and asked why they had a newspaper from 1968 in the news stand. "Is it some kind of holiday or tribute or something," she challenged.

The cashier snapped back, "This is today's paper. What kind of dope are you on honey?" She turned toward the other people in line half laughing and jested, "Darn hippies." Some of the people in line giggled.

"No, I'm sorry. Come on. What's the joke? Why do you have newspapers about the Viet Nam war dated April 17, 1968 in those news stands," she asked half smiling wanting in on the joke.

"I don't know what you're on honey but you'd better get some help and I mean now," the cashier restated not smiling anymore and nodded to the store manager who ran into his office.

Getting very frustrated, Jennifer ran her fingers through her hair and staggered back over to the news stands and looked at the paper again. She read it very carefully then sat on the floor holding her head and rocking trying to make some sense of this.

Within a few minutes you would have thought the store was being robbed. Police cars came from everywhere with their sirens blaring and their lights flashing. Several of the younger officers came running in the store with their guns drawn looking like Barney from the reruns of the Andy of Mayberry show.

"Put your hands on your head, ma'am," ordered one of the officers.

"You got to be kidding me," Jennifer groaned as she started to stand now feeling angry.

"Lady, do it now. Put your hands on your head and turn around," another officer demanded.

"Kiss my ass. What's the charge? I want a lawyer right now."

"I won't say it again. Put your hands on your head and turn around." The second officer repeated. "You'll get your lawyer at the station."

"You're serious," Jennifer asked as she turned slowly and started to put her hands on her head. The officer came up behind her and placed handcuffs on her. They quickly patted her down.

"Hey! Aren't you supposed to get a female officer to do that or is this how you get your thrills," she chided.

They removed her from the store and put her in one of the police cars. With the siren blaring they sped off to what she assumed would be the police station.

"Is the siren really necessary," she asked the older police officer sitting on the passenger side. He reached up and shut it off.

"Slow down Jerry," he told the other officer then looked back at Jennifer.

"So, what's your problem lady?"

"Nothing. I just asked that cashier a question and she gave me attitude then all of a sudden you clowns come out of the woodwork and treat me like I'm some kind of terrorist or something."

"A what? A terrorist? Are you stoned?"

"Stoned! Either you guys have been in the desert too long or you're dumber than dog shit," she shouted half laughing.

"Little lady, we'll see who the dumb one is here. Maybe a night in jail will help clear your mind and clean up your language."

"Yeah, well, I could use a good night sleep after what I've been through today. Do I get a hot shower with that room," she requested. The officers ignored her.

They arrived at the jail and sure enough they booked her then threw her into a cell where she would spend the night. She didn't even care about her one phone call at this point. She just wanted to lie down and figure out what the hell was going on. Aware there were other people in the cell with her the noise from their chatter didn't register as the events of the day ran over and over in her head. The realization of what might actually be happening to her was beginning to grab hold and she turned on to her side, pulled her knees up to her chest then began to weep. Not wanting the others in her cell to notice she suppressed it as much as she could but still the tears poured out.

"*Get hold of yourself Jen,*" she thought. But, it was too much. She felt alone and that was a very foreign feeling to her. She wiped the tears away from her eyes only to be replaced with new ones.

Finally, regaining control of her emotions, she fell deep into thought replaying the day once again in her mind. It didn't make any sense. Her head was beginning to hurt and she couldn't think about it anymore. Feeling mentally and physically drained her body, no longer able to stay tense and stiff from sheer fatigue, gave way and relaxed. She drifted off to sleep.

In the morning Jennifer felt more like her normal self. She got a newspaper with her breakfast and sure as shit it read April 18, 1968. "*How could this be happening? This has to be some kind of nightmare or something,*" she wondered. Once again she thought, "*It's just like that shit that only happens in the Twilight Zone or the Outer Limits shows.*" But as she read the paper and the morning went on she realized this was no nightmare. This was really happening. What was she going to do? The first thing she needed to do was get out of this jail but how.

After lunch, Jennifer was taken to the courthouse where she was charged with loitering and disturbing the peace. The court appointed lawyer told her if she pleaded guilty she would have to serve ten days then be set free or she could post bail for a thousand buck and wait fifteen days for her trial. Since she only had what was left of the twenty Marvelle gave her she opted for the ten days. She needed the time to figure out what she was going to do.

Arizona State Prison—Yuma – Elisaio "Ravin" Munoz
Fall 1991

Walking out the front door of the prison, the guard who had escorted thirty year old inmate Munoz called out to him, "The next time you try to bring drugs into our state we'll be sure to be waiting for you and we'll be more than happy to put you up in our establishment again. So, don't disappoint me convict and hurry back." Then he blew Munoz a kiss in a cynical gesture.

"Oh, I'll think twice before coming back here you fat piece of shit and I'll make sure I plan things a little better next time. There's no way you're going see me again," he stated unemotionally while raising his hand over his head, giving the finger to the guard as he walked toward the front gate.

Elisaio Munoz, 'Ravin' as his homeboys called him, had just finished serving a fifteen year sentence, cut down to seven years for good behavior, for smuggling drugs across the border of Mexico into the U.S with the intent to distribute or sell.

Seven years earlier he had made it through the Arizona/Mexico border check point but had made the stupid mistake of running a stop sign at the end of the first off ramp he came to. He was tired and hungry and just wanted to get something to eat at the Denny's there. He had been so pleased with himself for getting through the border without incident he didn't even notice the police officer behind him as he turned right.

Seeing the lights come on he pulled into the Denny's parking lot knowing he had no chance of running and waited in the car for the officer to approach. He was asked to step out of the car and when he refused a backup police car showed up a few minutes later. This refusal gave the officers probably cause to search the vehicle and hidden professionally under the back seat they found 10 kilos of cocaine. He was arrested, tried, and convicted.

Now, 11:20 am in southwestern Arizona, he was free and wanted to get as far away from Yuma as he could. He had arranged for his parole to be back in California close to his hometown in El Monte. He just had to get there and check in with his parole officer within 72 hours.

29

There was one small problem. He only had the fifty dollars the prison gave him. His family and friends had refused to pick him up or help him make arrangement to get home. Knowing that a few weeks earlier, he had already decided it would be easier to hitchhike home. This would give him a little time to get used to his new freedom, see a little of the country, and think about his future. Besides, he had hitchhiked all over California when he was younger. It was no big deal. So he walked out to the highway, stuck his thumb out, and started his journey home.

He had about a hundred miles north to go on Hwy 95 before reaching Interstate 10, then it would be a straight shot all the way back home. If all went well he should be home in a couple of days.

With no cars in sight in either direction Ravin noticed some dark clouds building up in the northwest but they looked like they were moving away from him and the temperature was still comfortable.

"This is going to be a long day," he uttered then started walking north.

* * * * * * * * * *

"Thanks for the ride man," Ravin grunted as he stepped out of the car at a truck stop west of Quartzsite on Interstate 10. Walking toward the restaurant he mumbled to himself, "What the fuck's wrong with these people? They zip by like I'm not even fucking standing here in the middle of the fucking desert. Do I look like some pinche' criminal or something? Shit man! Six fucking hours to go one hundred miles. It'll take me a fuckin year to get home at this pace."

He grabbed a quick bite to eat and went back out to the freeway and started walking again. He managed to hitch a few short rides and made a little better time. Walking again just outside Ehrenberg toward the bridge which crosses over the Colorado River in to California it started to rain.

"Fuck me! Why did that mother fucker have to drop me off three fucking miles from town," Elisaio yelled. He started jogging now hoping to get over the bridge and into Blythe before he drowned in the rain. Flash floods were common in the desert so when the clouds opened up it felt like buckets of water coming down. This was not a good start on his new life.

Lightning was cracking all around him now. The storm came over him quickly and fewer vehicles were on the road. No one was stopping in this rain to pick him up. He could see the town up ahead and thought he'd be able to take cover in another fifteen minutes or so if he didn't get blasted by one of those bolts.

It hit so fast, Ravin didn't feel himself hit the ground. He laid there for a moment trying to catch his breath. When he opened his eyes and sat up he was shocked at the heat and brightness of the sun. "*Holy shit man! I must have gotten knocked out or something and slept here all night,*" he thought to himself.

"Son of a bitch," he yelled looking down between his legs. "Who the fuck would steal someone's clothes when they were laying helplessly on the side of the fucking road?" He stopped himself and began to smile remembering he had stripped some bum, passed out in an alley one night, when he was a teenager just for the hell of it. Now he was laughing hysterically.

"OK," he laughed standing up and brushing the sand off of his ass. "I deserved that. What now?"

He started walking toward town watching for cars and hiding as they passed by. "This is going to be interesting, a fucking Mexican walking into town naked. These fucking patties will have my ass back in jail for sure. I'd better think of something quick," he mumbled almost laughing at the thought of it.

He managed to get into town without being seen and found some old clothes in a box next to a dumpster. They didn't fit well but it was better than nothing. He was now able to move around town a little more inconspicuously and after a couple of hours managed to scrounge up something that fit him better.

He came to the decision he needed to quit fucking around and get his ass home. He would have to get some more money though. It should be quick and easy in this little shit hole town. No one would ever catch him because he'd be gone before anyone knew what he'd done. The rest of the day he gathered up some junk he could use to make a shank. He waited until nightfall, held up a convenience store just outside of Blythe close to the freeway, stole a car, and headed for home.

TC Laboratories, California – Dr. Rajiv Ramakrishnan PhD.
Summer 2005

"Did you see it? Did ya? Oh my God! It was amazing. T.E.S.S. did it. It just vanished. Did you see it, doc," screeched Tim. He was jumping and dancing around screaming.

"Tim, you must calm down. We need to make sure we get all of the data from T.E.S.S. and review everything. We have to duplicate this to make sure it was not just a fluke. Tim! Are you listening to me," Raj insisted trying to get Tim's attention.

"Sorry doc. I can't believe we did it. Did you see…?"

Raj interrupted, "Tim, I need you to calm down and focus. Let us get this recorded and we will try it again this afternoon. OK?"

"OK doc. I'll get all of the data together in the next hour then we can review it."

"It is going to be lunch time in an hour. Let us meet back around 1:00."

"OK doc. One o'clock," Tim laughed as he realized what he just said rhymed then ran off.

Raj sat in his chair and was now smiling. He had done it. He made that ball disappear, but to where? He needed to come up with a plan, a way to corroborate T.E.S.S.'s ability. He needed to know for sure that the ball didn't just disintegrate. But how would he do that?

Raj had theorized early on that only organic material could pass through time. Earlier experiments with non-organic material burned or disintegrated where organic substances had much less damage. Using leather material yielded greater successful results. Now he had to verify the leather ball actually traveled through time but how.

For the next twenty minutes Raj typed as fast as he could, writing notes in his journal, all of the details from the experiment. He looked up several times thinking, trying to remember step by step what he did then suddenly stopped. "T.E.S.S.," he whispered jumping to his feet then rushed over to the generator to survey its position and portability.

T.E.S.S. is a generator he developed, several years ago, to produce an electrical charge with the quality and form of a non-angular emission, a straight bolt of electricity if you will. He called it "The Electrographic Symmetry Stabilizer." He wanted to use the same acronym he used for his time machine from childhood. It was silly but only he knew its true meaning. Raj believed that if an electrical discharge could be straightened out the powered driven light could travel slightly faster than the speed of light thereby opening up a time portal. The natural form of energized light is to zig zag causing it to slow down. He just needed to find a way to straighten it out to prove his theory and it looks as though his T.E.S.S. generator has done just that.

He walked back to his desk, grabbed the phone, and dialed maintenance. He spoke into the phone, "Could you have someone bring up a floor jack right away? Thanks you." He hung up and ran back over to the generator. He tried to push it but was unable to budge it. It was just too heavy.

He ran back to his desk and dropped into his chair. He started typing even faster than before and wrote more notes in his journal while he waited for the jack. He looked at the door several times over the next fifteen minutes expecting Maintenance to walk in with it. He was getting impatient. He started to dial the number again when a young man walked through the door pulling the jack behind.

"Someone called for a floor jack," announced the young man as he swung it around.

"Yes, yes. Thank you. Just leave it over there," Raj directed pointing to T.E.S.S.

The young man left the room and Raj walked over to maneuver the jack under the apparatus. He raised it a couple of inches off the floor, just enough to move it about three feet toward the wall. He lowered the generator and ran back to his desk and entered several more pages of notes before stopping. He removed a sandwich from his lunch bag, sat back in his chair, and took a deep breath then exhaled it out. "Let us see if that will work," he sighed. He then ate his lunch while walking through the process in his mind.

* * * * * * * * * *

Tim was back fifteen minutes early with a stack of printouts in his hands along with a DVD disk. "Here ya go Raj. Where do you want to start?"

For the next three and a half hours they went over the data, journal notes, and made several new entries and changes in to the computer. They were just about ready to try a second test.

"Tim. I have an idea of how to test the time movement of the object. If we reduce the power and increase the velocity of the charge I believe we can shorten the duration of time travel. I moved TESS about three feet toward the wall too. If we modify the data to the minimum settings I believe we can track the ball."

"I don't follow you Raj," Tim replied with a puzzled look.

"If we put another ball in the chamber, transport it, and move T.E.S.S. back to its original position, the ball should be under T.E.S.S. because T.E.S.S. was not in that position a few hours ago when the ball appeared. Do you follow me," Raj asked.

"Nnnnot really," Tim stuttered.

Raj walked over to the jack and raised T.E.S.S. up enough to see under it. He pointed, "Look. There is nothing under T.E.S.S., Right? When this test is done what ever we transport will end up under T.E.S.S. because T.E.S.S. was not in this position earlier today so it will drop to the floor when it appears."

"OK Raj. I think I got it. Let's just try it and see," Tim suggested somewhat unsure.

Within an hour they were ready to start the test. Raj placed his wallet in the chamber instead of the test ball. "What are you doing Raj? Why don't you use the ball," Tim asked wondering what Raj was doing.

"I do not want there to be any question as to the authenticity of the object transported. My wallet is one of a kind. It contains items that only I have. It is leather and that should validate my hypothesis."

"At least take your money and credit cards out of it," Tim urged.

"No, I want to see what effect this has on everything in it. Besides, it is just money and cards. They can be replaced, right?" Raj placed the open wallet into the chamber.

"OK Doc. If it doesn't work I'll buy you dinner," Tim responded with a cynical smile.

"Just start the generator," Raj grinned as he closed the chamber.

Tim threw the breaker and T.E.S.S. began to whir. In a minute the generator was turning at maximum speed building up power. The power level dial showed twenty percent and climbing.

Raj was busy entering in the final changes to the data settings into the computer. The noise from the generator was getting louder and Raj moved his ear plugs into place. Tim followed Raj's action and when Raj moved his protective glasses from the top of his head to down around his neck, Tim did the same. A few moments later, Raj moved his glasses over his eyes and walked over to the chamber. They were ready to make history.

Tim put his glasses in place and Raj placed his hand on the discharge button. He looked at Tim and gave him a nod indicating his readiness to go. Tim nodded back and Raj pressed the button.

The flash was incredible. Even through the protective glass of the chamber Raj could feel the power of the straight bolt of light pass by his wallet as he stepped back. In less than a second the wallet was gone.

Raj signaled Tim to cut the power. The generator spun down as they both stood there staring into the chamber. The wallet was gone. No residual material from the wallet was visible but there were a couple of melted plastic items and charred paper. When it was safe they removed the debris from the chamber and examined it. The plastic was indeed Raj's credit cards but only part of the credit cards. Apparently the part of the cards completely covered by the leather was missing and only the exposed portion did not transport. The charred paper looked like pieces of photos. Again, these portions which were not completely surrounded by the leather did not pass. Raj believed his theory was correct. Only organic material or things completely surrounded by organic material could pass through the time portals.

Raj signaled Tim to raise T.E.S.S. up with the floor jack. They pulled the generator back to its original place and lowered it. They walked around each end of it almost afraid of what they were going to see.

"There it is," Tim screamed jumping and carrying on as though he had just won the Lottery. Raj's wallet was completely in tact. No burns, no smoke, and no signs of damage at all.

Tim stopped jumping for a moment only to reach down for it but Raj stopped him. "Let us check if for radiation or contamination first."

Tim ran to the other end of the lab and grabbed a radiation monitor. "Nothing," he proclaimed. Not so much as a twitch registered on the needle of the gauge. Raj picked up his wallet and it was room temperature. It should be. Who knows how long it had been there. He opened it and everything was there just as he had left it except the missing portions of the credit cards and photos that used to protrude from it.

Tim began to scream again with excitement and hugged Raj enthusiastically saying, "You did it Doc! You did it. You did it. You did it. But how did you know for sure the wallet would be there?"

"I did not for certain but it seemed a logical conclusion it would be."

Raj explained to Tim how there was nothing occupying that space when the wallet appeared after it had been transported back in time. So it simply fell to the ground. But when he moved the generator into that same space they would not be able to see the wallet until after the test and they moved it back. Tim understood.

There was a long pause of silence between them. Raj broke the silence by asserting, "We have a lot of work to do first thing in the morning. We need to start working on a way to measure time, power, and durations to get a better handle on controlling this. You go home and I will stay and close up."

Tim yelled with excitement, "Are you kidding? We just sent an object back in time and you want to close up shop for the night. I couldn't sleep tonight if my life depended on it after this."

"I know Tim, but we both need time to calm down and digest what just happened. I think a fresh start tomorrow will be better for both of us. I need some time alone to think about what our next step is going to be. So let us call it a day and I will see you early tomorrow morning."

"OK…. You're the boss. Call me though if you change your mind. I'll be back here in a flash."

"OK Tim. I will see you tomorrow. I will be in at 6:00."

"I won't sleep so I'll be here early, waiting for you."

Tim grabbed his pack and left. Raj was still in shock. He could not believe after thirty-five years he had finally done it. He always knew it could be done but never imagined it would be him that did it and this soon. He cleaned up the lab and shut it down for the night. Tomorrow would be the start of a different yesterday.

Vail Hospital, Colorado – Wyatt Coleman
Winter 1970

The nurse had just left the room when Wyatt jumped up then winced in pain. He waited a second sucking up the pain then disconnected his IV and went to see if anyone else was close by. He opened the locker to see if his clothes were inside and saw nothing. He walked over to the window and saw snow everywhere. "*Must have been an early freak storm,*" he thought. He opened the bathroom door and saw a door that lead to another room. He slowly opened the door and saw a patient sleeping in the hospital bed. He crept into the room and opened the locker. He grabbed the clothes hanging there and went back into his room. He heard someone coming so he shoved the clothes into his locker, jumped into bed, and quickly hooked up his IV.

"Well, good morning and welcome back! My name is Nurse Koller. Do you know where you are," greeted the full figured woman in a tight fitting nurses uniform.

Clearing his throat Wyatt growled out, "Hospital?"

"Yes, you are at the Vail hospital. You were found unconscious in the snow by Loveland Pass. Do you know what happened," she asked as she began to check his vital signs and write them down in his chart.

"Not sure. I think I was involved in a collision with my truck."

"Well, you're doing fine now. You have a nasty bump on your head, a few broken bones, and some cuts and bruises but you'll live. Can I get you anything? Water, juice," she inquired checking his pulse now. "Your pulse is a little fast but not knowing what's going on probably has you a little excited."

"Some apple juice would be nice," he requested watching the nurse look at his IV.

"OK. Let me finish up here and I'll go get you some."

"How long have I been here," Wyatt asked looking at the nurse's face. She looked to be in her mid thirties, relatively attractive, and a little heavy but still nicely shaped.

"I think you came in five days ago." Looking at the chart she pointed to the upper section, "Yeah, you came in on March 3rd."

"March third! I've been here a lot more that five days," he protested trying to sit up.

She lightly placed her hand on his shoulder and pushed him back in to bed, "Don't try to sit up dear." He didn't resist. "No, you were checked in at 6:45 Sunday night. That was March 3rd." She closed the chart and put it back in the holder on the wall.

"I don't understand," he mumbled. "It was the middle of October when I had…"

"No sweetie. You're a little confused. That bump on your head is probably making you a little fuzzy. I'll call the doctor in to take a look at you. I know she'll be glad to see you're awake. In a couple of days things will be a little clearer. I'll be right back," she interjected as she headed out the door.

"*March? Why would she say that,*" he wondered. "*Is there something they are not telling me? Was I in a coma all this time?*"

A few minutes later a young attractive woman came through the door with Nurse Koller. "Hello there. I'm Doctor Levanthal and I've been treating you the past few days. How are you feeling," she asked while looking at his chart not really making eye contact.

"A little confused at the moment," he replied as she started to look him over.

"Well, that's understandable. You've been unconscious for the last five days. Do you know where you are?"

Wyatt nodded, "Vail hospital."

"Good. Do you know what happened to you?"

"That's where I'm a little fuzzy."

"After a day or so you should start to remember things more clearly. Do you need anything?"

"He asked for some apple juice," cut in nurse Koller.

"I don't see why you can't have a little to start. Let's see how you feel after that. Are you feeling nauseous or have any abdominal pain now," she inquired feeling his stomach.

"No. Just feels like someone beat the hell out of me that's all," he responded half joking and smiling.

Looking at the nurse she stated, "Well, we can talk about that later. Do you feel like answering a couple of questions and clearing up a few things for us?"

"Sure, if I can."

"Great. First off, we were unable to find any identification on you at the scene. Do you know your name?"

"My name? Yeah, it's Wyatt. Wyatt Coleman."

"Mr. Coleman. I'm very pleased to meet you." Now turning to Nurse Koller, "Nancy, would you make the changes to his chart and change his status from J.D. to Mr. Coleman?"

"Yes doctor." Nurse Koller took the chart from her and went out the door.

"Mr. Coleman. Do you think you are up to talking to a State Trooper to help clear up what happened to you on the pass?"

"Sure. I'm not really sure what happened myself."

"Well, anything will help them right now because frankly it's a mystery as to how you ended up at the bottom of that hill. I'll let them know they can talk to you this afternoon if that's OK with you. Maybe by then, and after you get something in your stomach, you'll be thinking a little more clearly." She turned and headed toward the door.

"Doctor?"

"Yes, Mr. Coleman."

"What's the date today?"

"Date? Oh, I'm sorry. Yes. It's Friday March 8th."

"I'm a little foggy, the year?"

"Why, 1970, but I'm sure you knew that. Right? As I said you've been unconscious for five days. You should begin to feel a little better after you eat. You'll have to excuse me. I have another patient I need to see. We can talk more later." She hustled out the door.

El Monte, California – Elisaio "Ravin" Munoz
July 1984

Not wanting to attract any more attention to himself Ravin drove just under the speed limit the rest of the way back to El Monte. During the drive he became aware, from listening to the radio and switching from channel to channel, that the date was seven years earlier and it was eight months ago, from now, from then, confusing as it was, that he had been arrested crossing the border. Here he was though, back in 1984. This changed everything.

The total drive to El Monte took him five hours. It took him three hours just to accept the fact that he had some how traveled back through time. He could only figure out it must have had something to do with the lightning bolt that almost hit him. Nothing else made any sense and there was nothing he could do about it now. Ravin always had the knack of looking at the brighter side of things.

The last two hours of the drive he tried to imagine the benefits of this whole phenomena: He was not in prison; He was older, stronger, and smarter; He knew things that were going to happen; He knew the future trend of the drug market; He learned who the major players for connections were from some of his co-inmates; and all of this knowledge would make him unstoppable. The greed of it all consumed him. He could take over his old territory and become "King Shit" and no one could stop him. This is, was, a great thing that was, is, happening to him.

A little more than a half hour from El Monte he entered Ontario. He decided he needed some extra cash so he could lay low for a few days, once he got home, to get his plan clear in his head. He also needed the time to build up a little capital to get things going forward. This would be the start of it all. He pulled off the freeway at Fourth Street and turned into the 7/11 close to the off ramp. It was a few minutes after 3:00 o'clock in the morning and he robbed the store with no resistance from the eighteen year old, pimple-faced clerk. He thought about shooting the kid just for practice but decided he would be generous because of his new life.

He hit two more stores, one in Pomona and the other in West Covina, just for the hell of it before arriving in El Monte. With a little over three thousand in cash he checked into the BIG 6 motel on Pico Boulevard and settled in for the night. He would need to move around for the next few days and ditch the car so as not to get busted. The adrenaline was still pumping and he couldn't sleep fanaticizing about his future power and wealth.

TWO

TC Laboratories, California – Dr. Rajiv Ramakrishnan PhD.
January 2006

"I'm sorry Raj, but six freaking months is just way too long to sit here doing nothing. We're already into the New Year and those bastards have our hands tied here when we could be moving forward on this project. How many damn balls do we need to send back in time before they realize what we've got here? We need to get started on trying to send living specimen? I just don't see why the executive board is waiting," Tim ranted pacing back and forth in front of T.E.S.S., completely pissed off.

"Tim, you must be patient. I know it is hard doing nothing but these things take time and I have been told we should be able to go to the next phase in a couple of weeks, probably by February," Raj explained trying to calm Tim down.

"They've been saying 'a couple weeks' for the last four months. Let's just do it and take our chances later."

"I know how you feel. But, if we wait we will have carte blanche on this project and we will be able to do as many tests as we deem necessary rather than do one test and spend the rest of our lives in jail or off the project all together."

"We're just wasting too much damn time waiting for these political bureaucrats to figure out how much money they are going to make off of this. That's what this is all about you know," Tim criticized.

"Money is what is paying for this project my friend so let us just wait a few more days and if they do not give us the OK by then I will start making some calls to some of my contacts in Washington."

"Alright, but just a few more days," Tim agreed then stomped off toward his desk.

Tim was right. The executive board was holding this project up trying to determine how much money could be made from this discovery. They were frantically putting together lists of potential clients. They were anxiously trying to decide how it could be used to set in motion their potential power control over other companies and possibly other countries or how it could be used as a weapon. Raj was almost sorry he had pursued it and shared his idea with T.C. Enterprises but at the same time he was excited to see the potential benefit it could yield. He needed to keep things under as much control as he could. Fortunately, he did have the support from the president and CEO of the company and that gave him some reassurance the right things would be done. However, if this project landed in the wrong hands it could prove detrimental to all concerned.

Raj called out, "Tim, wait a minute. I have something I want you to do for me. I have got some research I want you to start working on since we have the time right now. It will involve gathering data I think we are going to need in the next few months."

"Sure, doc. What do you need me to do?"

"I have been toying with an idea. Now, mind you, it is just an idea that came to me but I think we need to look into it. I have been thinking this type of thing has probably happened before," Raj implied walking around his desk then sitting back in his chair.

"What thing," Tim asked now sitting in the chair across from Raj.

"Time travel. I have a notion, a theory if you will, that I want to investigate."

"What are you suggesting? Someone else has already built a time machine?"

"No, no! Nothing like that! I just think it is possible Mother Nature may have been doing this over the centuries but no one has really thought to link it to what I am considering."

"What are you saying Raj?"

"I am saying I think people have been sent back through time before with the help of electrical storms. Lightning bolts similar to what we have created with T.E.S.S. but to a much greater degree." Raj pulled some photos from his desk and tossed them over to Tim. "I have been looking at some meteorological photos of electrical atmospheric activities over the last 50 years and I have seen, only a few mind you, lightning bolts that were symmetrical and non angular at the base of the strike." He pointed to one of the photos.

"You think some of these straight bolts sent others back in time," Tim asked staring at the photos.

"Obviously not all of them but yes, that is exactly what I am thinking. I believe if someone happened to be close enough to the strike and the bolt was straight enough to generate a displacement portal, they could quite possibly have been sent back in time. How far back? I do not know."

"Why haven't there been indications or signs of this before with evidence of large craters in the surface where everything close to the strike would have vanished, or thousands of people reported missing, or sudden unexplained appearances of mounds of material? I haven't seen or read anything like that."

"I have two thoughts about that. The first one is, what we do here in the lab is conducted under a controlled environment. We are focusing primarily on a single object, the one in the chamber, where there is no electrical interference inside or outside of the chamber and the bolt we create is not strong enough to send an object that far back in time." Raj stood up and moved around his desk. He continued, "The other one is, in an open environment there are several factors that could interfere or prevent the surrounding area from being transported. With the conductivity of a charge the earth serves as a ground so anything directly in contact would not be affected. However, human beings wear shoes and depending on the type of shoes they have on it may shield them thereby preventing a good ground. If they are close enough to a straight bolt strike they could potentially be transported back in time through the displacement portal. How far back? I do not know. That would depend on their close proximity of the bolt, the power of it, and its degree of non-angular symmetry."

"That still doesn't explain the lack of missing persons," Tim responded considering the possibility.

"As you know we had a heck of a time producing a straight bold here in our lab. My guess is that the rarity of natural straight bolt strikes and the chances of someone being close enough to one when it strikes is an infrequent occurrence. That would make the number of incidences very low over a long period of time, possibly one to two people every five to ten years. When electrical activity increases it is possible there could be more cases."

"OK, that kind of makes sense. So what is it you want me to do or what kind of data do you want me to start gathering?"

"Well, I am thinking we can work backwards on this by compiling a list of missing persons from the last fifteen to twenty five years focusing on areas where lightning storms are frequent. I am thinking if we confine it to the western region of the U.S. we could get a large enough sample of missing persons. Now, I believe the list may be quite extensive if we try to cover all of that territory, so perhaps you should start small and expand the territory outward as needed. I do not want to get bogged down with too large of a sample."

"Extensive Doc? It will be in the thousands if we pull data on all missing persons over the last fifteen years, and it will take months to go through and investigate all those names," Tim replied expressing concern.

"I was thinking about that too. If we narrow the search criteria down by eliminating all criminal references such as kidnapping, abductions, etc. and restrict it to Arizona and California to start, let us see what we get to work with. If the results are too many we can refine the criteria more and if we come up short then we can extend the search to include New Mexico, Nevada, and so on. We can always modify the criteria until we get a good test sample to work with. I would like a final sample containing approximately thirty or so viable names with no explanation for their disappearance. If these people were sent back in time I want to try to locate them if at all possible and talk to them. That is if they survived the trip. We have not gotten that far with our little time machine tests yet to see if living material can be sent back but if it turns out living matter can be sent back I want to get a jump start on this. This could give us some very useful information when we try to transport live specimens."

"If they did get transported back in time why would they want to talk to us? Especially now! It's probably been years for some of them," Tim asked standing, ready to go to his computer to start the search.

"Good question. I do not know that they would. Some of them may be completely acclimated to their new life or some may be in psychiatric wards, pumped up on Thorizine or something like it and diagnosed as delusional. Who knows what condition they might be in now? Would you have believed it a year ago if someone came up to you and said they had just come from several years in the future? Probably not. I would imagine they are going to be very hard to find even after we have their names."

"How soon do you want this doc?"

"As soon as you can put it together. This will give you something else to focus on while we wait for the approval from the executive board."

"Well, at least it's something to get us moving forward."

"That it is my friend. That it is."

Blythe, California – Jennifer Tomas
Spring 1968

Ten days had gone by quickly. The days were starting to get hotter and six hours each day picking up trash along the desert roads, well that was long enough for Jennifer. It did give her time though to think about what she might do and to accept the fact she was back in 1968. The rest of the afternoons she rested in her cot.

Evenings in the jail were another story. Some of the women in the cells were too busy trying to prove to the others they were bigger, badder, and tougher. This would go on most of the nights with frequent outbreaks of fighting and screaming. Jennifer wondered how these women functioned during the days with so little sleep. She managed to get enough sleep in the afternoons to sustain her while she just cat napped at night keeping semi-alert to unwanted advances from some of the others. She kept to herself and most of the ladies left her alone.

Today she was to be released. After a quick lunch, Jennifer was sent to Out Processing where she was given a change of civilian clothes, twenty bucks, and a taxi credit to take her anywhere in town. She was escorted to the front entrance by her arresting officer and released. He told her to stay out of trouble and asked if she needed a ride somewhere but she declined. She shook his hand, smiled, and walked out the door.

Jennifer knew there was no way to get home with twenty dollars. She wasn't really sure she wanted to go home just yet. She knew there was no one she could go to or call. If she called her folks they would think she was some nut on the phone because in 1968 she was only five years old. She thought to herself what the conversation would sound like, *"Hi daddy. This is Jen. This may sound funny but I'm twenty-nine years old now and I came back to 1968. Can you come pick me up at the Blythe jail?"* She laughed because it sounded ridiculous to her but here she was.

Jennifer pretty much decided a couple of days ago that she needed to get some kind of a job in town in order to make enough money to get her back to Anaheim on her own. Once back in Anaheim, she would find another job, maybe go back to school, and hopefully try to figure out what she was going to do with the rest of her life, this time around.

The idea of starting her own business floated in and out of her mind. She had a unique advantage now. She had a pretty good idea where technology was headed. She knew the names of a lot of companies that would evolve and make it big. She was vaguely familiar with the general rise and fall of the economy. She wished she had paid more attention to what was going on in the world but felt she had a good enough base knowledge. She just had no idea how to make it work for her yet. College was definitely something she needed to look into when she was able to. In the sixties and seventies, college degrees were highly looked upon.

Jennifer had always had it easy. Her parents tolerated her wild side hoping she would outgrow it by the time she was twenty then twenty-five then thirty then… Well, time kept passing with no change. She liked to party, go dancing, and go water skiing every chance she got. Blythe was the preferred location for skiing because of the smooth glassy water, all day, and the lack of large crowds.

In 1968, Blythe had a different look and feel to it. This was going to be home for a while and she needed to figure out how she was going to make this work. She needed to find a job but her job skills were few and far between. After high school, she managed to take some college class here and there to keep her parents off her back but never put any effort into them. Her grades proved that. She worked every kind of menial job available and was fired from each for either coming in late all the time or just not showing up at all because she was at the river skiing or hung over. She was indeed spoiled and now realized it. She never had to take anything seriously and wished she had.

Well now she was serious. If traveling back in time twenty-four years doesn't get your attention, nothing will. Jennifer came to that realization a couple of days ago and was determined she would put her life together. She looked around then asked herself, "OK Jen, where should we go?"

A few days had gone by. At night, she would sit in a booth drinking coffee at a 24-hour coffee shop reading the paper looking for jobs and getting caught up on the news. During the day she would wander around town taking naps under trees, in the park, or after school hours at the local elementary school.

She eventually took a job as a waitress at a "choke and puke" as the locals called it. It was a truck stop off of the 7th Street exit. She was able to convince the manager she had previous experience because she did, even though it was only two weeks but he didn't need to know that. He hired her for the graveyard shift at two dollars an hour plus tips. She found a local dive motel close by for eight dollars a day. She gave the job her all.

The first week was hard. She messed up a lot of orders, dropped several meals on the floor and on a couple customers. She got stiffed a couple of times from non-paying customers, and lost her tips one night. But she was determined to make money and get the hell out of Blythe. Within a short time she got the hang of it and turned out to be a pretty good waitress.

Making on average twenty dollars a day plus thirty dollars a day in tips Jennifer was able to save about a thousand dollars a month. As long as she was at work the manager let her and the other waitresses eat at the middle and end of their shifts for free. The food wasn't that good so she ate just enough to sustain her. At the beginning of her shift she usually bought a cup of coffee and had a piece of pie or toast with it. The motel was her only other bill other than the occasional shopping spree at the local Yellow Front for clothes.

After six months of working seven days a week, Jennifer had become one hell of a waitress. She learned how to live on just the basic necessities and now she had enough money to go home and start rebuilding her life in more familiar surroundings. She knew October would be a good time to leave Blythe and find a new job in Anaheim. This time of year companies would start hiring for the upcoming holidays. She gave her notice, bought a one-way bus ticket, and finished out her last week in Blythe.

On the bus ride, Jennifer felt a sense of accomplishment and pride within herself. She also felt sad because she was now leaving the place where she had begun this new journey and was not comfortable leaving her new home as it came to feel. She left behind some new friends too, along with her regular customers. The manager tried to convince her to stay and offered her more money but she had to leave. It was time. She now understood what her parents had been trying to teach her for the last ten years. In the last six months, Jennifer had become a responsible, caring, self-sufficient human being. It felt good.

As soon as she got back to Anaheim, she found a cheap motel, got a job as a waitress at Sambos, and started looking into restarting her life. She had six thousand dollars in her pocket and in 1968 that was a pretty good chunk of change.

Two weeks into her new job Jennifer tried to buy a used car and discovered right away she could not use her own identity. She realized being Jennifer Tomas in 1968 was going to be difficult. It was going to present some interesting problems and possibly raise a lot of questions for her younger self in years to come. She had to think of something.

She started searching through the major newspapers in the obituary sections looking for young women that fit her general description and age. Once she narrowed her list down to a couple of names she was able to find most of the information she needed to get birth certificates and Social Security numbers. She selected one of the new names that suited her. Everything after that was easy. She managed to get a drivers license fairly quickly. She just went to the DMV and claimed she lost her license where they simply took her picture and gave her a new one. She had the birth certificate in case they asked for it but there were no questions asked.

With the proper ID she then sent away for high school transcripts for her new name. They arrived in a few days. She had everything she needed now to start her new life as Kari Lynn Davis. She had changed jobs so she could use her new identity. She got hired at a finer restaurant, got an apartment, set up her utilities, insured her car, and started investing some of her savings.

During the next two years, Jennifer attended Fullerton Junior College during the days and worked evenings. She invested half of her earnings each month with an investment firm and steered them in the direction she knew would be beneficial to her. The more she learned about managing money and investments the braver she got with her investments. She had increased her total earnings a hundred fold in just a couple of years. She bought the restaurant she worked for and several others in the chain. Jennifer, now Kari, would never have to worry about anything again.

Vail Hospital, Colorado – Wyatt Coleman
March 1970

"Good afternoon Mr. Coleman. I'm State Trooper Dan Buckley." Dan walked toward the left side of the bed and stood over Wyatt in that silly police stance.

"Hello Officer Buckley. Doctor Levanthal said you might be stopping by." Wyatt replied trying hard to hold back his smile while looking away from the young policeman. It always amused him when police assumed that typical pose cops take when they try to look tough, standing with their legs spread wide apart as if their testicles were too big or shifted into the wrong position, and with their hands on their belt like cowboys waiting to draw on their opponent. He managed to suppress it and looked back at the officer.

"Yes. Well, how are you feeling today," Buckley asked noticing the smirk on Wyatt's face.

"Better, I think. The drugs they are giving me sure do help."

"I'll bet they do," responded Dan giving Wyatt a suspicious look. "Well, I'm glad you're feeling better. Listen, if you're feeling up to it I'd like to ask you a few questions if you don't mind," Dan inquired as he opened up his notebook.

"I'll do what I can. I'm still a little woozy but let's see what I can help you with." Wyatt tried to shift himself a little to get more comfortable.

"Good then, I guess I'll just ask you up front. Do you know what happened to you or how you ended up down that embankment?"

"I'm not sure. I've been trying to run it through my head and I just don't remember anything."

"Hmmm," Dan hummed scribbling something down. "Were you with someone?"

"I don't think so."

"There were no vehicles at the scene so I'm assuming someone had to have dropped you off there or left you there. Ring any bells?"

"Nothing. I'm sorry."

"Hmmm," he hummed and scribbled again. "Any thoughts as to why you had no clothes on?"

"I didn't have any clothes when you found me," Wyatt questioned surprised to learn that. It only added more to this mystery. "I wasn't aware of that."

"Not a stitch. There weren't any clothes anywhere in the area either. Can you explain that," Dan asked starting to get in Wyatt's face now and he could see Wyatt didn't like it.

"I'm drawing a complete blank. I have no idea how that could have happened."

"OK, let's try this," Dan asserted getting annoyed. "You say your name is Wyatt Coleman."

"That's right."

"Can you tell me why the FBI, DoD, and police files were unable to find a match for your finger prints or any record of you at all?"

"I don't know. That is my name though. Where and when did you get my fingerprints? Am I being arrested for something," Wyatt asked not liking the tone of these questions.

"We got them while you were unconscious and no, you're not being arrested at this time," Dan replied walking quickly to the other side of the bed. He stopped and pointed to Wyatt's shoulder then asked, "Why do you have a tattoo with the years '1977 – 1981' on a Marine Corp emblem?"

Wyatt shrugged and put his hand on his shoulder. "Ahhhh that. It was a joke. Several of my uh buddies and I got um pretty wasted one night and uh we all got them with those years. It was just a silly joke. Why do you ask?"

"Why those years," Dan asked while pretending to write fast in his notebook.

"Ummm, it was just something someone came up with. You know, guys just messing around, wanting something different." Wyatt didn't like where the conversation was headed and decided to end it. "Officer Buckley, I'm starting to feel a little nauseous right now. Can we finish these questions tomorrow?"

"I just have a few more." Buckley stated while reaching into his pocket for the ring he found.

"I'm really feeling bad. Can it wait?"

"I just need a few more minutes."

"I don't think I can," then Wyatt winced in pain over dramatizing a little to get Buckley to leave.

"Alright, I guess. I'll come back tomorrow." He shoved the ring back into his pocket. "That ought to give you time to think about it and maybe come up with more answers by then," he renounced slapping his notebook closed and putting it back in his shirt pocket.

"I'm sure I'll remember other stuff and have more for you by then. I just can't think right now."

"I'll be here first thing in the morning." Dan turned brusquely then walked out the door and headed down the hall.

"Thanks Officer," Wyatt called out as Dan left.

Dan was irritated. Something wasn't right. He stopped a short way down the hall when he saw Paula talking to another doctor. He waited for her to notice him.

"Hello Dan. Did you get a chance to talk to Mr. Coleman," she asked as she scanned through a chart.

"Yes and he wasn't very helpful. He's hiding something. He knows more than he is saying." Dan motioned for Paula to sit with him on the chairs.

"Why do you say that," she inquired looking up at him.

"Because he says he can't remember anything. How convenient. Then when I started to push him he claims he's feeling sick then asks if I can come back tomorrow. Why would he do that if he wasn't hiding something? You would think he'd want to remember or know why he ended up here. I don't like it."

"He did have a bad concussion and was unconscious for several days. It only stands to reason he would have some memory loss right now. Give him a few more days and I'll bet he remembers a lot more and answers all of your questions."

"I don't know Paula. I think he's purposely holding back. I'd like to post a guard outside his door to make sure nothing happens."

"That won't be necessary. He's not going anywhere in his condition. Besides, there is a lot of staff here all the time and he would be noticed immediately if he decided to get up and move around. So let it go for now. Come back tomorrow and I'll bet things will be better."

"I guess you're right. Listen do you have time to grab a cup of coffee? It'll be my treat."

"Give me fifteen minutes and you can buy me lunch," she teased with a flirting smile.

"You got it," he beamed back very pleased with himself watching her walk down the hall.

El Monte, California – Elisaio "Ravin" Munoz
July 1984

"Que pasa Jav?"

"Hola Ravin! Holy shit man! You look like hell ese."

"I've had a few bad days. What can I say man?"

When did you get out vato? I thought you were doing fifteen in AZ."

"Well, let's just say I got a second chance homi. You holding?"

"Si ese. How much you need? You hurtin? I'll fix you up man."

"No, nada vato. I wanted to see if you were still dealing. I need to talk to your dealers. Can you set up a meet. I've got something I want to run by them."

"What kind of something you talkin' bout ese? You know I need to watch my homies back. Entiende?"

"Si ese. I understand. Let's just say if what I have in mind works we can all get very rich if we do this right."

"Yeah?"

"Si ese."

"OK Bro! You talking my kind a something. When you want the meet?"

"Soon as you can set it up. You think they'll want to meet?"

"We'll see vato. Where can I find you?"

"I'm at the Star on Rowland in room 21. I'll be there for 2 more days then I'll be at the Vista Inn for 5. Give me your number and I'll call you if I relocate sooner."

Javier "Jav" Ortega is a cousin of Ravin's several times removed. In the Hispanic culture second, third, fourth, and fifth cousins are all treated like first cousins. La Familia. The two of them were born in East Los Angeles about a year apart with Ravin, born in 1963, being the elder. Their families moved to El Monte when Ravin was three hoping for a better life.

Growing up the boys were like brothers always seeing each other at family

50

get togethers, which were often, at least every Sunday. They also went to the same school so they were together every day. Jav did everything Ravin did.

At an early age they joined their neighborhood gang called Los Vatos Locos. Within a short time they were selling drugs for the older members and earning lots of money for themselves. They worked their way up through the ranks and did everything that was asked of them. At eighteen, Ravin got off the streets and began getting involved in the dealing end of the business. He had a very logical mind and was able to see and correct problems immediately. He developed a keen business sense and envisioned himself, one day, being his own boss. Jav, on the other hand, stayed with the selling end of the business and over the years had established a large enough phone clientele where he didn't need to be on the streets anymore and risk getting picked up. They were good at their jobs.

Ravin knew most of the hangout places Jav might be. He had gotten lucky on this day. Jav was at the first hangout he checked, El Mercado Pico. They used to steal cigarettes and alcohol or what ever they could carry from the store until one of the older members of the gang bought the place a few years ago. After that, they just hung out on the benches in front of the store smoking and talking shit.

Ravin knew Jav would get the meeting set up in the next day. Ravin also knew once he found out who Jav's current dealers were, he could learn who he could trust then he could start making some real money. Once he got his plan into motion he could take full control, eliminate the head guy himself, and eventually become "El Jefe", the Boss, a title he felt would show real authority. He had it all figured out and no one was going to stop him this time.

TC Laboratories, California – Dr. Rajiv Ramakrishnan PhD.
February 2006

After three weeks of pain staking research Tim managed to compile a viable list of twenty-eight names from five states. These people were still listed as missing, all had disappeared sometime in the last 30 years during an electrical or thunderstorm, and there was no criminal evidence connected to any of their disappearances. They were all from various education levels and professions. There was nothing in common at all about them. Two cases had eyewitnesses where they actually saw the individuals vanish and Tim highlighted them with a single asterisk. They would be the first to be investigated. In some of the cases there were empty vehicles, stranded bikes and motorcycles, and a rowboat. Tim identified them with two asterisks. There were other cases where clothes were left at the scene but the highlighted names were the ones Tim thought Raj might want to start with first.

Robert David Berke
** Marvin Allan Carnes
** James Wyatt Coleman
Stephen Joseph Exle
Jennifer Lynn Falk
Bryce Andrew Farley
Adolf Henry Heelenberg
Jacque Micha Iverson
Allen Robert Jeffers
Angelica Marie Kimball
Harold Lewis
Elisaio Guillermo Munoz
Burtrom Harrison Myers
** Robert Lee Niesen

* Juan Luis Ortega
Nathan Ellis Ortiz
Michael Gregory Padilla
** Sherrie Melissa Poole
Kevin William Raub
Jean-Paul Maurice Rosch
Gary David Sharp
Kathryn Joanne Simmer
Christopher Gordon Stevens
Marcus Antonio Thomas
* Jennifer Amber Tomas
Roger Vincent Van Muir
Joel Anthony Wilcox
Kim Li Young

"OK, Tim. This is a good base. Let us start with the two cases where there were witnesses then look at the other four you marked. After we exhaust those let us work the rest of the list from the top down. Do you have copies of the police reports?"

"Yeah, family, friends, and witnesses along with their addresses and phone numbers, it's all inside."

"Good. More than likely the contact information is no longer valid for most of them but it is a good starting point. We should be able to check with postal records to track their movements through mail forwarding."

"You make them sound like a herd of migrating elk," Tim joked.

"You know what I mean."

"Yeah doc. Just having a little fun with you."

"We will see how much fun you are having next week," Raj replied with a slight smile.

"Why? What's happening next week?"

"We received the OK to start testing live specimens and between managing the schedule we have with the tests and chasing these people down we are going to be putting in some long days," Raj reported offering a congratulatory handshake.

"It's about time," he exhaled accepting the handshake. "Are there any restrictions we have to abide by?"

"Other than the obvious, no, not really. They have set some guidelines as to the order of specimens we should start with but we are not bound to them. I have to prepare a schedule with realistic timeframes for the specimens we plan to use. They have left the door open to make recommendations for changes in our schedule but again we can either implement their recommendations or ignore them. We will review them and make those decisions when we are confronted with them. Besides, we are almost a year away from completing the new T.E.S.S. in order to experiment with the larger specimens anyway."

"I've been meaning to ask you about that. What idiot came up with that new name anyway, "Project STR-8 BOLT"? What's it stand for again?"

"To be honest Tim, I came up with the first part of it, "STR", several years ago. It stands for Symmetrical Transportation Reactor and 8, because it is the eighth prototype I developed. T.E.S.S., for lack of a better acronym, was just a name I came up with many years ago and the board did not much care for it in a scientific research environment. But now that this is real they wanted another name."

"As for BOLT, I had nothing to do with that. We do work, indirectly, under the Bioelectrical Research department but we control our own budget and research. They felt they deserved some recognition for their new part in this project and the executive board approved it, so they came up with the acronym BOLT (Bioelectric Operations using Light Technology). I know, I know. It is silly but they are now allocating funds to support this project so let us just appease them for now then we can worry about trying to change the name later on."

"Project STR-8 BOLT? I like TESS better," Tim declared.

"Get over it. STR8 BOLT is what we call it from now on. We have more important things to worry about. So, let us get started. Who is first," Raj asked looking at the list.

"Mr. Juan Ortega. He and about twenty others had crossed over the border from Mexico in August 1996. The witnesses stated they were looking for a place to camp for the night when a summer storm came upon them suddenly. His brother, Jorge, indicated to authorities Juan dropped back to go to the bathroom. After about five minutes, Jorge headed back because he didn't want to lose his brother. He stated as he cleared the top a small hill he could see Juan walking in his direction when a lightning bolt struck behind Juan. He claimed the bolt was quite large and the energy from it knocked him down. When he got up Juan was nowhere in sight. He ran down to where Juan had been and saw his clothes spread over the area. No sign of Juan though."

"Check with Immigration. I doubt if we can find this Jorge. He probably had fake ID and that was the name he used when giving the report. But follow up on it anyway."

"You never know doc. He may have been so upset at the disappearance of his brother he might have given his correct name."

"Maybe, see what you can find out. Also, get me a list of all of the Juan Luis Ortega's. How old was he when he disappeared?"

"Let's see. Ahhhhhh, nineteen."

"OK, only search for those over the age of twenty-eight. If he did get transported back in time there is no telling how far back in time he went. He would have to be at least twenty-eight by now. Also, check for them in California and Arizona first. Compile a separate list for those in Mexico."

"Why twenty-eight," Tim asked with a perplexed expression.

"Based on our tests with the time pieces and the leather balls that we used to measure how far these items traveled back through time and the power we used to transport them with TESS, I came up with an untested formula to help us determine an approximation for how far back in time these people may have traveled. It is simple and very basic but it works for what we are trying to accomplish right now and in such a short period of time."

"Ok Doc. I know you are going to explain it to me so lay it on me." Tim sat down and listened.

"We know from our tests what different power levels we were able to generate with TESS. We also know that with those different power levels we were able to open up the time or transfer portals. Let us call this part of the equation (P) for now. We know by using different duration intervals for prolonging the lightning strikes it too produced transfer portals. Let us call this (D). Finally, we know the experiments were successful because we were able to verify and prove the time pieces we used had different dates and times on them compared to what they were when we sent them through the transfer portals. If we break these down into seconds we have our time. We will call this (T). Are you with me, Tim?"

"Yeah Doc. I'm following you. (P) Power, (D) Duration, and (T) Time. Got it."

"Good. Putting this all together we find P times D is very close to equaling T. I am sure there are other more intricate variables that need to be considered for a more accurate result but for simplistic purposes this will do. Now, not knowing the exact (P) and (D) of the lightning strikes these people were exposed to, we can estimate it by using the data we have from studies of actual lightning bolts thereby giving us an approximate range for (T) until we gather more data from our tests. Based on this formula I have determined the probable minimum travel range for these people should have been somewhere around 10 to 15 years. That is why twenty-eight. Once we figure out how to measure the straightness of the bolt we can decrease the variance down to within weeks."

"OK. If it works for you it works for me. You're the Doc. So, what are you going to do," Tim asked as he stood and gathered his things together.

"I am going to start on the other highlighted name. I think I will start with Jennifer Amber Tomas."

* * * * * * * * * *

Sitting back in his chair Raj waited and listened to his headset as the third ring began.

"Hello!"

"Mr. Tomas?"

"Yes."

"Hello Mr. Tomas. My name is Doctor Rajiv Ramakrishnan. I am a researcher at the TC Laboratories in Twenty Nine Palms. I was wondering if I could ask you a few questions about your daughter's disappearance back in 1992?"

"What's this about doctor Ramakak....?"

"Please, you can call me Raj."

"OK Raj, what's this about?"

"I am investigating disappearances related to or as a result of electrical disturbances and the circumstances involved in your daughters disappearance caused her name to come up in our search."

"Do you have some new information about her disappearance?"

"No Mr. Tomas. I wish I did. I am just trying to collect some information about the electrical storm that was present at the time she disappeared. I am investigating several other individuals who disappeared under similar circumstances as well. So, if there is any additional information you could share with me it would really help my investigation. Is there anything you can tell me?"

"I wasn't there. All I know is what her friends told me and what I read in the police report. They said they think she was hit by lightning and it vaporized her or something. They didn't find any trace of her except her ski and bathing suit."

"I know this must be difficult for you but it will really help my research if you can give me the names of her friends who were with her that day, and their phone numbers if you have them."

"Aren't they in the police report?"

"Yes, but after this much time I am sure the information is not current. If you are still in touch with any of them it would save me a lot of time trying to track them down."

"OK, let me see here. I've kept in touch with one of the boys, 'CJ', Charlie Johnson. He's still in town. He's a real estate agent for a local outfit. He may know where the others are. His office is on Ball Road. I think I have his number somewhere here. Oh yes. Here it is. 555-7300."

"Thank you Mr. Tomas. I am sorry for disturbing you."

"Doctor, Raj. If you find out what happened to my daughter, will you let me know? No matter what it is?"

"Yes, of course I will. Thank you again."

Raj hit the disconnect button and quickly dialed the number for Charlie Johnson.

"L & L Realty. How can I direct your call," asked the perky young female voice.

"Mr. Charlie Johnson, please."

"Charlie, yes, hold please."

The sound of static music from a local radio station blared into the headset. The music was from an oldies station. "*This music will live forever,*" Raj thought humorously and remembered hearing it when he first came to America.

"Charlie here. Can I help you?"

"Mr. Johnson. My name is Doctor Rajiv Ramakrishnan and I am calling you from the TC Laboratories in Twenty Nine Palms, California."

"Please call me Charlie. What can I do for you Doctor?"

"Oh, OK, Charlie. I was just speaking to Mr. Tomas, Jennifer Tomas's father, and…"

"Jennifer? What about Jennifer?"

"Mr.Jo…, Charlie. As I said, I am with TC Laboratories and I am a researcher investigating electrical phenomena related to or resulting in the disappearance of individuals. If I could ask…"

"What do you want? I told the police everything I knew about it a long time ago. They didn't do a damn thing about it."

"I know Charlie. I have nothing to do with the police. As I said I am doing some research and there were a few pieces of information I did not see in the report that I thought you or one of the others in the boat that day might be able to help me with."

"What are you hoping to accomplish with this research?"

"There were similar cases where electrical storms were in progress or somehow involved and I am trying to see if there is any correlation between it and the disappearances."

"Ahhh… alright. I'll help if I can. What do you need to know?"

"I know Richard, your brother, was driving the boat and you were the flagman. So I assume you had the best view of what happened."

"Yeah, that's right. I was watching Jen finish up a set. She had stopped to look back at the storm which was coming up from behind us pretty fast. Those summer storms always popped up in the late afternoon for some reason. Anyway, this one had a lot of lightning with it. The lightning was pretty active and Jen gave the thumbs up to try and out run it. I leaned over to Rick and told him to nail it. Just as I looked back I saw a huge lightning bolt strike close to the shore behind her and on her right. Everyone in the boat felt it. I even felt the hair stand up on my head and arms. Next thing I knew the rope handle was bouncing in the water and Jen's ski shot out to the left. We thought she fell and turned back to get her. We couldn't find her anywhere. At first I thought the current pulled her under a log or something but there were no ripples in the water like there usually is when a log is lodged below the surface. We found her bathing suit floating, not too far from where we picked her ski up."

"How far back was she from the boat?"

"Jen skied on a pretty short rope. I think she was skiing on a sixty five foot line that day."

"Can you describe the lightning bolt to me?"

"Like I said, it was huge. I'd never seen one that close and that big before."

"What did it look like?"

"What did it look like? It looked like a damn lightning bolt."

"I mean was it angular similar to a normal lightning bolt or did it have an unusual shape? Did anything about it strike you as abnormal?"

"I was kind of weird. It was, for the most part, a pretty straight flash of light. It was slightly angled to the west, but for the most part, straight. It was real thick too. It looked like it may have been four feet wide. Kind of like a giant white telephone pole leaning slightly to the right. Why is this important?"

"Like I said, I am investigating electrical disturbances in relation to disappearances. You are the first person I have talked to. Do you or can you estimate how far she was from the lightning bolt?"

She was hanging out to the side of the wake and like I said it hit close to the shore so maybe thirty to forty feet. You think this may have had something to do with Jen's disappearance?"

"That is what I am trying to determine."

"What else do you need to know?"

"When you found her bathing suit and ski were there any signs of burn marks on them?"

"No, none. It looked as though she had just taken them off and let them go in the current. Is that important?"

"It could be. It is very early in my investigation to place any importance on any of these details."

"Well, I'd like to know what you find out and I'll help in anyway I can."

"Thank you. Just one more question."

"Shoot."

"Can you recall any strange letters, phone calls, strangers, inquiries regarding Miss Tomas before or after the incidence?"

"What do you mean?"

"I mean has anyone tried to contact you about Jennifer that struck you as very strange or misplaced?"

"This might sound weird but when I was younger, about sixteen, I got a weird phone call from some older chick. She claimed she was taking some kind of survey on the belief in time travel and did I think it was possible or not. She said she was doing research for a book she was writing."

"Why would someone call a sixteen year old boy about time travel," Raj asked.

"I was a big fan of science fiction and subscribed to several magazines. On occasion I got calls about new magazines or books and being the sucker I was I usually bought them."

"Why did you think this particular call was strange?"

"She called me 'CJ' twice."

"Was that unusual?"

"Yes, since there were only three people that call me that. My brother Rick, Jeff Becker, and Jen. There was something else. Around that same time I kept seeing this woman just about everywhere I went for little more than a week. Then I never saw her again."

"Why is that significant?"

"She looked a lot like Jen but she was in her forties. The only reason I remembered was because she looked like she could have been Jen's twin sister. I never spoke to her. It just seemed like she was following me. Then, like I said, she was gone. Jokingly, I told Jen I saw her twin sister walking around town but we never saw her again."

"Well, thank you for taking the time to talk with me Charlie."

"Did any of this help? I mean did you find what you were looking for about the weird things I mean?"

"Yes. That is exactly the kind of things I was asking for. If you remember anything else please call me. Again, I am at T.C. Labs and my number is, are you ready?"

"Yes, go ahead."

"619-555-2000 extension 9390"

"I sure will. Thanks Doc."

"Thank you Charlie. Good bye."

Raj wrote notes in Jennifer's file for about ten minutes then got on the phone again.

"Al! Good, you are in. This is Raj. I need you to do me a favor and get me everything you can find on a Jennifer Amber Tomas."

"Just something I am working on."

"Just Southern California for now."

"How about 1965 to 1990." Raj had estimated the years based on the information Charlie gave him.

If Jennifer was indeed a victim of Mother Nature's time travel she must have gone back to somewhere between 1965 and 1970 because if she were in her forties when Charlie was sixteen and being twenty-nine when she disappeared, that would place her there around that time period.

"What ever turns up. Send it all."

"Great! Al, could you rush it for me?"

"Thank you."

Pomona, California – Rajiv Ramakrishnan
September 1970

Raj had returned from his summer vacation in India to an apartment next to the college. He had rented it in advance before his trip. He was so happy to have been able to spend the last 2 months with his family but was eager to get back to his studies. Raj had a full year planned working and studying with his mentor and professor Dr. William Fetzberg in the physics department.

His time last year, with the Weston's, was a great experience. He learned more about American life from the kids than he could have learned from all of the books ever written on the subject. He felt he had become fully Americanized. J'Dub, the oldest boy, and Raj became very close. They spent hours talking in Raj's room about India, Raj's boyhood pranks and stories, and Raj's studies at the college. When Raj talked J'Dub would correct his accented pronunciation of English words. By the end of the year Raj had mastered the English language with the constant corrections from J'Dub to which Raj was grateful now. Raj promised to write and stay in touch with all of them this coming year. He planned to call them next week after he got settled into his new apartment.

Raj walked to the Registration building at Cal Poly to sign up for his second year of classes. The lines were long but he expected them to be. His plans this year were to hit Statistical Methods in Engineering and Physics, Managerial Statistics, Analytical Geometry and Calculus, Organic Chemistry, Geometric Dimensioning, and what ever else he could work into his busy schedule of studies. He knew the other students wouldn't be fighting to get in line for these courses. As a matter of fact the college had a hard time getting enough people to register for these types of classes as it was. But, with five or more they usually started the class hoping for student adds to get the numbers up. To help break up his hectic studies, he took a part-time job as a waiter at the 'Off Campus Bar and Grill'. Now if he could manage such a chaotic schedule he'd be in good shape.

Vail Hospital, Colorado – Wyatt Coleman
March 1970

Just after 1:00 am, Wyatt moved around in the darkness of his room putting on the clothes he had taken from the patient next door earlier that day. He found a wallet in the breast pocket of the jacket and there were a couple hundred dollars and credit cards in it. He needed to get as far away from Vail as possible before morning or at least somewhere Officer Buckley couldn't find him. He kept the wallet and made a mental note he would return it along with the money and cards as soon as he could. The Colorado driver license inside of it was for James Allan Bolaire born February 15, 1931. He quickly did the math in his head and deduced James would be 39 years old if this was indeed 1970.

"Sorry Jim," Wyatt whispered as he looked toward the patient's room.

Wyatt finished dressing. The pain was killing him but he kept going. He needed a crutch or something to lean on to help take the weight off of his broken leg. Having one arm in a sling didn't make it any easier. He hobbled his way to the door and peered out looking both ways to see if anyone was in the hallway. At that moment there was no one. He ducked back into his room and made the bed look as though he were still in it and asleep in case someone walked by after he had gone. He didn't want to alert the staff he was gone any sooner than necessary.

He was just about ready. He quietly went through the next door patient's room one more time to see if he could find anything useful to lean on. There was nothing there he could use. He hobbled back to his room.

"OK Wyatt, suck it up," he whispered to himself as he exhaled from a deep breath.

Wyatt took several more deep breaths then started toward the door but froze in mid step. He heard voices approaching. Someone was coming. "SHIT," he breathed aloud. He quickly slid in behind the door leaving it half open and held his breath. Two nurses walked by his room and looked through his half opened door. One of the nurses paused then pushed his door open just a little more as she surveyed the monitors and IV. The door had stopped just as it touched the tips of his toe. She looked at the patient then around the room. After a long pause she let the door go then continued walking down the hall. He waited a moment longer before exhaling then moving out from behind the door he cautiously peered out and watched as they turned the corner at the end of the hall. He hopped through the doorway and went in the opposite direction.

At the end of the hall were a set of double doors which stopped him. He pushed them slightly open to peer through and saw the way was clear. Once through the doors he hopped using the wall as much as he could to help support himself. So far no one was around. Sweat was beginning to form large droplets above his brow. The pain in his leg and arm were like electrical currents shooting up and down his body. Reaching another set of doors again Wyatt peered through and noticed an office area where a young woman was on the phone talking. She was turned facing away from his direction and probably wouldn't notice him if he move slowly past the office. Walking was not going to happen without making too much noise so he decided to crawl. As he bent down it was all he could do to fight the urge to groan from the pain in his leg as he moved it into an awkward position with the cast on. He managed to get it into a position he could maneuver around in. He could see another hallway up ahead on the right. As he crawled past the nurse he rounded the corner and spotted the elevator. He knew he was on the second floor from the view out of the window in his room. Wyatt pulled himself up to his feet and hit the elevator button. The door dinged and opened immediately. Wyatt jumped back but no one was inside. He went in then fell to the back wall and rested a moment before pressing the Lobby button.

The elevator was very slow which gave Wyatt time to catch his breath and wipe away the sweat from his forehead. Again, the elevator dinged and the door opened. He carefully looked out to see if it was clear. Over to his right were two people sleeping in chairs in the Lobby area and a security guard sitting at his station watching a portable black and white TV. They did not look in his direction. Wyatt was not sure how he would get by the guard without making too much of a commotion. He leaned back in the elevator to think. He looked out again. Then he saw them, leaning against the wall by one of the people sleeping in the Lobby, a pair of crutches. He needed those crutches.

The front door was way over to the right of the Lobby and the guard was straight across from Wyatt's location. Unfortunately, the crutches were against the wall between the guard and the front door. He had to move fast before someone discovered he was missing from his room. Sucking up every ounce of strength and energy he could Wyatt walked upright on both legs as smoothly and slowly as possible in order to not draw attention to himself and to not distract the guard from his TV.

The pain was incredible and Wyatt thought he was going to pass out a couple of times before reaching the crutches. The young lady sleeping next to the crutches stirred. Wyatt stopped only for a second, she settled then he grabbed the crutches and headed for the exit door. Every step was more painful than the previous one. He could feel himself getting light headed and was fearful he would faint or stumble before he made it out the door. Finally reaching the door he leaned on it to catch his breath. The guard started to turn toward the door trying not to miss what he was fixated on with the TV and quickly glanced at the door. Wyatt had already pushed the door open and walked out. The guard only saw the door closing as though someone had just walked out. He didn't give it much attention and went back to his TV.

The ice cold air slapped Wyatt in the face and snapped him out of his weakened state. He got a sudden burst of energy and put a crutch under each arm and began to walk out toward the street. The crutches were set up for someone much shorter than he but it would do for now. The pain in his leg began to subside in the cold air. Wyatt was having a hard time using one of the crutches because of his broken arm. He wrapped his thumb around the handle and got the hang of it in short order. There was a light snow falling and the sidewalks had been plowed earlier in the evening so he could see where it was. He noticed the street sign up ahead, Meadow Drive.

It was a short walk down the deserted street until he reached Vail Road.

From there he could see the freeway a short distance to the left. He turned and continued to walk toward it. He looked up and saw the moon shining through the clouds. It helped light his way making it less likely he would trip over something. He walked through the underpass and headed up the onramp of the freeway. He could here cars and trucks driving by but not too frequently.

Wyatt stopped to adjust the crutches then walked about a half mile before a trucker saw him and pulled over to offer him a ride. Wyatt was shivering and the warmth inside the rig was a welcome feeling.

"Where ya headed buddy," the trucker asked yelling over the noise of the diesel engine.

"California," Wyatt replied.

"I'm headed to Salt Lake so that'll get ya bout half way."

"Thanks. I was beginning to wonder if I would get a ride or not."

"Well, what the hell are ya doin out in the cold in the middle of the night anyway? Ya must need to git to California real quick or ya need to git out a Colorado real quick. Which is it?"

"I need to get to California. I have some business to take care of right away."

OK buddy. I believe ya. Let's get ya outta that cold and git ya there.

The truck went through its gears and was passing the Minturn exit when the trucker announced, "JJ."

"What," Wyatt replied somewhat confused by the statement.

"JJ. That's my handle. My name. Who might you be," he asked Wyatt looking at the cast on his leg.

"Jim."

"Well Jim, it's gonna be a long drive. Ya look like hell and could probably use some sleep."

"I'm completely worn out."

"I bet ya are. Why don't ya catch some Z's and we kin talk bout those injuries ya have later. I'd like to know what kind of trouble I might be gittin myself inta."

"There's no trouble but yes we can talk about all of this later."

"OK buddy. Git some sleep."

Wyatt leaned back in his seat and rested his head against the window. The familiar movement of the truck rocked him to sleep almost immediately. He would figure out what to tell JJ after he could think more clearly.

Anaheim, California – Jennifer "Kari" Tomas
September 1970

With transcripts in hand proving she had an Associates degree in business from Fullerton Junior College Kari (Jennifer) walked through the parking lot of Cal Poly, Pomona, toward the registration building to enroll in the business classes she needed in order to work on her Bachelor's degree.

The lines were long but the excitement of the students created a charged atmosphere of energy and this excited Jennifer too. She looked at the handwritten banners over the tables at the front of each line. Some of the lines had department names like Psychology, Chemistry, Physics, etc., written on the banners but they were across the promenade. The other lines for registering were in alphabetical order by last name with A – D, E – H, I – L, and so on. She subconsciously jumped in the line marked R – U. A moment later she remembered her last name was now Davis and moved to the correct A – D line. Feeling somewhat silly and uncomfortable she looked around to see if anyone had noticed. She saw a young, what looked like, Indian student looking at her. She smiled and gave him an embarrassed wave-off then turned to face the banners as if she knew what she was doing. As she turned she bumped into the man standing in front of her and almost fell to the ground. He grabbed her and was able to stabilize himself and her. He leaned on his cane to balance himself then quickly apologized to her thinking he had somehow bumped into her. She assured him it was her fault. They politely accepted each others apologies and went back to their business at hand.

Pomona, California – Rajiv Ramakrishnan
September 1970

Raj noticed an older girl moving into the A – D registration line then looked his way and made eye contact with him. *"Why was this pretty girl looking at me,"* he wondered in surprise. She smiled. Usually, Raj was treated like a geek by most of the women on campus and they laughed at him whenever he would try to make conversation with them. He smiled back and she nodded, half waved and turned back in line. Raj had to laugh as she almost knocked the gentleman in front of her over. He was leaning on a walking stick and the two of them almost fell but didn't. He understood her awkwardness because he was a new student last year and felt lost his first day too. She seemed to be a nice girl. Unlike most of the other women on campus she actually made him feel like a regular guy when she smiled at him. He truly felt, for a moment, like he was a normal American student. He liked that feeling. He knew this was going to be a great year.

El Monte, California – Elisaio "Ravin" Munoz
Christmas 1984

"Ho, ho, fucking ho, you piece of mierda," Ravin yelled as he stood over the body of his former employer. "You stupid asshole! You never give up the names of your suppliers to anyone you stupid fuck. I only smacked you around a little bit you baby and you start spilling their names. That's why you just lost your business. This is my business now. Entiende? You must think I'm stupid, huh Arturo? Treat me like some piece of dog shit you mother fucker! Who's the dog shit now pendejo," Ravin asked screaming then kicked the man in the face a couple more times.

Arturo looked up at Ravin with blood pouring from his nose and mouth and begged Ravin to forgive him. He pleaded, "You can have the business Ravin. I'll help you. I'll get you anything you need man."

"I have everything I need now asshole," sneered Ravin then he pulled a pistol from the back of his pants and shot his ex-employer in the head killing him instantly. He had completed the final phase of his plan and finally had his own business. He had no one else to answer to and there was no one left in his way. He had his connections in South America and Mexico now, and he had total control over Los Angeles and the San Gabriel valley.

Jav was surprised at how ruthless Ravin had become in such a short time. He had never seen him so calm and callus about killing someone. During his entire life, up to the point where Ravin went to prison, he admired Ravin because he was so smart and level headed but now he was different. Something had changed and it scared him but he trusted Ravin enough to know what he was doing.

"Jav, I want to meet with all of our dealers tonight. Entiende? I need to make it very clear I am the new Jefe now and if some of these vatos don't like it I'll get rid of them now. This is my hood and nobody is going to get in my way."

"Sure Ravin. I'll get them together."

"Call me Jefe. Everyone will call me Jefe from now on. You got it man?"

"OK Rav… Jefe."

Jav didn't know what to think. Maybe Ravin was just pumped up after killing Arturo or he was really speeding from all of the cocaine he had been using lately. He left Ravin in the alley standing over his kill staring at the wall with clenched fists breathing hard like a bull in the ring just after it gored the matador. *"Life would definitely be different now,"* thought Jav.

* * * * * * * *

In an old warehouse on Rowland Avenue in the industrial section of El Monte all of the top level dealers from the San Gabriel Valley and the Los Angeles basin were present except two from East L.A. They made it very clear they would not attend because they would not work for Ravin under any circumstances. This infuriated Ravin when Jav told him earlier of their response to being summoned to this meeting. Ravin made arrangements to deal with them at the right time then everyone would know he meant business with this takeover.

"Buenos nochas, Amigos," announced Ravin in a loud voice. Everyone quieted and turned in his direction. "Gracias! I am very happy you have joined me here tonight for this very important meeting. I know some of you have come a long way and I know too you have taken great risks in coming together like this. I will keep this short." He climbed up on some pallets. "Our former employer has met with a serious accident and has asked me to take over his end of the business from this day on. As far as you men are concerned business will continue pretty much as usual. I only have a few minor changes I will insist on." He folded his hands behind his back and gazed out over his newly acquired employees. "Any product you need must go through me with no exceptions. Next, from this day forward you must never use my real name. I will be referred to as Jefe from now on. This will protect you and it will protect me from the D.E.A. and the FBI. Last, I don't care how you run your businesses. That is completely up to you. But, I do care that you meet your quotas. The price of our product is going to go up over the next few years, Coca more than the others. There's a lot of money to be made and I intend on cashing in on this market. I am in this for the money my friends as are you. If you are not, then get out now. If you do what I ask I will help you when the heat is on and I will protect you. With that said does anyone have any questions?" He peered out over the men and looked very arrogant in his demeanor.

"Who the fuck are you vato to tell us we have to deal only

with you," someone yelled from the crowd.

"I am Jefe. I am your new patrón. I am your only source to the product coming in from across the border and believe me gentlemen you do not want to get on my bad side. So trust me when I say this is not up for negotiation," Ravin proclaimed in a self-important manner.

"This is bullshit man! We don't need you asshole. I have my own connections through East Lo vato," yelled another man.

"Ahhh yes. East Lo," Ravin chuckled with a smile. He nodded to one of his guards. "I thought someone might think that rumor was true." A door off to the left opened up where two men tied and gagged were brought in naked. Most everyone recognized them immediately as their associates from East Los Angeles. "You were saying something about East Lo amigo."

"What kind of shit is this you fucking asshole? You can't do this," the man shouted in a concerned tone.

"I can and I have. This, my friends, is what will happen to you if you try to go outside of my business." Without warning, Ravin walked over and shot both of the men in the back of the head killing them instantly. Several of Ravin's guards stepped forward with guns to protect him. Shock and acknowledgement was apparent on everyone's face. "Now, do you have any other questions or concerns my friends? Good. I look forward to doing business with all of you."

Ravin walked out of the warehouse. He knew he would have to look over his shoulder from this point on but he was prepared to do just that. To help protect him he had started building a force of body guards with some of his old homies from his childhood gang. There was no going back now.

TC Laboratories, California – Dr. Rajiv Ramakrishnan PhD.
February 2006

"There's just one more left on the list, Elisaio Guillermo Munoz. He's definitely around. He's been in the news and is in constant trouble with the law. I haven't been able to make contact with him yet. My gut tells me we should drop him from the list. I have a feeling he's nothing but trouble," Tim declared to Raj as he fumbled through his notes.

"What have you got on him so far," Raj asked.

"Well, we know he did seven years of a fifteen year sentence in an Arizona prison outside Yuma and was released in November of 1991. He was arrested and convicted for transporting drugs into the U.S. with the intent to sell. He lives near his hometown of El Monte, California and has been in and out of the news for suspicion of murder and drug dealings for many years."

"Why is he on the list," Raj questioned not hearing any facts indicating Mr. Munoz might be one of their candidates.

"In doing my research on him I found that while he was in prison for seven years, which I confirmed with the Arizona prison authorities, he was also in several news articles in the L.A. Times for being a suspect in three murders a little more than a year after he was incarcerated in 1984. I looked through some old news archives for the next several years after that and he turned up several more times with respect to his suspected dealings with drug cartels in South America. We know he can't be in two places at once. So, I'm pretty sure he is one of our time travelers."

"Very good Tim! He is someone we definitely need to talk to. Let me take over trying to track him down. I need you for another task right now."

"He's bad news doc. I think we should drop him from the list."

"Let me look into a couple of things and if I get nowhere then we will drop him."

"Alright, I guess so. So, what are these other tasks you want me to start on?"

"I want you to track down some old maps and building plans for this area, specifically buildings that were here before TC bought the land and built the complex. Depending on what you come up with I may have a test I want to conduct that could very well provide a huge piece of information that would accelerate the progress of our other tests. Can you get on that right away?"

"Sure doc. What kind of test?"

"I will let you know after I see the maps and plans."

"OK. I'm on it." Tim ran out of the lab.

Raj opened Mr. Munoz's file and read through all of the notes Tim had written about him and reviewed all of the documents that accompanied the notes. Raj's gut feeling told him he should drop this guy from their list too as Tim suggested but his case was definitely puzzling and needed further study. Raj picked up the phone and dialed.

"Al? Raj. Hello."

"I received it today. Thank you. Unfortunately, I have not had time to look through it. I do appreciate your getting it to me so quickly. I have another one for you to track down."

"No, this one is a little different. I know where he is but I need a complete file on him and I need to know how to get in touch with him to set up a meeting."

"You could say that but not in a popular way. He is a known criminal or at least has been accused of several crimes but I do not think there have been any convictions in the last twenty years."

"No no. I just need to talk to him and nothing more. He has some information I need and I would like to talk face to face with him. Can you arrange it?"

"Great! Let me know when you have it set up."

"Good. I will talk to you then. Good bye."

Raj hung up the phone and made a few notes in the file. When he finished he looked at the package Al sent him on Jennifer Tomas. Most of the people on the list were either ruled out or there was not enough information to be found. He had six pretty solid leads:

1. Jennifer Tomas disappeared August 1992 from Blythe California. Strangely enough there was a police record of a Jennifer Tomas being arrested in Blythe California in April 1968. No record of her after that;

2. Christopher Stevens disappeared in August 2001 from Las Vegas Nevada and through checking finger printed John Does a match was found where the victim was struck by an automobile and killed in 1988. He is still listed as John Doe LV882194;

3. Sherrie Poole disappeared from her backyard in 2004 in Casa Grande Arizona and through Jane Doe records a match was found for a victim that had committed suicide in December 1993. She is still listed as Jane Doe AZ930102;

4. Wyatt Coleman was reported as missing by a trucking firm he worked for. He disappeared in October 1999 from an area now known as the Eisenhower Tunnel in Colorado. Again, oddly enough Law enforcement records from 1970 showed the Colorado police had an APB in effect for several months on a Wyatt Coleman. He was never found and there is no record of him after that. A copy of the file had been requested but had not arrived at this time;

5. Elisaio Munoz disappeared in November 1991 and there is compelling data to prove he showed up again sometime late in 1984. The data is incomplete as to where or when he disappeared. The assumption is it was the same date he was released from prison and somewhere in Arizona. Waiting to interview;

6. Robert Niesen disappeared in July 1998 from Demming New Mexico and records of a person with the same name, currently in a psychiatric ward in Albuquerque, indicate he was admitted in 1985. He is diagnosed as a paranoid schizophrenic. He has been heavily sedated throughout his hospitalization and is not coherent. No additional information obtainable.

Raj opened the package on Jennifer Tomas and began to sort through the documents and photos inside. *"Al is very thorough,"* thought Raj as he began to read through the files. Facial recognition data from DMV files show a ninety six percent match to a Kari Lynn Davis. Raj looked at the photo of Ms. Davis and was startled for a moment. She looked very familiar to him but could not place where or why she would be. He shrugged it off and kept reading. He grabbed the last known picture of Jennifer and held them up together. They looked very similar but the age difference made it hard to tell. Jennifer was twenty eight in this photo and Kari was thirty six. The hair color and style were different and Kari was wearing glasses. "Could be," Raj mumbled to himself as if to lend credence to it. He continued reading.

Ms. Davis owned several fine dining restaurants in the Orange County area of Southern California. Bank records indicate she was very successful with the restaurants and stock investments. Her last known residence was Carbon Canyon in a very secluded area. MBA graduate from Cal Poly Pomona.

Raj laughed thinking how weird it was they had the same alma-matre then he noticed she graduated in 1974 while he was attending there. He wondered if he had ever seen her and looked at her picture again. She looked very familiar but he really couldn't say for sure. Business and Physics are different majors and he doubted they would ever have had any classes together.

She sold off all of the restaurants in 1980 and cashed in all of her investments. All records of Kari Lynn Davis ceased to go beyond that point in time. Raj knew this would require additional digging. He had a contact with the FBI and would call in a favor to have them follow up on this.

THREE

San Bernardino County Records – Tim MacCorrmack
February 27, 2006

Tim had spent the last four days going through hundreds of old site maps for the Twenty Nine Palms area where TC Laboratories was now standing. The property had been occupied twice before TC Enterprises bought it. First, by General Patton where he had several buildings constructed to serve as his command center in 1942 in order to train troops in preparation for the war in North Africa. Then in 1952, by the marines, the military converted the buildings to house temporary offices for the Marine Corps Air Ground Combat Center (MCAGCC). Twenty five years later the MCAGCC moved in to newer buildings on the base. In 1980, portions of the outer areas of the Marine base were sold off for commercial use. TC Enterprises bought most of it and started construction on the new buildings immediately. All of the old buildings were eventually destroyed. The TC Laboratories division was the last complex constructed on the exact site the MCAGCC had once occupied approximately twenty years earlier.

"I don't know what the hell Raj wants me to look for," Tim told himself as he tried to sort out all of the site maps and plans before him. *"Raj did say to limit it to the site where TC Laboratories was located,"* he thought and that is exactly what he had laid out on the table.

Tim studied the maps trying to figure out what Raj might have in mind but he could not come up with any reasonable explanation. The only things he could see were most of the buildings had been converted to warehouse

71

storage before the property was sold. "Oh well," he sighed as he gathered them up and went to the copy machine.

Cal Poly, Pomona – Wyatt Coleman
August 27, 1971

"We need to stop meeting like this. People are beginning to talk," Wyatt spoke interrupting the young lady standing ahead of him in the registration line.

"I beg you pardon. Do I know you," asked the young lady with a smile of embarrassment as if she should know the man.

"Last year, at this same time. You almost knocked me over in line. I caught you and apologized," he informed her.

"Oh my God, yes. That was you? I am so sorry about that. It was my first day here and I was …."

"It's OK," he stopped her. "It was my first day too. I wanted to talk to you but I could see you weren't really up to it. I saw you a couple of times during the year and was going to say hello but I didn't."

"Oh, I wish you would have. I never really did thank you for saving us both from total humiliation."

"It was my pleasure. My name is Jim, Jim Bolaire and you are?"

"I'm sorry, Kari. Kari Davis"

"It's very nice to meet you Kari. So, you're back for another year?"

"Yes, I'm working toward my MBA. I own my own business and I'm having a little trouble managing it but I think I'm getting the hang of it. So, what about you? You're back again. What's you're story," she inquired.

"Me, I'm just here to save young ladies from making total fools out of themselves."

Jennifer laughed and looked away still embarrassed by the incident. "OK! I admit it. I'm a klutz. You could have just let me fall and you'd be off the hook."

"No, no, no. Then I couldn't enjoy watching you blush," he teased.

"Alright! You win. I'm definitely blushing. Am I forgiven now?"

"Yes, I forgive you," Wyatt conceded, very please with himself.

For the past year Wyatt had been living as Jim Bolaire. He tried to make contact with the real Jim Bolaire only to discover he had passed away at the hospital in Vail shortly after Wyatt left. Wyatt was sorry he had taken the poor man's money but this was a perfect opportunity for him to keep his new found identity. He wrote the family and claimed to be a friend who served in the military with Mr. Bolaire and wanted to write an obituary in the armed forces paper, hoping the man served in the military. His assumption was correct and the family wrote back supplying him with all of the details. Wyatt was then able to get the documents he needed to assume the life of Jim Bolaire. He managed to get a California drivers license by using the Colorado license he took from Mr. Bolaire. By soaking the license in soapy water he was able to cause just enough damage to the picture of James Bolaire to make it difficult to see the picture was not of Wyatt. At the DMV Wyatt watched the clerks and chose one who didn't seem to be too concerned about doing a careful job. Wyatt got the license converted to a California license with no problem. He had a copy of the man's birth certificate and social security card, which he had just received in the mail, and was ready to produce it if the clerk asked for it but she never did. On that day he officially became James Allan Bolaire.

Wyatt too had made several investments during the past year and was in pretty good shape financially. He was able to live very comfortably on the dividends he received from those investments. He hired a company to invest half of his earning into new companies and he lived off of the other half. With some direction from him he managed to turn his net worth into several million in a short time.

His original reason for attending college was to try to get some scientific perspective on what might have caused him to travel back in time. He attended several physics classes but they didn't provide any valid explanation. They did however provide some answers to how this could be possible but there was no way this could be done by man with its current technology. It only confirmed what he already knew that it was a freak of nature and he was at the wrong place at the wrong time. Wyatt accepted the idea and decided this year in school he would concentrate of getting a business degree, rebuild his life, and not repeat what he did in his past life.

"So, what classes do you recommend? I have just this moment decided to change my major to business," Wyatt grinned looking at his class catalog.

Jennifer laughed then looked at his scribble marks on the catalog.

He jokingly pointed to the catalog, "I was thinking of taking…"

Industry Hills, California—Dr. Rajiv Ramakrishnan
March 1, 2006

"Welcome to my home doctor," Ravin greeted and directed Raj to a very large living room. "It seems you have some very important friends and I am very curious, why does a doctor of science want to meet with me so badly?

Who is this man who uses the FBI to make an appointment with me?" Ravin enunciated every word as if trying to sound smarter than he actually was. He also had an arrogant smile on his face and was strutting around like some important VIP. This irritated Raj right away.

"My assistant did try repeatedly to get in touch with you but to no avail Mr. Munoz."

"Is that this Tim fellow my people have been telling me about?"

"Yes, Tim MacCorrmack. He is one of my associates. I asked him to contact you but he could never get past your people, as you called them, or your voice mail."

"I'm sure you know, with your FBI contacts, that I am a popular and important man. Unless I know who you are or what you want I tend not to respond to such messages. But when my friends in the FBI tell me I need to meet with someone I usually do just to keep them happy."

"Well, thank you Mr. Munoz. I appreciate you taking the time," Raj replied with a little disdain in his voice then took a seat on the huge sofa.

Driving up the long driveway to Munoz's house Raj was sickened by the wealth this man had acquired from his drug dealings and criminal activities. And for this man to parade around the room and speak as if he were an aristocrat or someone important really put Raj off. In the village where Raj grew up there were several men like just like him. Raj and most of the other villagers were treated poorly by these men and Raj had no respect for people like this. Raj knew immediately he did not like this man.

Ravin sat across from Raj in a very large chair that was almost throne like. He could hear in the doctor's voice some contempt for him but he didn't care. "Please call me Jefe. Now, what can I do for you Doctor?"

"Mr. Munoz," Raj emphasized ignoring his proclaimed title. "I have some questions I need to ask you that may seem odd but they are for a study I am conducting on electrical weather phenomena." Raj wasn't too sure how he should ask his first question so he just went right into it. "I have a theory about people who have been caught in electrical storms, lightning storms to be exact, and I believe they may have experienced a rather significant change in their lives as a result of this encounter. Would you have any knowledge of this?" Raj stared at Munoz for some kind of reaction.

Ravin was absolutely floored by the doctor's question and it was all he could do to keep his composure. He gave Raj a condescending smile and declared, "I'm not quite sure I know what you mean Doctor."

It was obvious by the sudden change in Munoz's face and demeanor he knew exactly what Raj meant. Raj didn't like people who played games with him. "What I am asking you Mr. Munoz is, have you ever been exposed to an electrical storm or been in very close proximity to a lightning strike," he asked in a stronger tone again looking into his eyes to see what kind a reaction he would get this time.

Ravin began to fidget in his large chair. "Doctor, I don't know what kind of drugs you have been experimenting with but I have no idea what you are talking about," he stammered crossing his legs then began to nervously tap his foot in the air.

"This is no joke to me sir. I have a feeling you know exactly what I am talking about and I would appreciate an answer."

"What kind of a study did you say this was again, Doctor?"

"Electrical weather phenomena. People who get too close to certain kinds of lightning strikes experience a movement through time and I believe, Mr. Munoz, you know first hand what I am talking about."

Ravin stood up from his chair and walked around behind it looking back at Raj letting out a nervous laugh and obviously getting irritated with this entire conversation. "What makes you think I have first hand knowledge of something like that?"

Raj pulled out a folder from his briefcase and began to pull papers out of it and handed them to Munoz. Elisaio knew immediately what the doctor was showing him. There were news articles about him with circled dates. There were several photographs comparing differences in age and appearance. Then Raj handed him his prison records again with dates highlighted.

"Do you not see anything strange about these?"

"No, I don't. Why don't you explain it to me doctor," Ravin insisted with an irritated tone.

"You were arrested November 21, 1983 for bringing drugs into the U.S. for the purpose of selling. You were convicted January 16, 1984 and sentenced to fifteen years at the Arizona State Prison in Yuma. On January 2, 1985 you were brought in for questioning for the murders of three men during Christmas 1984. Can you explain how you were in a prison cell in Yuma and sitting in an interrogation room with the L.A.P.D. at the same time?"

"That's a mistake. That happened the year before," he fidgeted.

"No, you were in jail in Yuma awaiting trial the year before." Raj shuffled some papers, "On August 1, 1987 you were arrested for drug possession but the charges were dropped because of an illegal search. Can you explain this Mr. Munoz? These prison papers again indicate you were still in Yuma."

"I don't know why your papers show that. The D.E.A. is always trying to stick me with something. Maybe they forged those documents."

Once again Raj shuffled some of the documents around, "Here's a picture of you taken when you were out-processed from the Yuma prison on November 17, 1991 and here's a picture of you obviously several years older at a party in Hollywood on September 8, 1991. How did the D.E.A. forge this?"

"I think you have overstayed your welcome Doctor. I'm afraid I have to ask you to leave." Ravin stood and began walking toward the door.

"I just have one more question to ask you Mr. Munoz. Where were you when the lightning storm sent you back to 1984?"

It was apparent Ravin was very angry and he dismissed Raj, "Thank you for dropping by doctor. Have a nice day." Then he opened the door motioning for Raj to leave.

As Raj walked back to his car he was disappointed he didn't get the information he wanted from Mr. Munoz. He was sure though, after the interview, Munoz was definitely a time traveler and wished he had not let his contempt for this man thwart his objectivity in the interview. This was a propitious corroboration for his theory and made it more apparent to him that he needed to focus more attention on finding Jennifer Tomas.

Cal Poly Pomona – Rajiv Ramakrishnan
May 27, 1974

"… makes time travel quite possible but unfortunately with modern technology we can not travel at the speed of light nor do I see us being able to do so anytime in the near future."

Raj had heard Doctor Fetzberg present this lecture several times before and found it more fascinating each time. In theory traveling faster than the speed of light could create a portal, or door if you will, through which someone or something could pass through thereby sending them to another time. It was simple but technology wise we were hundreds of years away from accomplishing this.

Dr. Fetzberg and Raj had spent many evenings together hypothesizing various scenarios to which time travel could be achieved. Again, all of which were beyond modern capabilities. Raj only hoped that some day he could make a major contribution toward reaching that technology.

Before Raj could begin making his mark in the technological world he needed to complete six more classes in order to complete his PhD. But, he would have to cut his class schedule in half next fall because Mr. Weston had been killed in an accident at his work and Raj offered to help out Mrs. Weston until she got back on her feet. It was the least he could do since they did so much for him when he first arrived here from India.

Next week he would start a new job as a design engineer for a company called General Dynamics which was not far from the college and this way he would be close to both school and the Weston's making it a little easier to juggle all three. It would only take him another full school year to complete his PhD so taking this position would give him another year of low rent at his campus apartment and he could help Mrs. Weston financially before graduating. He was happy to do it.

Cal Poly Pomona – Wyatt Coleman
May 27, 1974

"So, what do you think about time travel Hun? Think it's possible," Wyatt whispered to Kari.

"Oh, I believe it's definitely possible. What about you," Jennifer inquired eager to talk about it for the first time in six years.

Both Wyatt and Jennifer had found out separately about this upcoming lecture on Time Travel several days ago from flyers posted around campus. They both plotted different ways to bring it up in conversation then would try to convince the other to attend it with them.

Wyatt's plan was to wait for it to appear in the campus newspaper then he would make some comment on it to Kari at dinner when they typically discussed items of interest. If she responded, which she usually did, he would ask her if she would like to attend. She probably would agree.

Jennifer too had a plan. She knew it would be in the paper but was unsure how to bring it up to Jim. He commented on most of the articles so she just had to make sure he noticed it. She laughed when she came up with the idea to tape it to her breasts and walk around the kitchen naked. He would definitely notice it, but would it get read? She decided that plan would be too obvious.

When it did finally come out a few days before the lecture she carefully placed the paper on the table with the article right on top hoping Jim would notice it right away. If he did he would read it for a minute or two then say something about it.

Wyatt sat down and saw it immediately. He hadn't seen the paper yet so he tried to think of something quick to say about it. He stuttered mentioning something about an interesting lecture set for this weekend on Time Travel. He suggested they go if they didn't have anything planned.

Jennifer was surprised at how quickly he noticed the article and when he asked about attending she immediately blurted out she would love to. It surprised her when she replied so quickly.

Wyatt was very pleased and surprised at her sudden acceptance. He had already decided he was going to go anyway but was happy he could get her to go with him because he was looking for some way to bring up the topic and tell her about himself.

Jennifer had the same concern.

Nothing more was said about it until that night except for a couple of reminders to each other to keep that evening free. Now, here they both were, listening to Dr. Fetzberg speak about something both of them knew was very possible in this day and age. They both knew Mother Nature had her own technology to make time travel possible.

"Allow me to introduce a student of mine who played a big role in helping me put together this and many other lectures on this subject, Rajiv Ramakrishnan. Rajiv came to us from India in 1969 and when I first met him he really stood out in my classroom asking me question after question, really putting me to the test on whatever topic I was lecturing on. Rajiv, stand up and take a bow please," announced Dr. Fetzberg.

Wyatt had taken several classes with Raj and had many conversations with him about various class projects but he had no idea that Raj was so knowledgeable on this topic. He would have to talk with him further about this in the future.

As the applause quieted Raj sat down and Dr. Fetzberg continued, "Rajiv will be graduating next year with his PhD but for now he is starting a new position with General Dynamic next week and we wish him all the best."

Doctor Fetzberg began his closing statements when Wyatt leaned over to Kari and asked her if she was ready to leave. She nodded yes. They slipped out of the lecture hall and headed for the parking lot toward Wyatt's truck.

"So, what did you think," she asked Jim.

"I think finding the technology to travel through time is a lot closer than they think."

"Why do you say that?"

"I don't know. I just think they are going to find out time travel is a lot more easier, technology wise, than they think."

"What do you know that they don't," Jennifer asked half kidding but knew Jim was so right.

"Some day I'll tell you what I know," Wyatt responded in a joking manner then pulled her close to him.

Jennifer pulled away and looked at Jim. "Tell me now," she demanded with a serious look on her face.

"I don't know what I'm talking about. I'm just playing around," he chuckled half considering telling her right here and now.

"No you're not. Tell me."

He hesitated, "I just have a feeling someone is going to discover time travel in the not too distant future."

She could see he was getting uncomfortable and decided to not press it further, at least for now. She smiled then teased, "If they haven't already but aren't saying."

Not really sure he wanted to continue this conversation in the parking lot he hesitated for a moment then asked, "What do you mean?" He was beginning to wonder where this conversation was headed.

Jennifer leaned in close to him, "What if someone had already traveled back in time. Imagine how hard it would be for them. They would probably have to live here unable to tell anyone for fear they would be labeled as crazy or they felt they were somehow part of an experiment that went wrong. People would have them hospitalized as some sort of nut case."

Wyatt interrupted, "Or someone might consider they were somehow caught up in some sort of natural freak occurrence of Mother Nature."

Jennifer stopped walking and pulled away. "Why would you say that," she asked.

Just coming off the top of his head Wyatt came up with an idea. "What if I was to tell you I heard about someone who claims to have traveled back in time because of a lightning storm he was exposed to? Would you think he was a total nut case or would you be willing to hear his story out?" There it was. His heart was racing. What was she thinking? Did she think he was serious or joking? He waited for her reply.

Very calmly she answered, "I would want to hear his entire story and form my own opinion." She stared into his eyes looking to see if he was serious.

He was relieved. But now what? He thought quickly, "I've had several conversations with someone about this and he truly believes he came from the future. He has quite a story to tell and he's pretty convincing. I almost believe him."

"Can I talk to him and see if I might believe him too," she asked very seriously.

"Yeah sure. I'll see if I can find him and set up a meeting," Wyatt replied breaking eye contact with her. His heart was pounding so hard he thought she would see it through his sweater.

"Alright. Let me know where and when," she stated with very little emotion then continued walking.

They quietly went to the truck and didn't say much the rest of that evening.

* * * * * * * * * *

Two weeks later Wyatt and Jennifer drove to Palm Springs for the phony meeting Wyatt had set up. The drive was lengthy and muted. Wyatt was nervous and Jennifer was quiet. Both of them had been acting strange ever since they decided to set up this meeting after the lecture but the day had finally come. Jennifer wanted to meet this man and see if he had indeed experienced what she had.

They arrived at the hotel an hour before the meeting was to take place. They checked into their room and Jennifer took a hot shower to help calm her self. Wyatt ordered a bottle of wine from room service needing some courage for what he was about to do.

Jennifer came out of the bathroom and saw Jim drinking a glass of wine. He lifted an empty glass asking her if she would like a glass as well. She said, "Please." Wyatt poured her a glass and handed it to her. "How long before he shows up," Jennifer asked.

"Should be any time now," Wyatt answered taking another gulp of his wine. "Come sit down beside me." He patted the cushion next to him on the sofa. She joined him.

After a few minutes of sipping their wine Jennifer asked, "Do you think he'll show?"

"Yes, I'm quite certain of it. As a matter of fact, he's already here."

Jennifer looked around the room for a second then looked back at him.

"I'm sorry I brought you here like this Kari but I didn't want you to not give me a chance to explain and tell you everything before you walk out."

"Go a head. I'm listening," Jennifer capitulated folding her arms and looking a little put out by the deception.

"I'm not quite sure how to explain this. Hell, I'm not real sure how it happened my self. Anyway, here goes." He took the last gulp of his wine. "About four years ago, I was driving in Colorado toward Denver. There was this really bad electrical storm. It was pouring down rain and I was trying to get to Denver before nightfall. As I came out of the Eisenhower Tunnel, which you may not even be aware of as yet, a huge bolt of lightning struck close to or may have even hit my truck. I'm not really sure. Anyway, it threw me from my rig. The next thing I knew I woke up in a hospital several days later."

"What does this have to do with you bringing me here to meet someone who claims to have traveled back in time Jim," Jennifer asked with a perplexed look on her face.

"My name is not really Jim Bolaire. It's Wyatt Coleman and it was 1999 when that lightning bolt threw me from my truck."

There was a long pause. Jennifer did not move or say a word. She just stared at Jim/Wyatt. Tears started to well up in her eyes and she could not take her eyes off of his. He couldn't look away either. Finally she dropped her face down into her hand and began to cry.

Wyatt put his arms around her and she fell into his lap crying. Wyatt didn't know what to do. She cried long and hard. He just kept rubbing her back and saying he was sorry. "I know this sounds crazy but it's true. I've wanted to tell you so many times but didn't know how," he pleaded trying to lift her up but she resisted.

All of these years and she thought she was alone. The emotions inside of her erupted at the news he told her and she broke down. It felt like a tremendous weight had been lifted from her chest and she was able to take her first deep breath. At that moment the love she felt for him consumed her and she knew she could share her secret with him too but not now. This was his time. There would be plenty of time for her later.

Finally after what seamed an eternity to Wyatt, Jennifer looked up, grabbed his face, and gave him a long passionate kiss. Still holding his face she pulled back and looked into his eyes and said, "I love you Jim," then kissed him again.

Wyatt embraced her and pulled her to him relieved he had not lost her. He kissed her several times on the mouth and on her face. "Does this mean you believe me," he asked with an expectant look.

Jennifer smiled and commanded, "Shut up," then pushed him down on the couch. She put her knees on the couch around both sides of him and sat on his lap. She kissed his neck and face and started to unbutton his shirt.

Wyatt was a little surprised but got in the mood quickly. He tenderly reached around her then sliding his hands slowly down the contour of her back he moved his hands inside of her jeans and pulled her into him. She let out a slight moan of pleasure then she began to rhythmically but slowly move her hips on him. She could feel him growing with each movement.

With his shirt opened she leaned down to kiss his chest and suck on his nipples. His response excited her. She sat up and he lifted her blouse off releasing her swelling breasts then took her erect nipple into his mouth. She arched her back and neck welcoming his devouring of her breast. She amplified the undulating movement of her hips up and down on him and could feel him becoming very hard under her. She wanted him inside of her.

Pulling her in tight against him Wyatt picked her up and carried her to the bed. He gently laid her down and began to remove her clothes very slowly, kissing every exposed part of her body as he did. As she lay there nude, Wyatt was completely taken in by her beauty as he always was and leaned down to kiss her. She reached for his pant and unbuttoned them. He helped her pull them down and off then he laid down beside her.

For a moment they just held each other close and looked into one another's eyes. A light tender kiss and they both knew they would always be together. Kissing once again they took each other and made love.

TC Laboratories – Tim MacCorrmack
February 28, 2006

"Great job Tim! This is exactly what I was looking for," Raj praised as he examined the site plans Tim had copied from the county records. "Yes, yes. I think this could work," he mumbled.

"What could work," Tim asked somewhat feeling left out.

"I am sorry Tim. Let me explain why I had you do this. I needed these site plans because I developed a theory I wanted to consider testing. I was thinking we might try to establish a communication link with the past and I think it might work."

"What! That's nuts Doc. How can you communicate with anyone in the past?"

"It is really quite simple Tim. We have a time machine. Am I right? By sending messages through it to the past we can communicate with it."

"But, how do they talk back to us?"

"That is what I want to try to substantiate."

"You lost me Raj. Substantiate what?"

"Let me explain how I expect this to work."

"OK. Lay it on me doc."

Raj smiled at Tim's puerile idiom. "We know we can send objects back to a fairly specific point in time to within a couple of weeks which we have demonstrated through our testing with the time devices. Correct?"

"Correct."

"OK, I asked you to get those site plans because I want to send a message back in time to this location and verify it can be retrieved in our time."

"But, how do we…"

"Hold on Tim. We know this exact location was occupied by the military until TC Enterprises bought the property in 1980. The buildings on this exact site were used as storage until they tore them down in 1985/86 to build this building. We also know, in theory since we have not really tested it yet, this STR8 BOLT model can generate enough energy to send an object back in time about 30 years give or take five. The new STR8-BOLT generator being built next door will increase that to 100 years. I propose sending a message back in time to myself approximately twenty-five years. If I get it I should have an instant memory of it right after we send it."

"Why would you have any memory of receiving a message from yourself when you haven't sent yourself any message yet and you can't remember receiving a message that you haven't sent. God, I can't believe I just said that."

Raj laughed, "The reason I have no memory as of yet is because I have not sent it yet. But once I do send it and I receive it in the past I will suddenly and instantaneously remember receiving it, now, in the present, and who would not remember receiving a message from the future."

"OK, let me get this straight. You can't remember getting a message from yourself because you haven't sent yourself the message yet. But when you send the message you will suddenly remember receiving it in the past."

"Yes, that is exactly it," replied Raj pleased with his explanation.

"Why didn't you say so, I thought this was going to be much more confusing," Tim moaned shaking his head as if he had just been hit.

Smiling, Raj instructed, "OK Tim, this is what I need you to do. Run a model and get the coordinates we need to send a small package back in time as far back as we can before 1980. With the five year margin of error we need our package to arrive before they empty and destroy the old buildings. I also need you to find some vintage postage stamps for that time period. I will prepare the items I want to be included in the package. Let us try to set up a preliminary test in a couple of weeks."

"Whoa! Postage stamps," Tim questioned.

"Yes. If you found a package lying around, unopened, with an address on it would you not take it to the Post Office or try to make sure it got delivered?"

"You're going to mail it to yourself?"

"Yes," Raj replied with a big grin on his face.

Tim left the lab shaking his head.

Industry Hills, California – Elisaio "Ravin" Munoz
March 1, 2006

"I want that son of a bitch dead. You hear me. Dead! He's trouble and I know he's going to fuck me up big time," Ravin screamed at his trusted bodyguard. "I don't care how it's done. I want that mother fucken pendejo dead by April 1st. You hear me. April 1st!"

"Come on Jefe. He's a fucking big time doctor. You kill him and all shit is going to break out man."

"Then make it look like a fucking accident. I don't care. He came into my house and called me a liar. Who the fuck does that cock sucker think he is? I want that asshole dead!"

"OK Jefe. I'll get the doctor killed. I know the right vato to use who can make it look like an accident. I don't understand how this doctor is going to fuck you up. He just asked you some silly questions and you told him you didn't know what he was talking about. End of story."

"He's trouble. I don't want to have to deal with him later. So get it done."

The bodyguard left the room then Ravin paced back and forth cursing the doctor. He was trying to figure out how Doctor Rajiv found out about him and how he could ruin everything he had built up. Could he somehow reverse what has happened? Could he prevent him from going back in time all together? What does this doctor know that could change everything? He told himself he was right. He needed to eliminate the doctor right away and kill any chance of fucking up his life.

"Have you set it up yet," he yelled to his bodyguard who was on the phone in the other room. There was no answer.

* * * * * * * * *

"I know ese, but he's freaking out man. He wants the pinche doctor dead by April first," insisted the bodyguard to someone on the other end of the phone.

"OK. I'll tell him it's done. Don't fuck this up Asesino. It will be both of our asses you know."

"OK. Call me when it's done."

The bodyguard went back into the room where Ravin had just sat down in his chair. "Well. Did you take care of it," Ravin asked.

"Si Jefe. It will be done by the first."

"Good. The sooner, the better."

"I will let you know when it's done."

Ravin nodded then decided he needed to calm down, "OK. Now get the fuck out of here. I need to relax. Send Carmen and Gloria in here then turn the hot tub on."

Palm Springs, California – Wyatt Coleman
June 11, 1974

It was almost noon. Wyatt and Jennifer had slept through the entire morning and would still be asleep if the maid had not awakened then trying to get into their room to clean it. After chasing off the maid Wyatt jumped back into bed and took Jennifer into his arms and said, "Good morning." Jennifer bid him a good morning too. "Sleep OK," he asked her. They both had had the best sleep they've had in years.

"Wonderful," she exclaimed with a beautiful smile as she put her arms over her head and gave out a sensuous moan and stretched. Wyatt was so captivated with her beauty he just stared in awe at her.

"What" she asked looking back at him wondering why he was staring.

"God, you are so beautiful. I am so in love with you and I can't put it into words enough to tell you how much."

"So, what you're saying is if I were ugly you wouldn't love me as much," she asked with a flirtatious grin.

"Oh, you're OK looking. I was talking to myself. I didn't realize you were listening. I'd say you're average cute."

Jennifer gave him a love tap on the shoulder and scolded, "You're mean."

Wyatt grabbed her and pulled her close to him. "OK, I was talking to you. You're beautiful too."

Again, she gave him a light tap on the shoulder then hugged him. "What do you want to do today," she asked. Jennifer had planned to tell Wyatt about her life when they woke up but it was already early afternoon and she knew Wyatt wanted to give her more details about himself. She would have to wait to tell him her story later.

"Let's get up, get some breakfast, and go for a walk." Wyatt wanted to take her out for the day and talk about what he had been through. She threw the covers off of them exposing their naked bodies and playfully teased Wyatt trying to lure him into the shower with her as she crawled off of the bed. It worked.

After breakfast they walked around the town a little bit then decided to take the Palm Springs Aerial Tram to the top of the San Jacinto Mountain and went for a long walk in the pine forest. Wyatt gave Jennifer all of the details of his life and what he went through, how he got out of the hospital in Vail, how he hitchhiked to California, how he made his money, why he went to Cal Poly, everything. He didn't hold anything back and Jennifer just listened, sympathetic to everything he told her.

The day passed by quickly. It was beginning to get chilly so they made their way back to the Tram to descend the mountain. On the ride down Wyatt had finally stopped talking and just held Jennifer close to him and enjoyed the view feeling the warmth of her body close to his. Jennifer could feel him hold on tight and she didn't want him to let go. She loved that security, that feeling of closeness to him. They decided to go back to the hotel, get cleaned up, and go out for a nice romantic dinner. When they got back to the room they decided dinner could wait and made love.

"Thank you for listening to me ramble on all day," Wyatt said in a low voice as they sat down for dinner.

"Thank you for sharing everything with me," Jennifer replied. Everything Wyatt had told her she wanted to say to him like "I know" or "I did the same thing," but she didn't. She knew when the time was right she too would be able to tell him everything but right now was not the time.

"So, what do you think about all of this. I've been talking pretty much non stop and haven't let you say anything. Does all of this sound crazy to you," he asked her.

"No Honey. I don't think it's crazy at all. I've always felt time travel was possible and you are living proof."

"I am so amazed at how easily you accepted what I told you. I think that's what attracted me to you when I first met you. I got the feeling you would be someone I could confide in and would believe me."

"I do believe you Jim and I love that you trusted me enough to tell me."

"So, where do we go from here," he asked.

"I don't know. Do you still want to try and find out how or why this happened?"

"Not anymore."

"Do you want to find a way to fix it and go back?"

"Absolutely not! I love my life here with you. But even if I wasn't with you I'd already exhausted all my efforts on that and I have accepted the fact that I am here to stay."

"I would help you if that's what you wanted?"

"Nope! I'm here with you and I don't want to be anywhere else."

With a sigh of relief Jennifer asked, "What now?"

"I think we need to get away for several months and really get to know each other. You up for it?"

"What did you have in mind?"

"Do you trust me?"

Jennifer nodded yes.

"OK, leave everything to me. I'll make all of the arrangements. All you have to do is show up."

"OK. I'll be there. Just let me know where and when."

"Alright! I'm going to hold you to it."

"It? I would hope you'd do more than hold me to 'it'," she teased with a clever smile.

"Check please," he called out to their waiter.

TC Laboratories – Raj and Tim
March 21, 2006

"It is fine Tim. I would like to narrow down our time difference to a shorter margin if possible. Weeks are more preferable than years but days would be even better," Raj directed as they reviewed Tim's data for the tests they were going to perform in the next week. "We need to do a few more experiments to pin-point the time and output levels but we need to go further back in time to make it more accurate."

"OK. I'll get it set up for tomorrow," Tim complied as he jotted down some notes.

"We need to see what we can do about sending a timer back far enough to gather more accurate data. We also need to find some way to protect the timer to insure it gets back here to this time without interference. Do you have any ideas Tim?"

"I don't know Raj. If we had something that couldn't be moved or opened that was here then and now we could probably do it but I have no idea of what."

"I will think of something tonight," Raj acknowledged as he looked back down at the data. Several minutes later Raj noticed Tim looking around not quite sure what else he could do. He pushed his paperwork aside and called out, "Why do you not go home to your wife. You have been working late almost every night."

"It's OK Raj. She knows I am working on something big."

"I know but I need you fresh tomorrow so please go home to your wife and spend some time with her."

"Are you sure you don't need me?"

"Yes, go home. I will see you in the morning."

"OK Raj. Do you need anything before I go?"

"No my friend. Go."

Tim ran out the door and Raj continued to study the data. After entering several notes in the files he sat back at his desk trying to figure out a way to protect the timer they planned to send back in time to keep it secure until Tim and he could retrieve it. Several ideas came to mind but none were viable. He stared out and around the lab for several minutes then it came to him. He jumped up from his desk and ran to the wall next to the STR8 BOLT generator. He moved his hands along its surface and pounded on different locations. He ran back to his desk, picked up the phone, and dialed a five digit number.

* * * * * * * * * *

When Tim arrived that next morning he saw Raj standing by the STR8 BOLT generator with several maintenance workers hustling about. He noticed that a large section of wall had been removed from the backside of the machine.

"What's going on Raj?"

Raj turned startled at Tim's question. "What are you doing back here so soon Tim?"

"Soon! It's 7:30 in the morning. Were you here all night?"

"Yes, I suppose I was."

"What's going on," Tim asked again as he surveyed the workers.

"I think I figured out how we can secure our timer so we can send it back at least twenty years and retrieve it unharmed."

"I certainly hope so with all of this demolition work going on."

Raj looked around and laughed, "Yes, I would hope so too."

"Do you want to tell me what went on here all night?"

"Of course Tim. Let us grab some breakfast and I will explain all of this to you. I am suddenly very hungry."

With some food and tea in his system Raj let out a satisfied sigh and sat back in his chair.

"OK, can you tell me now what is going on," Tim asked still perplexed by the chaos he witnessed in the lab when he arrived this morning.

"Yes, yes, I am sorry Tim. After you left last night I was trying to think of a way to preserve our timer for a long duration in order for us to gather more accurate data when I saw it."

"Saw what?"

"Your idea about finding something that could not be moved or opened until we needed it."

"And that is…?"

"The wall," Raj declared proudly.

"The wall," Tim questioned.

"Yes, the wall. That wall was put up when they built this building originally in 1985. The other side of the wall was a storage closet. I cut a hole in the wall big enough for the STR8 BOLT generator to be moved over the same position. If we send anything back in time after 1985 from that position it would appear inside the wall. We move the generator back and it should be right there on the floor. No one will have touched it until we do."

Tim realized immediately what Raj had planned, "Good going Doc. The only problem I see now is how do we keep the timer going all of that time until we retrieve it?"

"I thought about that too. With the low drawing power of the timer and the new long life batteries they have now I think we will not have a problem."

"Well, what are we waiting for," Tim asked excitedly.

"You! I need you to enter in the power and time coordinates then we can see what we get. I think we should send the timer back in increments of five years. Each time we increase the years it will give us a more accurate reading on the time and power settings."

"Well, alright then. Get your butt up and let's get to work. Ooops! Sorry Doc. I didn't mean that. Shall we go to work," Tim kidded.

Raj let out a good laugh and they walked back to the lab expecting great results.

* * * * * * * * * *

"I think that should do it Doc. Ten tests with ten different settings should allow us to decrease the margin to within a couple of days."

"Excellent Tim. When can you compile the data and get it back to me?"

"I'll have it ready for you by Friday. We should be able to start sending messages back first thing Monday."

"Wonderful. I will leave you to it then. I think I will call it a day and I will

see you tomorrow." Raj was exhausted and needed to get some sleep.
"Yeah, what are you still doing here? Go home."
Raj smiled at Tim then went out the door.

Twenty Nine Palms, California – Manuel "Asesino" Gutierrez
March 22, 2006

Manuel Gutierrez was a hired assassin who primarily worked for Elisaio Munoz or 'Jefe' as he liked to be called. Manuel was a natural born killer. He grew up watching his mother kill chickens and the occasional pig for dinner just about every day of his life. At the age of four he begged his mother to let him kill his first chicken. It scared and excited him at first but after he did it he cried. She grabbed him and stated, "Everything has to die sometime mijo." She told him, "The death of anything thing is only justified if it is used for the good of the living." He knew what she meant, that killing the chicken was necessary for him and his family to survive, but he developed a taste for killing and modified the justification to include killing people for the good of him or his employer. Hence his nickname 'Asesino' was born, meaning 'Killer'.

Asesino sat outside of the TC Laboratories all night waiting for the Doctor to leave so he could follow him to his home. He liked to spend a few days watching his victims before he killed them. He liked to learn their habits and daily routines. He wanted to know something about them. It was well after noon when the Doctor finally came out of the parking lot. Asesino was beginning to think he had the wrong place but there he was. Asesino had never killed an Indian before and this thrilled him. He wanted to take special care in killing this one.

For the next several days he followed the Doctor to and from work. The Doctor went home just about every night, usually late between 7:00 and midnight, but was always home from 1:00 a.m. to 5:00 a.m. and that was about the only schedule that was fairly certain with this Indian. He decided the killing would have to take place at the Doctors home. That would be best. He would decide how when the time got closer.

After a week Asesino was ready. It was almost time and he needed to make the final preparations.

Diamond Bar, California – Wyatt Coleman
   June 21, 1974

"I don't care what it costs, I just want it done. Call me back when you have our itinerary finalized. Bye." Wyatt hung the phone up somewhat irritated then went out to the kitchen where Jennifer was cooking dinner.

"Who was that," she asked him.

"Travel agency."

"So, we are really going to do this then?"

"Yes. I want this time with you and I think you need it too. Are you going to be able to let your restaurants go for that long?"

"Sharon can handle everything. I trust her completely. When should I tell her I'll be leaving," she asked while preparing their plates.

"I have us leaving July 1st but that can be changed if we need to adjust our plans." Jennifer sold her home in Carbon Canyon and moved in with Wyatt six months ago mostly because they had been spending every available minute together and decided this arrangement better suited them. He had converted one of the bedrooms into an office for her similar to his office. She worked out of the house whenever possible while Wyatt worked from the house all of the time.

Wyatt bought this house within two years of his journey back here because he knew the housing market was going to take a big jump in the near future and his investments were producing large returns. So he bought this place in the 'Country Estates' which was a new gated development in Diamond Bar. The house sat on a couple of acres and it was semi secluded giving him the privacy he preferred.

"Can you tell me where we are going," she asked.

"I thought I'd let you stew a while longer before I tell you."

"See how you are? You are mean." She tossed a cooking mitten at him.

"I'll tell you if you really want to know."

"No. As long as we are together that's all I care about." She continued to prepare their dinner.

"Is everything OK," Wyatt asked as he walked around to where she was standing.

"Yes, fine. I was just thinking how different everything is now."

"How so?"

"Oh, I don't know. Probably because we, I mean you, already know what is going to happen for a good part of the future and we, sorry, you get to relive your life in a way that is, I would hope, better than your last."

"It is 'we' and my life is already a million times better than my last because of you."

"I feel the same way too, that my life is a million times better, because of you."

"Then nothing is going to be different. I'm happy. You're happy. We are together and that's the way it will stay."

She kissed him and asked, "So where are we going?"

Wyatt laughed, gave her a quick hug and proceeded to tell her his plans for the trip.

TC Laboratories – STR8 BOLT laboratory
March 28, 2006

"How will we know if it worked Raj," Tim asked.

"We will have to send several more packages to different times and hope that someone picks one of them up and takes it to the post office. If they open it, it will not mean anything to them so they may feel compelled to deliver it to the local post office. Once they do this, and my theory is correct, I should have an instant recall of it once we send it back. As of right now I have no memory of this package so we can assume it did not get delivered and we should try again."

For the next few days they sent several packages back to various times in the past and with each one Raj did not have any memory of them. These packages simply contained three items and they were addressed to himself in his past. The three items were a current picture of him, a copy of his birth certificate, and a letter explaining what this was all about. Raj knew that his younger self would understand what he was trying to do and keep it to him self.

"I don't know Raj. I don't think this is working," sighed Tim feeling frustrated.

"Yes, something is wrong. I should have had some memory by now. What are we missing," Raj asked scratching his head.

"Maybe we should…"

"Hold on Tim. I have an idea," Raj interrupted as he ran to the phone. He began dialing a number and Tim could not hear what Raj was saying to the person on the other end. When he finished the call he came back to Tim and asked, "Remember when we first sent the test ball back in time successfully?"

"Yeah, I think so."

"How did we prove the ball, or should I say my wallet, went back in time?"

Suddenly realizing what Raj was referring Tim replied, "We had to move

T.E.S.S. because T.E.S.S. was occupying the space we were doing our tests in. But I don't understand what this has to do with what we are doing now."

"Perhaps, there is something occupying this space in the times we have been sending the packages to. Maybe a storage shelf or a stack of boxes or what ever is in this spot." Raj pointed to the generator. "The packages we have sent back are most likely arriving inside of what ever was in this space and that's why no one is finding it."

"OK, so what can we do about it?" Just then a maintenance worker arrived with an electric forklift and Tim knew immediately what Raj had in mind. With the modifications they made to the STR8 BOLT generator over the last several months it became larger than T.E.S.S. had been originally and required something with a little more muscle to move her around. They finished moving the STR8 BOLT generator to another location in the lab and set it up to try several more tests.

Finally, after moving the machine several times, it was late, almost Midnight, on March 31st. Raj and Tim sent one final package for the day back and Raj suddenly got a little light headed. Tim grabbed Raj by the arm to help support him and asked if he was OK. Raj began to smile and chuckle then replied, "Yes." He suddenly recalled receiving a package when he was in the first year of his employment here at TC Laboratories. "Tim, we did it. I remember getting this package. I received it on September 9th 1988 my first year here." Raj could not stop smiling. The feeling of suddenly realizing he had communicated with himself in the past was exhilarating. The benefits from this could be limitless.

"Tim, we need to get all of this data recorded and processed tonight before we go. I want to go over all of it tomorrow and be ready to do more tests on Monday. We have some serious work to do next week."

"Oh hell, it's only Midnight. I wasn't going to go to sleep anyway. I'll get on it right away. What are we going to do with all of this now that we know it works?"

"I have not thought that far ahead yet Tim. That is what you and I need to talk about next week. We need to brainstorm and see what kind of possible uses we might have for this."

"I'll get this recorded and start the processing then let it run through the night. I'll come in early and make sure it's done so we can look at it first thing in the morning."

"Very good my friend. Excellent job today," Raj commended Tim patting him on the shoulder

For the next 90 minutes they both attended to their own tasks then called it a night.

Twenty Nine Palms, California – Manuel "Asesino" Gutierrez
April 1, 2006

It was 1:45 a.m. and the Doctor was just leaving the TC Laboratories parking lot. Asesino had been waiting since 6:00 p.m. to fulfill his contract on the Doctor. His plan was to follow the good doctor home then early in the morning break into his home and kill him, making it look like a burglary gone bad, but this was even better. *"Early in the morning, on a deserted highway, what could be more perfect,"* he thought

There was an area on Highway 62, heading toward Palm Springs, which was notorious for fatale accidents. He was an expert at running people off of the road and causing their deaths. Everything was falling into place as if it were fated. Knowing how much Jefe had this thing about killing people on holidays, Asesino wanted the killing to be executed on April Fools Day. He knew Jefe would appreciate the humor in it.

The drive from Twenty Nine Palms to Yucca Valley seemed to pass by quickly mostly because there was very little traffic at that time of night and they were able to drive just over the speed limit. He remained far enough behind the doctor so as not to arouse any suspicion. It would only be a few more miles before they started down that steep grade toward Interstate 10 and Asesino was getting energized.

At the right moment he would pass the Doctor and force him to run off the road down into one of the deep crevices along that stretch of highway ending the Doctors life. He could feel the adrenaline beginning to rush through his body. This was the best part about killing someone, the Adrenaline Rush.

"Here we go," he said to himself as they headed down the steep grade. He pulled up close behind the Doctor almost on top of him causing the doctor to increase his speed. "You read my mind Amigo," he called out talking louder now. He inched forward closing the gap between their two cars and it was obvious the Doctor was getting nervous. He was beginning to weave ever so slightly. "Ah si, si. You feel it too, don't you my friend?" Their speed was increasing even more. The sharp turn Asesino was waiting for was just up ahead. "OK Amigo. This is where you and I become espiritues pariente." Asesino pulled out to pass the Doctor and pulled up along side of him. The Doctor looked terrified as they looked into each others eyes speeding into the turn. Asesino pulled ahead just enough to tap the front end of the Doctors car and there it was. That long sound of silence that filled the air as the adrenaline rush hit him. The Doctors car swerved to the right and crashed through the guardrail. It flew into the air then down the deep gorge to an awe-inspiring explosion as it hit the bottom. Asesino almost ejaculated in his pants at the sight of it. "Whew," he screamed. "God damn it that was good. Yeah man!" He knew this rush would slowly subside so he continued to speed down the hill taking the sharp turns at high speeds to make the rush last just a little longer. When he reached Interstate 10 he was too excited so he drove back home without stopping. He could not wait to report his success to El Jefe.

29 Palms, California – Tim MacCorrmack
April 1, 2006

Tim had arrived early Friday morning to go over the data one final time before giving it to Raj for their brainstorming session on Monday. Tim had managed to get some sleep since he lived close to the lab. Raj on the other hand had a longer drive and would probably be in around 8:00 a.m. It was 7:00 now. He went through the data validation reports and began thinking about what kind of uses they might have for this newly discovered technology.

The morning was rushing by. It was 10:30 and Tim was beginning to get worried about Raj. He never came in later than 9:00 no matter how long they stayed the night before. Tim tried to call Raj on his TREO but there was no answer. Just then several people came in to the lab and Tim's heart fell into his stomach. He knew something bad had happened.

"Mr. MacCorrmack?"

"Yes. I'm Tim MacCorrmack."

"I'm Detective Dan Buckley. I need to ask you a few questions."

"Sure. What's up?"

"Can you tell me when you last saw Doctor Ramakrishnan?"

"Oh my God! Has something happened to Raj?"

"I'm sorry to have to tell you this but Doctor Ramakrishnan was killed last night on highway 62. Apparently he was run off the road."

"Oh shit," gasped Tim and almost fell to the floor. "How? Why?"

"We had an eye witness, a hitchhiker, who claimed he observed them speeding down the highway and indicated the second vehicle struck the front of the Doctors car sending him off an embankment. The speed of the impact probably killed him instantly."

Tim collapsed to his knees and began to cry. After a couple of minutes he composed himself and asked the detective, "What do you need from me detective?"

"When did you last see the doctor?"

"We worked late last night and we both left around 1:40"

"Do you know if the Doctor had any enemies or know of any one who wanted to hurt him or worse, wanted him dead?"

"No. No one. Raj was the nicest man I ever met. I can't imagine anyone wanting to hurt him."

"From the evidence at the scene it is almost certain this was a professional hit on the Doctor. Has he had any contact with anyone recently who might want to cause him harm?"

"I can't think of anyone."

"What time did you say the Doctor left here?"

"Like I said we both left around 1:40 or 1:45 this morning. We had just completed a critical experiment and wanted to finish processing the data before we left."

"Did you notice anyone or anything unusual when you left?"

"No. The Doc went West and I went East on 62."

"Was he going…"

"Wait," Tim interrupted. "I did see another car pull out of the parking lot shortly after we did. Not many people work late like we do. Does that mean anything?"

"Maybe. Did you get a description of the vehicle?"

"No, like I said I went east and both of them went the other way. I didn't give it any thought."

"Is there anything else you can think of that may help?"

"No, I wish I had more."

"Well, if you think of anything else here is my card. Call me, no matter how insignificant you think it might be."

"Yes detective. I certainly will. Thank you."

The detective left with his associates and several TC employees stayed behind to talk to Tim and mull over possible reasons for Raj's death, none of which made any sense. After the last employee left Tim sat at Raj's desk and had a good cry for his friend. When he cleared his tears away he saw the folders of Jennifer Tomas, Wyatt Coleman, Elisaio Munoz, and Robert Niesen on his desk. He felt so bad because Raj had made so much progress on this and now it was over. The company would probably get someone new in to take over but no one would know as much about this as Raj did.

Tim opened the folders and glanced through the files of Ms. Tomas. He was all too familiar with its contents. He opened Mr. Coleman's and the same. He had prepared all of this information himself. He tossed them back on top of the others and several pages of notes fell out of the folder for Mr. Munoz. Tim half stared at them until he realized these were Raj's notes. He had not seen these. He started reading through them and discovered Raj had an interview with Munoz and during his interview he commented on how he made Munoz angry and was asked to leave. Tim read further.

* * * * * * * * * *

"Ah, hello. Detective Buckley? This is Tim MacCorrmack at TC Laboratories."

"Yes Mr. MacCorrmack. How can I help you?"

"You said if I had something no matter how insignificant it may be that I should call you?"

"Yes. Did you find something?"

"I believe so. After everyone left the lab today I started looking through Doctor Ramakrishnan's folders. I found a file regarding an interview he had with an Elisaio Munoz last month."

"The drug dealer Munoz from Los Angeles?"

"Yes, the same."

"What kind of business would Doctor Ramakrishnan have with someone like Munoz?"

Mr. Munoz had some information concerning an experiment we were conducting and I told Raj, Doctor Ramakrishnan, I didn't think it was a good idea to talk to this man but it looks as though he conducted the interview anyway. In his notes he indicates he met with him a few weeks ago and it seems he upset Mr. Munoz and was thrown out of his house."

"Knowing what I do about Munoz he does not like to be confronted or upset, as you put it, by anyone and with his temper it's a pretty good assumption he might be capable of doing something like this to the doctor." There was a short pause then he asked, "What was the interview about?"

"Well, I'm not at liberty to say but I can assure you there was nothing illegal about the information Doctor Ramakrishnan was trying to ascertain from Mr. Munoz. It was simply an information gathering interview about a situation Mr. Munoz found himself in many years ago."

"Could this situation have been something that Munoz could somehow feel threatened by and want to kill the doctor over it?"

"I don't see how but I don't understand the criminal mind."

"OK Mr. MacCorrmack. Is there anything else?"

"No. I just thought you should know they met."

"Well, thank you. I'll look into it further."

Tim hung up then reread every line in Munoz's file. This was one bad seed and Tim was sure he was somehow responsible for Raj's death but why? By 5:00 Tim was mentally exhausted and went home.

* * * * * * * * * *

Saturday morning, Tim went into work to clean up but mostly to just get away for a while. Everything was going to change now. He wasn't even sure if he was still going to have a job or not. *"What would happen to Raj's project? Would they put it on hold for a while or just reassign it to another scientist?"* These and hundreds of other thoughts raced through his mind.

Tim was moping around the lab opening and closing drawers, books, and folders. He kept wondering, *"Why would Elisaio Munoz want to kill Raj? What was in it for him or why was it necessary for him to have Raj out of the way? What could Raj do to him?"* Just then it hit him. "Munoz must have thought Raj was trying to find a way to send him back to his own time or prevent him from going back in time. That is the only logical reason for him to do this," Tim uttered aloud.

Something had to be done. He got an idea and ran over to his desk. He started looking through folders, print outs, and notebooks. He turned his computer on and began typing fervently on his keyboard then read the results of his query on the LCD screen. He scribbled notes in his notebook then continued this pattern of activity for the next couple of hours.

He hit the <ENTER> key in a concluding manner, grabbed Jennifer Tomas's file, and ran over to the printer. He anxiously paced around the printer impatiently waiting for the printout to finish. When it finally did he tore it off of the printer then ran toward the large double doors of the lab next door.

There it was, the new STR8 BOLT generator. Compared to the one Raj and he had been working on these last several months this one was immense. Tim approached it slowly as if it were some sort of a hallowed idol. "This is for you Raj," he spoke to it.

The preliminary tests had been completed earlier that week. Raj and Tim were prepared to start testing it for accuracy in a couple of weeks anyway.

Tim threw the main breaker and the generator roared to life. He entered in some essential data, punched in coordinates, grabbed a timer, and began a series of accuracy tests and processed the results.

Several hours had passed. Tim was just about ready. He grabbed Ms. Tomas's file and ran back to his desk and began typing. He copied several documents from her file and along with a two page letter put them all together in a small package. He wrote down the last known address they had for her on the package, placed several vintage stamps on it, and set it down on his desk. He replicated several more packages and stacked all of them together. He gathered them up and went back in to the larger lab. He fired up the STR8 BOLT generator once again, entered the co-ordinates from his notes, placed the first package in the holder and sent it on its journey through time. He set it up for the next package.

Industry Hills, California – Manuel "Asesino" Gutierrez
April 2, 2006

"It was a clean kill," Asesino yelled into the phone.
"No. The highway was deserted."
"I don't know man. I'm telling you it was just the Doc and me. No one else."
"What channel?"
Asesino walked to his living room and turned on the television. He didn't say anything to the other person on the telephone. He just listened.

"*...on the way to Palm Springs.*
According to our sources local law enforcement alleges the death of Doctor Ramakrishnan was not the result of an accidental hit and run. Inside police headquarters behind me they are at this time interviewing a young man who stated he was at the scene when the accident occurred. The witness, an indigent, hitchhiking to Laughlin Nevada said he observed another vehicle speeding down the hill almost pushing the Doctors car ahead of it. The vehicle pulled out to pass then hit the front of the Doctors car purposely sending it over the side of the road and into the ravine. The other vehicle continued down the highway never slowing.
The question of why someone wanted to kill this scientist from TC Enterprises has detectives concerned. We can only..."

"Son of a bitch! How the fuck...," screamed Asesino.

"I don't know."

"OK. I'll take care of it. Does Jefe know?"

"Shit! Tell him not to worry. I'll take care of it."

"I said I would take care of it ese."

"OK." Asesino hung the phone up.

"God damn it," he screamed throwing his fists in the air. He looked back to the television again and turned up the volume with the remote.

"...no comment from Detective Buckley.

It has also been reported Doctor Ramakrishnan met with known drug lord Elisaio Munoz and officials say they are looking into a connection. Munoz has on many..."

"Fuck! I may as well be dead. Jefe is no doubt going to have me killed if I don't clean this fucking mess up. But how?"

Asesino paced around his apartment trying to get his thoughts straight and to form a plan. What could he do? Killing the witness would only make matters worse. He wasn't sure what the witness actually saw. Did he get his license plate number? Did he get a good description of his car? The news wasn't saying. He decided he only had two choices. He could turn himself in and take the fall for Jefe, keeping his mouth shut and hoping Jefe doesn't have him killed in prison, or he could run. South America was big. Jefe had contacts there but they were only with other drug lords. He could hide out in a small village for several years or hide out in a large city and bury himself in the crowd. That made more sense. He had enough money to live comfortably and his chances of living longer were better in South America.

Asesino started packing everything he could take with him then made arrangements to get out of the country later that day. When he had finished he took a last look around his home. "Jefe is on his own on this one," he mumbled as he hurried out the front door.

29 Palms, California – Tim MacCorrmack
April 3, 2006

It was three o'clock in the morning before Tim had sent out the last package. He had no new memories about Raj, Jennifer Tomas or anything. "How will I know if this worked," he asked himself aloud. But nothing came to mind.

He tried to think of something else he could do. But what? He was exhausted. He shut down the lab and sadly headed out the door. Feeling totally ineffective he went home. Perhaps some sleep would help him think of something tomorrow. The short drive home seemed like an eternity.

FOUR

Wyatt cashed in some of his stocks from Zenith, IBM, and Texas Instruments but only because he knew they would be in a slump for the next couple of years. He would wait for them to bottom out and then buy them back when they started climbing up again in 1980. He remembered he should buy back IBM a little sooner.

With the money he received from the stock, Wyatt booked a four month trip for Kari and him. In Wyatt's past, or a few years from now, he had spent several months in the Indian Ocean diving and sailing while working on a project for the local government of the Republic of Maldives. He knew that area of the world would not be spoiled by tourism for at least another ten years and decided it would be the perfect place for Kari and him to plan their future together. Little did he know she planned to tell him about her tale during that time as well.

The Republic of Maldives is a small country about one thousand miles South of India in the Indian Ocean just north of the Equator. They have been trying to gain their independence from the British since the 60's and that would come in just a couple of years. The country is made up of 2,200 islands or atolls, which are circular coral reefs surrounding an island made up of ground coral forming lagoons.

Wyatt spent several months on the island of Male'. It would become the Capital for the Republic of Maldives but not for a few more years. The

Maldives is an Islamic country and they take their religion very seriously. Wyatt was all too familiar with their customs and the ways they dealt with non-Islamic people. As long as Jennifer and he followed their customs they would be very welcomed by the Maldivian people. His plan was to spend most of their time on the boat and only go ashore to get supplies.

Wyatt planned on making several stops before they arrived in the Republic of Maldives. He wanted to take Kari to Tokyo for a few days simply because neither one of them had ever been there before. Then they would fly down to Singapore to do some last minute shopping before heading on to Sri Lanka. There, they planned to start their four month sailing cruise out of Columbo.

In finalizing their plans they could not decide if they wanted to take a tour of Sri Lanka before departing on their sailing cruise or do that after they returned giving them time to re-acclimate themselves back into the world. They opted to make that decision once they arrived in Columbo.

Jennifer knew her businesses would be in good hands. She would check in with her managers once a week if possible to make sure there were no problems or anything she needed to be involved in. She was very confident Sharon Fortinelli, her senior manager, would make the right decisions for all of the restaurants in her absence.

* * * * * * * * * *

The day had finally come for them to leave on their trip. They had just arrived in front of the TWA terminal at Los Angeles International Airport (LAX) and it was 6:00 am. Wyatt had rented a limousine to take them to the airport. He promised they would travel in style on the entire trip. Jennifer loved this because she had never really taken any time to enjoy the fruits of her success and who better to enjoy it with than the man she loved, a man who shared the same kind of life she did. He just didn't know it yet.

Not a lot was said during the limo ride. They just sat, wrapped in each other arms and took pleasure in the quiet ride. As the driver maneuvered to park Wyatt asked Kari, "You nervous about leaving everything for so long?"

"No, not at all. I love the fact that we are getting away for a few months. I didn't realize how badly I needed this until we actually left the house this morning. Now that we are on our way, I am cherishing every moment. How about you? Are you ready to spend all this time alone with me and only me?"

"I'm ready to spend the rest of my life with you if you'll have me," he proclaimed almost as if proposing.

"Well, let's see how the next four months go lying around naked, making love, drinking expensive wine, and talking about all of this then we'll see," Jennifer responded then smiled and gave him a quick kiss.

"Are you folks ready," the porter asked as he opened their door.

Jennifer grabbed her handbag from the Limo and replied, "Absolutely!" She took Wyatt's hand then walked with him to the check-in counter.

* * * * * * * * * *

Seated in First Class, Wyatt was appreciating how comfortable the seats were and how nice and polite the attendants and staff were compared to what the airline industry would evolve into in the future when gas prices soared, employment was cut in half, ticket prices shot up out of control, and service and comfort were just about non existent. He started to tell Kari about his observation when...

"What would you folks like for breakfast after we take off," interrupted the stewardess.

"I'll have the Eggs Benedict with Hollandaise sauce. What about you, ummm Wyatt," asked Jennifer still not used to his real name.

"I'll have the same but can you put the sauce on the side?"

"Yes sir. Very good," replied the stewardess. "Would you care for some champagne before we take off?

"Yes please," responded Jennifer.

"Bloody Mary for me," ordered Wyatt.

"Thank you. I'll bring those drinks right out for you." The stewardess went in to the galley.

You're still not used to calling me Wyatt, are you?"

"I'll get it. I've been calling you Jim for the past two years and it just seems a little strange. I'll get it though."

"I've been thinking about that and maybe you should just call me Jim. That is the name I have on my passport and drivers license. Anyone who knows me knows me as Jim so why not keep it that way. Besides, I've gotten used to it too so why change now. I don't know if I ever told you this or not but my real first name is James. I just never liked it and chose to go by my middle name of Wyatt since I was a teen."

The stewardess returned and placed their drinks on the center tray.

"I like Jim. You look like a Jim," she affirmed taking a sip of her champagne.

"What's a Jim look like," he asked smiling.

"Well, Jim's are sexy, handsome, and love women who look like me. They look like you." She kissed him.

Several minutes after reaching their cruising altitude the Stewardess brought them their breakfast and for airport food it was not too bad. As they ate Jennifer asked Wyatt, "So how big is this boat we are sailing on?"

"It's a 40' foot catamaran. I thought you'd be more comfortable on a boat that stayed flat for the most part and it travels a lot faster than a sailboat does so when we go island hopping the trips will be quick. That way if we encounter any tropical storms we can get around them and get to port before they hit."

"I like that. I have to tell you I am a little nervous about sailing since I've never done it."

"You're fairly familiar with boats. You've been boating since you were a teen. Granted, a water ski boat is not a sailboat but you have a basic knowledge of boating. I'll teach you everything else you need to know on the cat. I've sailed all up and down the coast of California and Mexico on a 20' foot cat by myself and I can handle this boat very easily with your help. We'll be fine." Wyatt could see Kari was pretty nervous. He suggested, "Maybe I should have the broker in Columbo get his people to sail it to Male' for us then we can pick it up there. That way you won't have to worry about being out on the open water and trying to learn the basics of sailing right off the bat."

"That would make me feel a lot more comfortable."

"OK then. When we get to Tokyo, I'll call ahead and arrange it."

"I love you Jim." Jennifer leaned in close to him and whispered, "Wyatt."

* * * * * * * * * *

Their time in Tokyo was short. After two days of dealing with the crowds they were ready to leave. They had had their fill of sushi too. It was time to go to their next destination Singapore.

Singapore was much more exciting. After arriving at the Marco Polo hotel they checked into their room then quickly headed out for an early dinner. They were met outside of the lobby door by several Rickshaw drivers and decided to hire one to take them to a restaurant. Once they were seated in the Rickshaw they asked the driver if he could recommend a good place to eat and he replied, "I take you good food. You like. Yes?" They agreed and the young man took off running, towing them behind.

Rickshaw drivers were incredibly strong. They could run at a steady pace for long periods of time and use the Rickshaw to help them rest simply by shifting their weight forward or backward when going down gradual slopes. It was a very impressive thing to watch.

The city was beautiful and the architecture was unbelievable. The young Rickshaw driver pointed out several landmarks as they traveled through downtown. It was obvious to Wyatt and Jennifer the young man was giving them the long tour and was working very hard in hopes of receiving a good tip. They were not in a hurry and enjoyed the young man's enthusiasm. As he turned down Orchard Avenue toward Chinatown, Wyatt remembered being in this part of town many years ago. Well, actually a few years from now. Either way it looked the same.

Thirty minutes into the run the young man stopped in front of a beautiful building. He spoke in his broken English, "You eat good. You eat here." Wyatt generously tipped the young man and they went inside.

After dinner Wyatt wished he had given the young Rickshaw driver a bigger tip. The food was by far the best Chinese food he had ever eaten. Full and satisfied they walked around the city, went into several shops, bought some personal items, and ate some fruit off of a little food stand. They walked by the Boulevard Hotel and went inside. It was a brand new hotel and had some of the most modern technology for its time. It was getting late so they caught another Rickshaw back to the hotel then went in for the evening.

Early the next day they took a taxi to the top of Mount Faber and the view of Singapore was magnificent. The ocean, the city, the ships, all of it was breath taking. They decided to walk down so they could enjoy the beauty and ambiance of their surroundings. It was a perfect day.

The next several days were just as pleasurable. They went out for a sunset cruise in the harbor, visited the zoo, went out on a SCUBA trip, and lounged around the hotel pool. The rest of the world was fading away.

On their last day in Singapore they went to the Singapore Botanical Gardens. As was everything else in the tiny country the gardens were lovely. Beauty everywhere you looked. Rare and exotic plants were all around them. It was the ideal end to their stay in Singapore. They had an early flight to Columbo so they returned to their room early that afternoon to prepare for their departure. They decided to go on to their final destination of Male' and take the tour of Sri Lanka upon their return.

Anaheim California – Sharon Fortinelli, Restaurant Manager
July 5, 1974

The mail usually came just after 1:30 p.m. Today was no different than any other. The restaurant was filled to capacity with its lunch crowd and Sharon, along with her staff, continued rushing about taking care of their customers. The postman walked into the front door thumbing through his bundle selecting the restaurant's mail. He placed it on the counter, gave a quick wave to Sharon then went back out the door to his next stop. Several minutes later Sharon walked by the counter and picked up the mail. She mechanically fingered through the stack not really looking at it while walking to her office. As she was about to reveal a package addressed to Kari Davis, one of her servers called to her for some help. Sharon put the mail on Kari's desk and went to help the caller. She didn't notice the small package with the word URGENT stamped on all sides of it.

Later that evening, at 10:35 p.m. the last customer left the restaurant and Sharon locked the door behind them. The last of her evening servers were finishing up their duties, dividing their tips, and preparing to leave. After letting out the last employee Sharon locked the door, turned out the main restaurant lights, and headed back to her office to finish out the days paperwork and prepare her deposit for the bank drop.

It was after 11:00 p.m. when she finally leaned back in her chair letting out a long exhale thinking she was done for the day when she noticed the stack of mail on Kari's desk. "Oh crap," she exhaled. She debated whether or not to go through it now or just wait until morning when she was fresh. She noticed an URGENT stamp on the package under the stack of mail. She pulled the package out and saw it was addressed to Kari Davis. Kari was OK with Sharon opening any mail sent to the restaurant but this package was not the typical business mail. It was hand written and looked very personal. Sharon wasn't sure if she should open it or not. If it had been from a vendor or one of their suppliers she would have opened it without giving it a second thought as she did so many times before. But this package was from someone she did not recognize. She knew she was going to hear from Kari next week sometime. Perhaps she should wait until then. She started to open it but at the last moment decided it could wait until she talked to Kari first. She had no way to get in touch with Kari anyway so she put it back on Kari's desk and went home.

Male, Republic of Maldives—Wyatt and Jennifer
July 11, 1974

"There's a several second delay Sharon. It helps if you say 'OVER' when you've finished what you were saying so we don't keep talking over each other. OVER." Jennifer was having a very difficult time understanding Sharon on the telephone because the connection was so bad with static, echo, and about a four second delay between their conversations. They kept interrupting each other when they began speaking. The operator suggested they say OVER between conversations and that would help prevent talking over each other.

"No. Male'. We are going back there for a week before we return home. OVER"

"Probably the end of October. OVER"

"Yes, it's absolutely beautiful. I'm looking forward to getting to our first port at Vadoo. OVER"

"Maybe a week then we'll head for Farkolo Fushi. OVER"

"Yes, I know. It was all I could do to learn the names of those first two islands. Hopefully I'll know them all before the end of the trip. OVER"

"We will. OVER"

"I'm sorry. A what? OVER"

"What kind of package? OVER"

"Who? OVER"

"I don't know a Tim MacCorrmack. What's the address? OVER"

"Nope. I don't know anyone in Twenty Nine Palms. It's probably junk. OVER"

"Urgent? Did you open it? OVER"

"Then leave it until I get back. If he sends another one or contacts you then open it up or let me know what it's all about next time I call. OVER"

"OK Hun. I'll check back with you in a couple of weeks. OVER"

"Bye."

"What was that all about," Wyatt asked.

"Oh Sharon wanted to know where we were and if I was having a good time."

"I got all of that. What was that about a package?"

"She said I received a package marked urgent from someone named Tim McSomething. I don't know anyone named Tim and I told her it was probably junk or some advertising packet to solicit our business. I told her if another one shows up to just open it and tell me about it the next time I call. Otherwise, it could wait until we get back."

"Why didn't you tell her to open it now?"

"Because I didn't want to deal with it now. If it was from someone I knew I would have but since I've never heard of this Tim guy I figured it could wait. Wouldn't you agree?"

"You're right. If it had really been important he would have sent it certified mail or called."

"See. We think alike," she grinned.

"OK. You have everything?"

"Yes Captain," Jennifer saluted in a cute manner.

Assuming a playful role as Captain, he ordered, "Then let's get the sheets to the wind and make way."

"Aye aye Captain," she saluted again.

They took their food supplies and incidentals to the harbor section of the island. Even though the boat was fully stocked they picked up these few items just to give them a sense of being ready to go.

The Columbo yacht broker, Ali Manoku, was there to greet them and to show them where all of the tack, sheets, and equipment were located on the boat. He went through all of the compartments in the galley, berths, and heads.

After a couple of hours Ali bid them a bon voyage and helped cast them off. They were on their way to the island of Vadoo. It was only a four hour trip using just the main sheet to pull them through the calm sea.

Dolphins played in the late afternoon sun jumping out of the water, flipping and splashing about. It was the best conditions for Jennifer to learn about sailing. Wyatt ran her through several of the maneuvers and each time they performed it Jennifer became more confident. They pulled into the small lagoon of Vadoo, dropped anchor, and settled in for the night.

Early the next morning, the Harbor Master boarded their boat. Wyatt presented their papers and passports. They were given in return the necessary documents to put into any of the ports within the Maldivian borders. After a light breakfast they went swimming, snorkeling, and basked in the beautiful tropical weather. Each of the days, on all of the island ports they put in, were similar but at the same time different with their distinctive specialties. At Farkolo Fushi, which would later become Club Med, they enjoyed lobster every night. On the other islands, Uhurra, Vellisaru, Korumba, Furana, and Gilaavaru they enjoyed local dishes, customs, and festivities, all unique in their own way. The weeks were passing by too quickly.

Nine weeks into their trip and everything was going perfectly. Their businesses were functioning well in their absence, the people they left in charge were making good decisions, and there were no other urgent packages from Tim MacCorrmack which Jennifer had forgotten all about. They were having the time of their lives but Jennifer realized they were already over half way into their trip. She needed to tell Wyatt about her time travel experience because if she didn't do it soon their vacation would be over before she got the chance. She decided she would tell him today.

They had just finished a swim and were lying on the trampoline sunning them selves. Jennifer interrupted the silence, "Honey, I need to talk to you about something." She was feeling very nervous.

"Sure sweetheart, what's up," Wyatt asked sitting up.

"First I want to say I am having the most wonderful time with you and I love you so much for bringing me here. I can't believe nine weeks have already gone by. I had hoped to do this earlier."

"I love being here with you too. Do what? What's wrong Kari?"

"That's just it."

"What's it," Wyatt asked getting a little concerned.

"Remember when you told me you weren't Jim Bolaire?"

"Yes, when we went to Palm Springs. Why?"

"You said there was someone you met who claimed to have been sent back in time when we were at the lecture of Dr. Feltzberg's."

"Yeah, I needed time to prepare how I was going to tell you about myself so I set up the fake meeting."

"Well, that night of the lecture I was going to talk to you but you surprised me with that and I didn't get the chance. Now, its a few months later and I need to tell you what I wanted to tell you then."

"OK Hun. Tell me." He gave her his full attention.

Her eyes were opened very wide and staring right into his. Her heart was racing. She took a deep breath and paused for a moment then she took his hands and speaking a little bit fast she blurted out, "My name is not Kari Davis. My name is Jennifer Tomas and I was sent back in time just like you but from 1992 to 1968. I'm sorry I didn't tell you sooner Jim. I just… I don't know. You were so happy after you told me your story I thought I should wait but I never expected to wait this long." She stared at him waiting for his reaction.

There was a long silent pause. He cleared his throat then replied, "I don't know what to say to you Kari."

"Say you love me and that you understand." Her eyes began to well up.

"I do love you but I'm not sure I understand why you couldn't tell me this sooner."

"I told you, you shocked me and the right opportunity didn't present itself until now."

"Well, I'm shocked now." He stood up. "Let me have a few minutes to clear my head."

"I was so happy when you told me in Palm Springs Jim. I wanted to tell you so many times but there just wasn't a right moment," she repeated.

He stood at the edge of the boat and asked again, "Just give me a minute, OK?" He jumped into the water and swam away from the boat then stopped about a hundred yards away.

Jennifer began crying. She knew she had hurt him by not telling him sooner. She looked at him floating in the water looking away from the boat. She was sure she had lost his trust. She cried again. Every few minutes or so she would look at him but he never looked back at the boat. She finally stopped crying and turned to her side wondering if she should have told him.

Fifteen minutes later he swam back to the boat and climbed up the swim step on the back of the boat. He walked right by her and went down below. She didn't move. A few minutes later he came back up with a couple of ice cold beers in his hand. He handed one to her and said, "OK, tell me everything."

Jennifer jumped on him almost knocking both of them over the side and gave him a long kiss. He carried her to a deck chair and sat down. She sat on his lap facing him and told him her entire story. Wyatt didn't say a word. He just listened.

Night had fallen. Wyatt had only gotten up a couple of times to refresh their drinks. Jennifer was just about done with her story. Wyatt asked, "You hungry?"

"Famished," she exclaimed.

"Let's go down below then you can finish up while I make us something to eat." He started down through the hatch to the galley.

"That would be great." She stood and called down to him, "I'm going to take a quick dip and I'll be right down."

They talked well into the early morning hours. Wyatt had many questions and Jennifer was eager to answer them if she could. They went back to their berth and lay down. Their heads felt like they were about to over flow. They talked for a while longer then fell asleep in each others embrace.

The next morning, feeling refreshed, they compared experiences then laughed and cried at some of the problematic situations each of them had been in. He jokingly called her a convict and she retaliated by calling him a fugitive. They were completely comfortable with each other and agreed to not keep anything from the other from now on.

The next several weeks went by very quickly. They spent a lot of time talking about their future plans, investments, and occupational direction. Jennifer agreed she should sell off her restaurants and invest the money into stocks and companies they knew would grow. They talked about starting their own company which could develop some of the technologies they knew would be emerging in the future. Their opportunities were endless.

Industry Hills, California – Elisaio "Ravin" Munoz
April 2, 2006

"Do you see this, God Damn it? Do you? How the fuck did Asesino screw this up so bad man," Ravin screamed as he watched the news on the TV.

"I don't know Jefe. He said he would take care of it," the bodyguard responded a little frightened knowing Ravin's temper and what he was capable of doing when he got pissed off like this.

"How the fuck is he going to take care of it. They're already using my name and calling me a suspect. They also know I met with that fucking doctor last month."

"So you say you met with him. So what man," the bodyguard replied wishing he hadn't.

"So what! I'll tell you so what. The fucking FBI set up the meeting. That's so what. They probably know exactly what we talked about too. Hell, they probably sent that little fucking pendejo here to set me up." Elisaio was stomping around the room looking for something to take his frustration out on.

"But you told him you didn't know anything about what he was asking you Jefe. How can the FBI use that against you," the body guard asked slowly stepping back and out of the way in case Elisaio threw something.

"Yeah, well, I don't. I'm sure they'll find some way. He probably told those pinche FBI guys I got pissed off and threw him out. That gives them a fucking motive to pin this on me. God damn it man. Where's that fucking Asesino now?"

"I don't know Jefe. He said he was going to take care of this and to tell you not to worry. I guess he's on his way back to Twenty Nine Palms."

"When he gets back here you tell that son of a bitch I want to see him right away. If he doesn't clean this up I'm going to kill that mother fucker myself for getting me into this."

"OK Jefe. I'll try to get in touch with him."

Ravin threw one of his expensive art pieces at the large flat screen monitor hanging on the wall. "Fuck," he screamed. The bodyguard ducked down then noticed the debris sliding across the floor. He ran over to pick up the rubble but Ravin yelled at him to leave it alone. "Just get that fucking Asesino back here now. I'll try to straighten this mess up myself." He stormed off to his office.

Elisaio turned the television on in his office and started watching the news again. News reporters were camped out around the TC Enterprises complex in Twenty Nine Palms. A smug reporter on the TV was speaking as if she had uncovered the top story of all time.

"...according to unnamed sources at TC Enterprises. Dr. Ramakrishnan had been working on several prototypes for the past several years and was about to begin work on the final product next week. They call it the Straight Bolt, spelled STR8 BOLT, project. We have not yet been able to get information from our sources as to its exact function however this Top Secret project is said to be going forward despite the death of Dr. Ramakrishnan. Police investigators say they are looking into a possible connection to his death with L.A. drug lord Elisaio Munoz because of a reported meeting between the two men several weeks ago.

Tim MacCorrmack, who is the Associate Director of the project, will most likely continue as the new director in charge so our sources tell us. Mr. MacCorrmack, who has been working under Dr. Ramakrishnan for the past several years, is the most logical choice for heading up the project. This is Karen..."

Ravin turned the television off and wrote down the name 'Tim MacCorrmack' and 'STR8 BOLT' on a notepad. "So this is what the good doctor has been working on. I knew that son of a bitch was working on something that would fuck me up. Now this little cock sucker MacCorrmack is going to take over. Maybe I should pay a visit to our young Director here and see if he's going to be a pain in my ass too," he stated aloud. He sat down at his desk then began typing away on the keyboard and searching the Internet for whatever information he could find on Tim MacCorrmack.

TC Laboratories – Tim MacCorrmack
April 3, 2006

Tim wasn't sure why he was driving into work on Sunday. He did everything he could think of the day before. He didn't know what else to do. He pulled into the parking lot and sat in his car for twenty minutes before exiting. He walked in to the lab and sat at his desk for a couple of hours analyzing everything, pushing his intellect to its capacity. What else could he do? He decided to send out a few more packages using a different approach. Maybe one of these would get to Jennifer Tomas.

Columbo, Sri Lanka – Wyatt and Jennifer
October 28, 1974

"I don't know Kari. He just said he wanted to meet with you personally. I told him you wouldn't be back for another couple of weeks. What do you want me to do," Sharon asked over the phone.

"He wouldn't say what it was about," Jennifer asked.

"No. Just that it was very personal. That's it."

"If he calls again Sharon, tell him I'll be in on the fourth and I'll meet with him then. If he doesn't call then I'll call him when I get back."

"OK. Well, I bet you look gorgeous with a golden tan and sun bleached hair. I can't wait to see you," Sharon changed the subject.

"Yeah, I'm ready to come home I think. We have had the greatest time and I don't know how I will react to being back in the normal swing of things."

"Well, everything is going great on this end. You won't have anything to do when you get here so you can work back into it slowly."

"I may do that. Jim and I have several things we need to do when we get back and that may take up a lot of my time for a while. I'll fill you in when I see you."

"OK Kari. I can't wait to see you. We missed you."

"Thanks Sharon. I'll see you next week. Bye."

"Problems," Wyatt asked.

"No. Sharon said some guy has been calling trying to set up a meeting with me but wouldn't say why."

"Was it that Tim guy who sent you the package a few months ago?"

"I forgot all about that but I don't think so. She said she never got the guy's name and he insisted it was very personal and that he would only meet with me. I wonder what it's all about."

"Well, we'll see when we get home. For now we have our limo waiting to take us around the country. Shall we go?"

"Yes. I'll deal with it when I get home."

Over the next four days Wyatt and Jennifer traveled through the country of Sri Lanka. They left the Intercontinental Hotel and headed toward Kandy where they spent a couple of days. On the way they stopped at Kadugannawa Pass and took a couple of pictures posing with Bible Rock in the background. They continued on and took a quick tour through a spice garden where they learned the history of Ceylon Tea. They arrived at their hotel, the Citadel, on the Mahaweli Ganga River. The view from their room resembled that of looking from Tarzan's tree house in the jungle with all of the jungle sounds to go with it.

The next day they toured the Temple of Tooth in Kandy. It was an ancient temple built by monks around a giant elephant tusk. Then that evening they watched a fire walking ceremony after dinner. The next morning they went to another botanical garden. Later they visited the Kandy museum, did a little shopping in town then went back to their hotel. The next day they left Kandy and toured southern Sri Lanka. After several days of exploring villages and Sri Lankan history they went back to Columbo for one more day. It was a wonderful ending to a beautiful voyage. Tomorrow they would head back to civilization.

TC Laboratories – Tim MacCorrmack
April 3, 2006

Subsequent to sending out several more packages Tim was not satisfied he had done everything he possibly could. He still did not notice or feel anything had changed. He felt like he had failed Raj. He sat back in his chair and tears welled up in his eyes. He wiped them away then looked around the room as if lost or searching for a way out. He noticed a large envelope in the mail basket and walked over to it then opened it. The envelope was from the Colorado State Troopers Office. The file inside was for Wyatt Coleman, no middle name. He read through the file and noticed several pieces of information that could be very useful when applied to his own data on Mr. Coleman. Colorado did not have the information available that he had on Mr. Coleman because in 1970 Mr. Coleman didn't really exist yet or at least not as an adult. He grabbed a notepad and began to take notes.

First, the reporting officer was a Daniel M. Buckley. The name seamed very familiar to Tim. He rummaged around his desk and found the business card of Detective Buckley had given him Friday. There it was, Daniel M.

Buckley. "What are the odds of this," he asked himself. He placed the card in the folder and continued to write down other important details.

Mr. Coleman allegedly stole a wallet from another patient at the Vail hospital, a Mr. James Allan Bolaire, but no record of any credit card use had been indicated. Mr. Bolaire passed away shortly after the incident. Without the Internet and no record sharing capabilities prior to 1985 it would have been very difficult for the police to track down suspects across states and that would have made it easy for Mr. Coleman to assume the identity of Mr. Bolaire with very little chance of being discovered.

"This is nuts," he declared out loud. "I'm really grasping at straws now. I'm sure the police would have followed up on this lead themselves." But there was no indication they had. The more Tim thought about it he knew he had nothing else to go on so he continued to sift through the file.

There was an identifying mark that would single out Mr. Coleman and that was the Tattoo the police had a picture of in the file. Studying the tattoo Tim said aloud, "I don't know about you Mr. Coleman but I think I just found me another time traveler." With this new information Tim began to run searches in his database for everything he could find on James Allan Bolaire.

Anaheim, California – Jennifer Tomas
November 4, 1974

"Yes, I'll be here," Jennifer spoke in the phone.

"Yes of course, I'll see you in two hours. I look forward to meeting you too sir."

Jennifer hadn't been at the restaurant more than 10 minutes when she received the telephone call from the gentleman Sharon told her had been trying to get in touch with her. The urgency in the man's voice was compelling so much so she agreed to meet him today. Now she was beginning to worry and considered calling Wyatt to ask him to join her for the meeting but the more she thought about it the more she decided not to.

Her desk was clean like she had left it in July and she wondered why she even bothered coming in at all today. She grabbed the books from Sharon's desk and reviewed the restaurants business over the last few months and everything was good. She opened drawers and closed them, stood up and sat back down. If she hadn't agreed to that meeting in two hours she would have got up and went home. She got up once more and went out into the restaurant and observed the early morning crowd filtering in and out as her staff raced about doing their jobs. She walked back to the kitchen and it was the same there with cookware clinking and clanging as staff hustled in and out. She went back to her office and Sharon was in there sitting at her desk looking over some orders she had placed with their vendors.

"Are you glad to be back," she asked Kari.

"I feel so out of place. I feel like I'm in the way."

"You're being silly. You're probably still tired from the trip and need a few days to get your sleep cycle back on track."

"Yeah, you're probably right. Is there anything I can do for you while I'm here?"

"Nope. We're fully staffed today and everything is going smoothly."

"I was afraid you were going to say that," Jennifer nervously laughed.

"Oh come on Kari. You just got back. Relax. By next week you'll be back to your normal self, running around wishing you were back on that boat."

"You're right. So, did I miss anything while I was away?"

"Business was good and the vendors were great getting our orders here on time."

"Alright! I'll stop," Jennifer groaned as she leaned back in her chair.

Sharon laughed then asked, "So, tell me. What's up with you and Jim? Should I be planning some special parties anytime soon?"

Jennifer laughed quietly, "Keep your party hat in the drawer for right now. But I would say keep it dusted off."

"I knew it. You two look great together. You guys were made for each other."

"You don't know how right you are."

"I'm so happy for you Kari."

"Thanks Sharon."

"So, did you bring pictures with you?"

"No. I have to take the film in to be developed later today. I'll bring them with me when I come back."

"I am so jealous of you being able to just take off like that and sail all over another part of the world."

"I'll tell you Sharon. I'd do it again in a heart beat. Jim wants to sail around the Mediterranean and Aegean seas next year."

"Do you need a Cabin Girl to do the washing and cleaning?"

"There probably won't be much washing. We weren't wearing clothes most of the time."

"That's OK. I'll have an easier job then." Sharon put her hands together as if praying and curled her bottom lip begging.

"I'll see what I can do," Jennifer responded in a dismissing but joking manner.

Sharon leaned back in her chair and insisted, "Go home."

"I can't. I set up a meeting with that guy who has been trying to get in touch with me. The guy you told me about last week."

"Oh yeah. When's he coming?"

"In about ninety minutes."

"Did he say what this was all about?"

"No. Just like he told you he said it was very personal and needed to talk face to face with me."

"Do you want me to sit in the meeting with you?"

"No. I'll talk to him here. I don't think there will be any problem. He sounds like a nice man. You saw him and he didn't look creepy or anything right?"

"Yeah, he was a very nice looking man."

"Well, I'll see what he wants then go home afterward."

"Alright Hun. Say good bye before you head out."

"I will."

Sharon stood up to hug Kari. "I'm glad you're back. I should get back to work."

"OK Sharon." Jennifer picked up the phone as Sharon walked back out to the restaurant.

Diamond Bar, California – Wyatt Coleman
November 4, 1974

"Yes I have the business license and I need you to file and publish the fictitious business name in the local paper. We want to start printing up stationary as soon as possible," Wyatt instructed his lawyer on the other end of the telephone.

"Great. Thank you."

"Listen, I need to run. There's someone knocking at the door. I'll call you later today," Wyatt told his lawyer then hung up the phone. He grabbed his coffee then got up to see who was knocking. It was the mailman who usually brought the mail to the door when there was too much mail to fit in the box. Wyatt thanked him and thumbed through the stack as he walked back to his office.

There were the usual bills, investment magazines, catalogs, and junk mail. There was also a small package. Wyatt tossed the package on his desk. He sorted through the rest of the mail and took Jennifer's mail to her office then put the small pile on her desk. He returned to his office with the rest of the mail and considered going through it later after Jennifer got back from the restaurant because he knew she would be tucked away in her office busy preparing the sale of her restaurants. He set the mail down and leaned back in his chair recollecting their time together on the sailboat. He smiled as the memories flashed through his mind. Jennifer and he had so much in common that it was as if they were destined to be together. He glanced down at her picture on his desk and started to reach for it when his hand brushed the package. He unthinkingly picked it up and turned it over a couple of times before he became aware he was holding it. His attention changed to the package and he opened it up.

Wyatt had the contents of the package laid out over his desk in front of him unbelieving what he was looking at. There was a copy of his medical record from Vail, his driver's license before he disappeared in 1999, his driver's license as Jim Bolaire, the police report from the Colorado State Troopers, various other pictures, and a letter from Tim MacCorrmack. Wyatt was in shock wondering how anyone could have put all of this together or even had access to his 1999 driver's license when he would not have gotten it for another twenty years. He sat there staring at the documents on his desk for several minutes. Finally, he picked up the letter visibly shaking and began to read it:

April 3, 2006

Dear Mr. Coleman,

I know this package will be received with understandable surprise but I have nowhere else to turn and I need to ask you for your help.

My name is Tim MacCorrmack and I work for a research facility called TC Enterprises in Twenty Nine Palms, California, in the year 2006. I work in the TC Laboratories division of the company.

My Mentor and friend Dr. Rajiv Ramakrishnan was murdered two days ago. We were experimenting with time travel, due in part to your experience in 1999 of being sent back in time to approximately 1970 due to a lightning strike you had the misfortune of being too close to. I could go into detail about how we discovered this and our experimentations which lead up to being able to replicate it but I have neither the time nor energy at this moment.

I can tell you we have discovered there are several other people who have experienced the same thing you have over the last fifty years and we have been able to track some of them down. Unfortunately, as I am sure you are aware, since you found it was necessary to assume another identity some of these other people attempted similar courses of action but did not fare as well.

119

There was one gentleman in particular, and I use that term loosely, who disappeared in 1991 and was sent back to 1984. I have included his information on the following pages.

Wyatt turned the page and glanced at the picture of Elisaio Munoz with several dates and text following each date. He turned back to the letter.

Dr. Ramakrishnan interviewed Mr. Munoz a month ago. The Interview did not go well and it was terminated quickly. Mr. Munoz is a known drug dealer and criminal and has been implicated in several murders over the past twenty years. The police are currently looking at Mr. Munoz as a major suspect in Dr. Ramakrishnan's murder.

I know this is going to sound crazy but I think I can prevent Dr. Ramakrishnan's murder with your help by preventing Mr. Munoz from ever traveling back in time. I know, you are probably thinking how can this be done? Please hear me out.

As you can see from the data on Mr. Munoz we know that on November 17, 1991 he was released from prison in Yuma, Arizona and disappeared somewhere between Yuma and El Monte after that date. We also know that on November 21, 1983 he was arrested smuggling drugs across the border on Highway 95 out of Mexico into Arizona. I believe these two points in time present an opportunity for us, you, to alter Mr. Munoz's history. If you can prevent him from being arrested or changing his course of action during that time it will prevent him from being at the location of the lightning strike. If you miss the first opportunity you will have a second chance by preventing him from repeating his journey home the day he is released from prison. Just the slightest alteration of either of those times should prevent him from being at the exact location of the lightning strike.

Again, I know this may sound insane but it's the only thing I can think of to help my friend. If Mr. Munoz is prevented from traveling back in time then he will not be in a position to murder my friend.
I have no way of knowing whether or not you ever received this package other than the outcome. I hope to see my friend here again.

Sincerely,

Timothy MacCorrmack

Wyatt was awe struck at what he just read. He read the letter again just to try and understand what had just been revealed to him and what was being asked of him. He read the several pages on Mr. Munoz and wondered how any of this was possible. Then it suddenly hit him who Dr. Rajiv Ramakrishnan was. After all of this time he only knew him as Raj. He didn't really know his last name. He had seen it in print several times but never really paid much attention to it.

"My God! Raj," he whispered. How could this Tim have linked Raj and him together, he wondered. He never really saw Raj much after college. Should he tell Raj, he pondered. No, it was over thirty years away and if he was able to do something he wouldn't know the results until then so it wouldn't make any sense telling him now.

For the next couple of hours Wyatt studied the documents, made some notes, and organized his thoughts. Since there was no Internet yet he would have to go to the library and research these items he made notes on or make telephone calls regarding them.

Wyatt put all of the documents back in the package and looked around his office not really looking for anything specific. Jennifer had not come home yet so he left her a note then ran out the door.

TC Laboratories – Tim MacCorrmack
April 3, 2006

It was late in the afternoon and Tim sat in his office reading through his notes and files. He heard the door open up and didn't look up right away. He said to the intruder, "Just give me a minute here while I finish this up."

Detective Buckley replied, "Take your time. I'll just look around for a while if you don't mind?"

"Sure, go ahead. I'll be right with you." Tim continued with his review.

Tim finished up and walked over to where Detective Buckley was standing. "So, what does this contraption do," Buckley asked.

"This is called the 'STR8 BOLT' generator. We use it to generate enough power to simulate a lightning bolt."

"Is it some sort of weapon? Something that can generate that much power could cause some serious damage or disintegrate anything close to it."

"It all depends on how you use it. I suppose if put into the wrong hands it could be used as a weapon but that's not what we are using it for."

"So what specifically are you using it for?"

Tim laughed then walked around the generator to face Detective Buckley. "This is only a smaller version of the real generator which we are or were going to start using next week."

"You mean you have something bigger than this one that can do the same thing?"

"Let me ask you this detective, have you ever had a case where you could not explain how or why it happened?"

Detective Buckley gave Tim a puzzled look then answered, "Yeah sure. I had a case once, early in my career when I was a State Trooper in Colorado. Some Perp or victim, we never really found out which one he was, appeared out of nowhere and disappeared the same way. He didn't really do anything wrong as far as I could tell but the whole situation was mysterious. He was definitely involved in something but we never found out what. There were no records of this guy ever living and every where I turned something even more unusual would come up, then he was gone. Not a trace of him ever again. For several months I tried to find out anything I could on this guy but all I could come up with were dead ends. According to all sources available to us at the time he never existed. What's this have to do with this machine?"

"This generator helps us to solve mysteries. You said Colorado."

"That's right. I was a state trooper."

"What brought you out here to the desert? I would imagine Colorado was a much nicer place to live and work."

"I got married and my wife and I were tired of the snow. An opportunity came up for us to move out here so we did. I'm sure you didn't ask me here to hear my life's story," Buckley asked somewhat bewildered by the questions.

Changing the subject Tim asked, "Have there been any new developments in Raj's case?"

"It was definitely murder. Our investigators were able to uncover evidence confirming the other car forced the doctor over the side of the ravine. We have issued an arrest warrant for Munoz to question him about all of this. It has all of the ear markings of one of his hits."

"When do you think you'll have him in custody?"

"It's hard to say. Munoz can be very hard to find when he knows people are looking for him but I anticipate we'll have him, with the help of the L.A.P.D., before the end of the week."

"Why do you think he did it? I mean why would he want Raj dead?"

"With people like Munoz it could be one of a hundred things. Perhaps the Doctor insulted him, maybe the Doctor threatened him somehow, or maybe he just got too close for comfort and Munoz just eliminated any potential problem.

This is his normal M.O., Modes Operandi. The problem is investigators have never been able to link him to any solid evidence in a crime he was alleged to have committed in the past. We don't have a lot right now either but after we talk to him we may find the connection or motive we need."

"Well, if there is anything I can do to help please let me know. I have full access to Raj's files and I'll keep looking for information. If I find anything else linked to Mr. Munoz I'll let you know immediately."

"You have my card. Call me," Detective Buckley instructed then left the lab.

Tim managed to get the information he needed from the Detective concerning the Wyatt Coleman report and it was as he suspected. Now he hoped the packages he sent back would somehow reach him or Ms. Tomas.

Diamond Bar, California – Wyatt Coleman
November 4, 1974

It was after 9:00 p.m. and there was no sign Jennifer had ever come home. The note he wrote was still where he left it. He called out for her and there was no answer. He wondered if she was still at the restaurant. He went back to his office, looking into hers as he walked by, then placed the small stack of papers he was carrying on his desk. He walked back to the kitchen and grabbed a beer from the refrigerator and sat down on the couch. He let out a long sign and took a moment to relax.

Jennifer walked into the kitchen startling him and he asked her if everything was OK. She opened the refrigerator, also took a beer, and sat down beside him then said, "What a day I had." She took in a deep breath then let it out.

"I think I may have you beat on this one, Hun," he advised as he pulled her close.

"I doubt it. My day could be right out of the Twilight Zone." She took a sip from her beer.

I was thinking mine was more in the line of the Outer Limits." She turned and gave him a quizzical look then he smiled and said, "You first."

She took a big gulp from her beer and began telling him about her day. "You know I went to the restaurant today, right?"

Wyatt nodded.

"Well, remember Sharon telling me when we were in Sri Lanka that some guy needed to meet with me face to face?"

Again he nodded.

"I set up a meeting with him this morning."

"Wow! That was quick. He didn't waste any time." He saw Jennifer begin to shake then she broke out crying. Wyatt grabbed her and held her tight. I'm sorry Honey. Are you OK?"

"I'm fine. I just still can't believe it."

"What? What can't you believe," he asked facing her with a concerned look.

She wiped her eyes and continued, "As soon as he walked into the restaurant I lost it and started bawling my head off. He ran over to me, held me close, and rubbed my back like he did every time I'd ever gotten hurt."

"Who," Wyatt asked very worried now.

"My father," she broke down crying again. "It was so wonderful to see him again after all of this time. He was so young looking but he knew immediately who I was."

"How could he have possibly found you or even known you were you?"

Jennifer handed Wyatt a small package and in it were copies of her driver's license from 1992 and now. "I had just gotten my license renewed before I went to Blythe that weekend. He had recent pictures of me and a letter explaining what this was all about. The package was sent to him at our house in Anaheim."

"What did you tell him?"

"After we both got over the shock we spent the entire day together and I told him everything that had happened to me. Of course he still knew me as a little girl living at home. But he was so loving and understanding. He asked me if there was anyway I could prevent this from happening. I told him that's all I thought about for the first few years until I met you. Oh, he wants to meet you."

"Did you tell him about me too?"

"No. I wasn't sure I should tell him. I figured we could always tell him later if we needed to. He knows you know about me though and he said you must be a very understanding man. I told him you have your moments," she laughed through her crying then gave him a hug.

"So, what does he think about all of this?"

"He said he couldn't explain it but he would help in any way he could. He said he needed time to tell my mother or find some way to explain why he was helping out a woman his same age that looked like his daughter," again she laughed shakily.

"Poor Sharon," she blurted out. "I need to call her and tell her everything is OK. She must have thought I had a nervous breakdown when I fell to the ground crying as hard as I did when my father came in the door and called me Jen. I told her to leave me alone. I hope I didn't hurt her feelings."

"I think Sharon will survive." Wyatt got up and she grabbed his hand.

"Oh there's more," Jennifer insisted pulling him back.

He raised his index finger signaling her to hold that thought. "I'll be right back." When he returned he handed Jennifer his package. "I believe you were going to tell me something about Raj."

"Yes. How did…?" She began looking at the items in Wyatt's package and it was very similar to hers. The only difference was the date at the top of the letters. Hers was one day earlier.

"What can we do about this Jim? I know you are close to him. I just don't know how we can help."

"That's what I was doing today after I got my package. I went to the library and got as much information as I possibly could about the prison, U.S. Customs, drug trafficking, etc. I picked up several maps of Mexico, Arizona, California, and several city maps for the Los Angeles area. I'm not sure what we can do either but we have about nine years to try and come up with something."

El Monte, California – Wyatt Coleman
Summer 1982

The kid was only fourteen years old and already headed for a life of crime when Wyatt started watching him. Wyatt had hired and provided information to a Private Investigator in the summer of 1975 to find Elisaio Munoz. Once they found him and knew where he lived, went to school, hung out, and people he associated with Wyatt began learning all he could about the young man.

Wyatt had bought an office building in Elisaio's neighborhood and used it as his base. He outfitted it with the latest surveillance equipment, KayPro II computers, which were the newest personal computers for the time, and police radios to monitor crime in the area.

In the first several days of surveillance Wyatt observed young Elisaio and a friend break into a small market then walking out with arms full of what ever they could carry. He saw them break into parked cars stealing radios and other loose items from inside of them. He watched him shoot at dogs and cats with the gun he carried around in his belt behind his back. The kid was working hard at being irresponsible and reckless. Wyatt knew early on to keep his distance.

Over the next few years Wyatt decreased his days of surveillance and redirected some of his attention to Jennifer's and his company. He had hired another detective agency to keep track of young Elisaio. By this time he had seen the young man graduate from a petty breaking and entry kid to an adult street drug dealer. He was surprised Elisaio had not been arrested more than he should have been with the number of crimes he had committed early in his life. He had learned more about the young man than he cared to know about anyone but understood the more he knew about him the better equipped he would be to carry out his plan when the time came.

Jennifer was also very involved plotting Elisaio's daily activities, routines, and people he kept in contact with. Together, they had gathered enough information on Elisaio Munoz they could almost predict his every move. They were just one year away from trying to stop him from being arrested in Arizona preventing him from ever being anywhere near the lightning strike which would occur seven years later in 1991. They were ready to start putting their plan into place.

During these past several years Wyatt and Jennifer also formed their own company which helped fund this elaborate plan and it was growing at an accelerated pace. They began it by buying interest in companies new and old such as Sony, Apple, Zenith, Toshiba, and many other technology based companies. Wyatt and Jennifer bought thirty to forty nine percent of these companies leaving the original principals in charge allowing those businessmen to continue on their destined course in life. Also, knowing in advance what impact these companies would have on future technology and how they would affect the world economics guaranteed large profits and success for their new company.

This last year Wyatt spent a lot of time in Arizona. He had been looking at property for their company and at the same time preparing for next years confrontation at the border. The company needed a lot of room to expand and property was very inexpensive in Arizona. He knew Phoenix would be going through its first big growth spurt in the next couple of years and this would be a good time to buy. Property values would soar increasing the assets of their company significantly.

Everything was coming together and they were just about ready. If they were going to save their friend they preferred it be next year. Otherwise they would have to wait another seven years before they could get a second chance to stop Mr. Munoz from going back in time.

El Monte, California – Elisaio Munoz
November 18, 1983

"Ahhhh, Bueno! Ravin, mi amigo. Viene aqui, por favor," Arturo Rojas greeted as he waved Elisaio to come toward him. Arturo was the current drug boss for the East Los Angeles territory. He was a large man in his mid thirties, always wearing black clothes and lots of gold jewelry. He looked like a pimp sometimes. All he needed was a large hat and long coat to complete the outfit. He held his hand out to Ravin, "I have a favor to ask of you amigo. Please, come, sit." Arturo's bodyguard stepped away from the door making way for Elisaio to pass.

Arturo had put the word out on the streets to have Elisaio meet him at his home. Elisaio had been to his home several times before and was always impressed with the wealth Arturo had acquired from the business. He could see himself living like this in the future.

"What's up Patrón," Elisaio asked as he sat across from Arturo.

"Would you like a drink, something to eat? Monica, bring some food and wine, por favor."

"No, gracias Patrón. Estoy bien."

"Monica will bring it anyway and you can eat and drink or not."

"Thank you Patrón. So why have you called me here?"

"I have a favor to ask but we can get to that after we talk and maybe eat. OK?"

"Si Patrón."

"How is your familia? Everything is good I hope," Arturo asked but really didn't care. He was simply making conversation.

"Si, mi familia es good. And yours Patrón?"

"Bien, muy bien. Your business is doing well I see. Product sales continue to grow steady. You're on time with your payments. You have proven yourself to me my friend many times over and I think it is time I rewarded you."

"Thank you Patrón. I have tried to do everything the way you want," Elisaio responded then sat back and relaxed.

Monica returned into the room with a large tray of food and wine then Arturo gestured to Elisaio he should help himself so he did. They sat quietly and ate some of the food and drank wine. A short while later Arturo asked if the food was good and Elisaio nodded his approval. Arturo talked a little about some of the artifacts in the room and told a few jokes just to make small talk until they were finished eating.

"See my friend, you were hungry and thirsty too. Good. I'm glad you had something," Arturo grinned as he motioned for Monica to pick up the tray. He picked up his wine glass then walked over to a chair next to Elisaio. As he sat down he took a drink and set his glass on the table.

Elisaio mimicked him and thanked him for the hospitality. He turned to face Arturo then asked, "Tell me Patrón, what can I do for you?"

"Right to business huh," he replied smiling then eased back in his chair. "I like that. Well my friend, I have a little problem with our delivery for this month and I need your help to bring in an emergency shipment to cover us until I get the problem resolved."

"Sure Patrón. I will do what ever you ask of me."

"Good. I knew I could count on you. I need you to go to Mexicali and meet with our people down there and bring a small shipment across the border. I need you to bring it in through Arizona though. Can you do that for me?"

"Yes Patrón. I will make the arrangements and have one of my guys do it right away."

"No my friend. I want you to do it. I need to know it will be done right. Will you do that for me?

"Of course I can do it but I have good men who…"

"I said I want you to do it. Entiende," Arturo insisted with a stern smile.

"Si Patrón, I understand," Elisaio conceded not liking the idea and wondering why he had to do it himself.

"I would like you to head down there tomorrow and be back here in four days. I need this shipment no later. Do I make myself clear?"

"I will take care of it Patrón."

"Excellent. I want to see you as soon as you get back. We need to talk about our future together." Arturo stood then looked at Elisaio as if dismissing him. Elisaio hesitantly stood up, thanked Arturo then left the house.

Arturo returned to his sofa chair and waited for his bodyguard to come back after escorting Elisaio out. Moments later he returned. "So, are we all set? Is everything in place," Arturo asked the bodyguard.

"Si. They'll be waiting for him at the border. They assured me he won't make it back. The police have been tipped and they'll have him in custody before he reaches Yuma."

"I don't want him getting back here. Do you understand me X? I want him out."

"I don't understand why you're taking him out now. He's your top dealer. He brings in the most money. Why get rid of him?"

"He's expanding too fast. He's gaining power and that's what I am stopping. In order to stay on top my friend you have to eliminate any potential threat before it becomes a real threat. That's what I am doing. Young Ravin will be out of circulation for at least ten years and that is just long enough to stop him from ever being a real threat to me."

"I don't know. You could always have him hit if he gets too close."

"That's too messy. This way I can get him back after the wind has been knocked out of him. I'll be able to control him better and he'll feel like he owes me for letting me down when he didn't get me my shipment when I really needed it." Arturo laughed, pleased with his plan. "I want you to make sure there are no slip ups. Get down to Yuma and see to it."

"You're sure this is how you want it to go down," the bodyguard reiterated standing by the door before exiting.

"Yes X. Call me as soon as it's done. Entiende?"

"Si Patrón. I'll call you the minute they take him in," confirmed the bodyguard then he walked out the door.

"Bueno! Then get your ass back here right away so we can start breaking in his replacement. You here me X" Arturo yelled to him.

"Si, si," his voice echoed back through the foyer.

* * * * * * * * * *

As Elisaio drove away from Arturo's home he began speculating as to why he had been selected for this. Arturo did say he wanted to discuss their future together. Could this mean he was being promoted to some higher position and given more territory? Several scenarios came to mind suddenly. Maybe Arturo was testing his loyalty or maybe he was testing his competence to see if he could do the job or maybe he was supposed to meet the people he would be dealing with in the future. He was beginning to feel confident Arturo was going to move him up in ranks but to where. It dawned on him too that Arturo may even be setting him up but couldn't think of any reason why. He had done everything Arturo's way and never talked out against him to the other associates. Elisaio dismissed the idea and continued thinking this was definitely a good thing.

He drove home and packed a small bag. He put enough clothing in it for three days. He figured he could get down there late tonight if he went down to San Diego then across to Mexicali, spend the whole day tomorrow talking to their people then drive back through Arizona the next day getting in late that night. He had made that drive before and this would be no different except he was doing this for Arturo this time. He grabbed his bag, headed out the door, and took off for Mexico.

Yuma, Arizona – Wyatt Coleman and Jennifer Tomas
November 19, 1983

Not having the greatest of accommodations in Yuma, Wyatt and Jennifer stayed at one of the nationally popular hotel chains on 4th Street which was, for its time, a very clean hotel. Wyatt had been notified by his investigators that Elisaio had left for Mexico yesterday and arrived in Mexicali last night. He had taken the southern California route. Jennifer and Wyatt flew in to Phoenix this morning then rented a car to drive down to Yuma. They were going to establish their base camp down here and wait for the investigator to contact them about Elisaio's activities and exact location.

"Did the detective give you any idea when he would call," Jennifer asked Wyatt.

"No, but I'm sure he'll call us as soon as he knows something."

The past nine years seemed like an eternity to both of them but they were ready for these next few days. They had run through several scenarios over and over and one way or another they would either stop Elisaio from crossing the Arizona border or get him through Arizona safely. He was not going to be arrested in Arizona if they had anyway to prevent it. Everyone was in place. They had several truckers with their rigs standing by. They rented several large vans with drivers, along with over thirty other vehicles and drivers. They were given specific instructions to protect Elisaio at all cost from getting arrested in Arizona. Once he crossed into California the Highway Patrol would be notified then Elisaio could be arrested and jailed there.

"Is everyone clear what they need to do if he gets through the border? Are they all ready to go? Have they all checked in on the radio," Jennifer asked very nervously.

"Yes. Everyone is on standby waiting for us to give them the signal to go. It's going to be fine honey. I don't see how we can fail."

The initial plan was simple. The Mexican police had been warned and paid off to look for Elisaio. They had been supplied with a complete file about him. All they needed to do was, at minimum, detain him for at least a week then release him in Tijuana. Wyatt was not ignorant to the corruption of the Mexican officials and knew not to trust them. So he had a full backup plan ready to go.

If Elisaio happened to get across the border they had in place several strategies established to get him through Arizona as quickly and safely as possible. The main concept would be to keep him surrounded with all of the vehicles which would be spread out over a mile traveling at his speed to keep the way clear and if a police car were to be spotted they would close him in tight to prevent him from breaking any laws and shield him. Once he was free from Arizona they would break off slowly and their mission would be complete. The chances of Elisaio being in Arizona seven years from now would be almost impossible and Raj would not be in a situation to be killed by him in the future.

"Why don't you try to get some sleep before it all goes down," Wyatt asked Jennifer.

"Are you kidding? There is no way I'm going to be able to sleep until this is all over. I hate just sitting here though. Isn't there something we could be doing?"

"Everything is in place Hun. We just have to wait."

"What if he still gets arrested? What if something goes wrong?"

"I don't like it but if he does we still have seven years from now to try again when he gets out of prison. We won't need as many people and it should be easier to get him out of here quickly. We'll have a lot more options available then."

"I know. I just want this over now," she sighed feeling exhausted.

"There's still one more option we haven't really discussed should everything fail. We can always tell Raj about all of this and we can help him do what ever is necessary to prevent it from ever happening."

"Yes, but we decided that would absolutely be our last option. Right?"

"You're right. We'll only do that if we can't stop Elisaio."

Jennifer sat on Wyatt's lap on the couch and hugged him hard and long. "Is it going to work," she whispered in his ear.

"I hope so honey."

Mexicali, Mexico – Bodyguard, Xavier del Torres, "X"
November 19, 1983

Xavier del Torres waited in the shadows of the alley for Elisaio to leave the warehouse in Mexicali. Xavier or "X" as everyone knew him, was a childhood friend of his boss Arturo in Guatemala then again, after following him, in Los Angeles. They were like brothers so he could talk to Arturo in a way other people in the business could not. Even though he disagreed on how to handle Elisaio he would do as Arturo asked of him.

It was almost 5:30 pm when Elisaio left the warehouse. The obreros were experts at hiding their product in vehicles. It had taken them a little over two hours and X could see Elisaio smiling as he drove away. Moments later X pulled in through the double doors and went to the office where several Dons were talking, enjoying cervezas and Cuban cigars.

"Hola amigos. Como estas?"

"Hola X. Viene aqui. Come sit with us and have una cerveza."

"Gracias my friends." He sat down with a beer and selected a cigar when it was offered to him. He lit his cigar and took several hits from it before taking a drink from his beer. "So, how did everything go with young Elisaio?"

"Bien X," one of the men replied. "I personally supervised the loading of the product and did a final check then sent him on his way." Several of the other men laughed.

"Any rookie cop should be able to spot it even with the windows closed," another man stated. They all laughed again then raised their bottles in a toasting manner.

"Arturo will be happy to hear that. Do you think our friend suspects anything?"

Another man replied, "He was so full of himself he had no idea we were leaving traces of the product all over his car." Then he took a drink from his bottle.

"Good. That's what I wanted to hear. Is everything else in place," X asked with his cigar protruding from the right side of his mouth.

"I told him we have him set up at the hotel for two nights if he wanted to stay. He said he would probably leave tomorrow. Carmen will make sure he stays the second night. She knows to give him the time of his life. She's going to slip him a little dope and really wear him out if you know what I mean?" They all laughed in a lecherous manner. "She will make sure he's good and tired before he leaves."

"What makes you think he'll take the bait?"

"My friend, have you seen Carmen? I don't care who you are. You can not resist this woman. She could tempt Jesus Christ himself." They all broke out laughing hysterically.

"She better if you know what's good for you."

"Trust me my friend. Carmen will not fail."

"What about the border agents?"

"They will notify the AZ policia the minute he crosses the border. They should pick him up before he gets five miles into the U.S."

"Bueno. Then we wait, si?"

"Si X. He's as good as wrapped."

Several minutes passed and one of the men cleared his throat. "X. Does someone beside you, Arturo, and the four of us here know about this shipment?"

"No. Why do you ask," X inquired leaning forward in his chair.

"Someone has been trying to buy off the Federales. Who ever these people are they want Elisaio stopped before he gets across the border. They want him detained for a week. What do you know about this?"

"Nada amigos. Do you know who it is?"

"All we could find out were several California private detectives had been coming down here for several weeks buying off every Federale they could make contact with and were told to pass the word that they would make it worth their while to hold Elisaio."

"Do we have a problem," asked X.

"No. We doubled what the detectives were paying them to let Elisaio pass. I have been assured he will receive an escort without even knowing he has one all the way across the border."

"See what else you can find out about these mysterious detectives."

"We were already on it but the detectives have stopped coming down so I am not really sure how far we will get with it."

"As long as Elisaio gets popped the minute he crosses the border I don't really care who they are but if he makes it you better make sure I find out who they are and I mean right away. Entiende?"

"Young Elisaio is going to be breaking in a new roommate real soon. I don't think we have a problem my friend."

"I'll take you at your word." X sat back to enjoy the rest of his cigar and beer.

Mexicali, Mexico – Elisaio Munoz
November 19, 1983

Elisaio pulled out of the warehouse with his car full of product. He was always impressed at how fast and expertly the workers hid the product and made it virtually impossible for anyone to detect it or find it unless they knew exactly where to look. Even the drug sniffing dogs could not detect the product because of the packaging techniques they used. He felt very confident he would have no problem getting the shipment back to Arturo.

Elisaio drove to the hotel where the Dons had arranged for him to stay a couple of nights. He didn't want to offend the Dons by not accepting their offer but at the same time he knew Arturo was in a hurry for the product so he checked in and decided he would turn in around 10:00 then get an early start in the morning.

As he was walking toward his room he noticed there were a lot of people in the bar celebrating loudly as he passed by the entrance. It was crowded and thick with smoke. It felt festive. He decided he would come back later and have a drink before turning in for the night.

Showered and feeling good he went down to the bar. He saw her sitting alone and smoking a cigarette. She had to be the most beautiful woman he had ever seen. She was sitting with her legs crossed and the open slit in her silky dress exposed her long slender legs. Without even trying she was so seductive and every man in the bar knew they didn't have any kind of a chance to be with this woman. Elisaio stared at her for a moment longer contemplating whether or not he should waste his time trying to talk to her. Then she looked at him making full eye contact. He smiled and she smiled back in a shy way looking back at her drink. He walked over and sat down on the bar stool next to hers.

"Buenas nochas Senorita," he greeted her as she looked at him.

"Buenas nochas," she replied in an incredibly sexy voice.

"Mi llamo Elisaio Munoz."

"Carmen. Mucha gusta."

"Habla Ingles," he asked.

"Yes, I speak English," she replied.

"Why is a beautiful young woman like you sitting here all by herself?"

"Because no one has come over here to talk to me, except you."

"I can't believe that. You must be doing something to scare all of these men off."

"Apparently I'm not scaring you."

Her eyes were amazing. Dark latina eyes with an extraordinary bright white surrounding them making her gaze almost hypnotic.

"Can I buy you another drink," he inquired.

"Black Tequila Rose please."

He signaled to the bartender and ordered the drink. "I've never heard of a Black Tequila Rose. What's in it?"

"It's a raspberry liqueur mixed with tequila rose. It is very smooth. It is said to inspire romance. We'll see. Yes?"

"But of course." He ordered a tequila shooter for himself. "You never answered my question. How come you're here by yourself?"

"I'm here visiting my mother. She had a little accident and is having a hard time getting around so I came here to help her out for a few weeks until she gets back on her feet. I needed to get out of the house for a while. That's why I am here by myself."

"Where did you come from? You said you were visiting."

"I came down from Phoenix. I moved there last year." The bartender set her drink down and put the tequila shooter next to it. She took a sip and he took his shot.

Clearing his throat, "What do you do in Phoenix?"

"I work at a hotel. What about you? Why are you here in Mexicali?"

"I'm here on business."

"What kind of business," she asked taking a bigger sip from her drink.

"Sales. I'm here making arrangements for a shipment."

"You seem very young to be traveling and making shipping arrangements for some company."

"I was recently promoted and this is my first assignment."

Carmen swallowed down the rest of her drink then asked, "Do you want to get out of here? I'm getting tired of this place."

"What did you have in mind," he asked putting ten dollars on the bar.

"I'm sure you can use your imagination being a big time salesman. Sell me on an idea."

Elisaio leaned over the bar and whispered something to the bartender then gave him a twenty dollar bill. The bartender gave him a bottle of Cuervo Gold. Elisaio told her, "let's go to my room then we can negotiate a merger of some kind."

"That's the best you can come up with, a merger? We need to work on your sales skills young man." Smiling she grabbed his arm and they headed toward his room.

Two days later Elisaio woke up exhausted and hung over. It was 11:30 am and Carmen was no where to be seen. Elisaio realized he couldn't waste time looking for her now. He had to get the shipment to Arturo today and he had to get going right now. He packed his bag and checked out of the hotel in less than thirty minutes.

He was sick. He couldn't remember ever being this sick from drinking too much tequila. He drove slowly to the border check and decided once he got through he would stop and get some coffee and food. After that, he would be able to make the drive straight through in order to get back on time.

Yuma, Arizona – Wyatt Coleman and Jennifer Tomas
November 21, 1983

"Where is he? Did he slip by us somehow," Jennifer yelled very upset.

"He's still in Mexicali according to the detective. He's been in a hotel and hasn't moved for the last two days."

"I think he's gone Jim. I think he slipped out without any of our people seeing him."

"Look. He's still there and our guys are watching for him. He didn't get by us," Wyatt insisted. The telephone rang interrupting them and he answered it.

"Yes."

"When?"

"Where is he now?"

"How long?"

"OK. Stay on him and keep me posted. Use the radios from now on. We're on our way." He hung the phone up and said to Jennifer. "He left the hotel fifteen minutes ago and is headed toward the border. The detective said it will take him about an hour and a half to get through the border check."

Jennifer jumped up, grabbed the bag, and headed for the car. Wyatt was right behind her. They drove to the border in forty five minutes and met up with several of the other members of their group.

"Everyone is in place Mr. Bolaire. If he gets through the border we'll pick him up immediately. He'll be wrapped up so tight no one will notice him."

"Good. If he does get through we need to get him to California without any problems. The California Highway Patrol has already been notified and they are standing by to nab him the minute he crosses the state line. I doubt anyone will notice him but I can not stress it anymore, the Arizona Police can not pick him up. Got it! Just keep him in the envelope and everything should go smoothly. Hopefully the Mexican police will pick him up and we won't have to worry about it. Let's just wait and see where this goes."

"We're all ready Mr. Bolaire. Everyone's on radio and standing by."

The next hour felt like an eternity. Wyatt, Jennifer and the others at the border stared at every vehicle coming out of the border check point even though they were in constant radio contact with the detective following Elisaio. They would know exactly when he crossed the border if he crossed at all. The Federales were contacted and given a full description of the vehicle and were told Elisaio was approaching the border check point. It would be all over in the next couple of minutes.

To the amazement of everyone Elisaio was passed right on through the check point. He never had to stop. Everyone was totally caught by surprise even though they knew this might happen. Wyatt was pissed. He knew immediately the border patrol and Federales took his money without ever intending to stop Elisaio. He decided he would deal with that at another time. Right now they had to move.

Wyatt radioed ahead to the trucker at the first off ramp to block the ramp so no one could exit. This is the off ramp Elisaio would have taken to the Denny's where he got arrested but not this time.

Wyatt was two cars behind Elisaio as they approached the off-ramp. Traffic in the right lane came to a sudden stop because the jack-knifed rig blocked the entire exit. Vehicles were trying to drive around it but could not. Elisaio sat there in the traffic for a minute then moved back out to the freeway and drove by the exit. Wyatt let out a sigh of relief. The next off ramp was ten miles ahead. They had passed the first major hurdle. Everything was going accordingly to their contingency plan.

Three miles into Arizona everyone was starting to settle back and relax for the long drive. They were moving at a pretty good pace at just over 65 MPH. Jennifer was much more relaxed and gave Wyatt a kiss on the cheek. She leaned back in her seat and looked out the window.

"Uh oh! We might have trouble," Wyatt interrupted. He got on the radio and let everyone know police cars were coming up fast. The group slowed down and closed in on Elisaio trying to shield him. He was trying hard to get around their fabricated traffic jam but they had him boxed in tight. The group tried to maneuver over to the right lanes allowing room for the police to pass but they did not. With their lights flashing and sirens blaring they weeded out the grouped vehicles one by one until they closed in on Elisaio's vehicle.

The police completely blocked all traffic while they pulled Elisaio from his vehicle. Wyatt and Jennifer watched in horror as their long term plan was obliterated in a matter of minutes. How could this have happened they both thought. Wyatt radioed to the group ahead to break off and wait for further instructions.

Highway 95, Arizona – Elisaio Munoz
November 21, 1983

"Come on you fucking people," Elisaio screamed at the traffic around him. He was so pissed off because some stupid truck driver jack knifed his truck at the off ramp where he wanted to stop and get some coffee and food. He felt like he was going to vomit if he didn't get something to eat quickly. The next exit was ten miles and he decided he would stop there. A few minutes later and traffic was suddenly closing in on him. "What the fuck," he shouted. He couldn't budge. He tried to maneuver around them but they had him boxed in real tight. He kept looking in his mirror for a break then he saw all of the flashing lights approaching fast. He quit trying to pass and figured he would use the traffic to protect him. After the policed passed by he would try to get out of this traffic jam and get some food.

Elisaio could see the traffic behind him slowly pulling off to the right until the police were right on top of him. They had him surrounded and he had no choice but to pull over. He looked around the inside of his vehicle to make sure the product was still hidden then noticed a small trace powder on the floor of the back seat. "Fuck," he yelled. He knew he was busted and waited for instructions from the police.

Mexicali, Mexico – Bodyguard, Xavier del Torres, "X"
November 21, 1983

It was the strangest thing X had ever seen. First the jack knifed truck at the off ramp where the police were waiting for Elisaio was completely blocked. Half of the police scrambled to take care of the truck accident and the other half took off to catch up with Elisaio further down the freeway.

Then it almost looked as though all of the traffic ahead were trying to shield Elisaio from the police. If the police had gotten into too much of a hurry they might have pass right by him without noticing him in the bunched up traffic but they didn't. *"What the hell is going on,"* he thought.

He had heard from the Dons a couple of days ago that someone was trying to arrange for Elisaio to get busted in Mexicali at the border. Then today it looked as though someone were trying to protect him from the Arizona police. This was weird. It didn't matter anymore. He could see the police pulling bags of cocaine out of Elisaio's vehicle and there was no way he could get out of this mess. His job was done. He waited for a chance to cross over the median and go back into Mexico to take the southern route back into Los Angeles. He would call Arturo after he crossed the border.

Highway 95, Arizona – Wyatt Coleman and Jennifer Tomas
November 21, 1983

Jennifer could not believe what she was seeing. She could not stop crying. Wyatt just held her in his arms and said nothing. He needed time to think about what they were going to do next. Radio messages kept coming in but they ignored them. Finally, Wyatt told everyone the mission was aborted.

Back at the hotel Jennifer broke down and cried long and hard. Wyatt was sad too. They failed their friend and didn't know what they should do to help him. She cried herself to sleep and Wyatt drifted off too for a few hours. They were exhausted and had no place to go or anything to do for the next seven years.

The next several weeks were quiet. Jennifer and Wyatt didn't talk to each other much. It was just the usual good morning, good night, and the occasional conversations on major news topics they had lived through once before so long ago. Then the news about Elisaio's conviction made the news and it was as it was, fifteen years with the possibility of parole in seven. Nothing had changed. Wyatt was sick of the whole thing.

Several more days had passed before Wyatt got real busy. He began making lots of phone calls, running out to the office several times a week, spending hours in his office at home, and acting like he had a new mission. Jennifer didn't take any interest in what he was doing. She went to her restaurants once in a while or just laid around the house depressed.

Another month had gone by before Wyatt approached Jennifer. "Get your ass up," he demanded. "We're not going to continue living like this. Pack a small bag with a couple of changes of clothes. We'll buy what we need later."

"What are you doing," she retorted lying on the couch.

"I'm saving us and our friend. Come on. Get up. You've got one hour to pack your bag and get cleaned up."

"Where are we going," she asked annoyed.

"Away from here. We need some time together and we need time to sort things out."

"I don't want to go anywhere. Just leave me alone," she whined pulling a pillow over her head.

"You get you ass up now or I'll drag you out the way you're dressed."

She threw the pillow at him and he caught it then tossed it on the floor. He walked over behind the couch and flipped it forward throwing Jennifer to the floor. "Hey," she yelled.

"I said get up. You have fifty eight minutes now."

"Where are we going?"

"Airport. Fifty seven minutes."

"Jim. This isn't funny."

"It's not meant to be funny. We have to get out of here and I'm making it happen."

Jennifer got up off of the floor and walked slowly to the bathroom. She slammed the door hard then heard Wyatt yell, "Fifty six minutes." She half smiled rubbing her sore butt.

TC Laboratories – Tim MacCorrmack
April 3, 2006

"Still nothing," Tim sighed. He had no sudden recollection. From what Raj had told him he should feel a sudden rush as the new memory formed in his mind. It was obvious the packages didn't reach Mr. Coleman or Ms. Tomas. There was no rush, no tingle, and not so much as a twitch. "What am I doing wrong?"

It was getting late. If he had to Tim was going to stay all night trying to fix this problem. With the technology Raj and he had developed there was no excuse for him not to try everything and anything to prevent this whole incident from ever happening. It was frustrating.

He called his wife and told her he was OK and that he was going to continue working. She pleaded with him to come home and get some rest but he insisted on staying. She understood he needed the time and didn't push him any further. He went back to reviewing all of the files and data trying to find something, anything.

Twenty Nine Palms, CA.—Elisaio Munoz
April 3, 2006

Elisaio left Tim MacCorrmack's home a few hours earlier. He had claimed he was a news reporter and wanted to talk to Tim about Raj for an article he was writing. Tim's wife, Laci, told him her husband had spent the day at the office and he might be able to catch him there.

Elisaio had considered having a little fun with Laci but wasn't sure when he would finish with Tim. He thought she was a very attractive young woman. He decided after he took care of MacCorrmack he would come back here and unwind with her a little before heading back to L.A. The police would determine her rape and murder were linked to MacCorrmack's murder. He'd get back home and establish a good alibi so no one would be able to connect him to their deaths.

When he left the MacCorrmack's home he drove to the TC complex and waited in the parking lot for several hours with no sign of Mr. MacCorrmack. He wasn't sure what building he might be in. There was only one car in the parking lot so he parked close to it hoping Tim would eventually come to him. It was starting to get dark and this would make it easier for him to take care of this guy without any one seeing him. All he had to do was wait.

FIVE

"Did I ever thank you for making me come with you on this trip," Jennifer asked lying in the lounge chair by the pool at the Ramada Hotel in Cairns. It was still summer in Australia and the warmth of the sun was soothing to her mind, body, and soul.

"No, but I'm sure we can work something out later," Wyatt teased in a playful tone.

They had flown into Sydney a week ago, bought clothes and all of the things they would need to travel for several weeks so they both heal emotionally. After two days in Sydney they flew here to Cairns to just lie around and bask in the sun.

Jennifer hit him on the shoulder and replied, "If that's all it takes then you owe me because I think I've thanked you in advance many times over." They giggled.

"Do you want another drink," Wyatt asked.

"No thanks Hun. I'm a little drunk already. I think I need something to eat. Do you mind if we go into town and have an early dinner?"

"Not at all. I'm hungry too. Why don't we go back up to the room and I'll let you thank me in the shower then we can go grab some dinner."

"What? Dessert before dinner? You'll get fat."

"So be it then. I guess I'll just have to get huge because I want to have dessert with you for the rest of my life."

Jennifer blushed and told him, "Then you need to make an honest woman out of me."

"I plan to very soon."

She looked at him with surprise and asked, "Are you going to let me know when this momentous event is supposed to happen?"

"You'll be the first to know."

Again she playfully hit him and they went up to their room.

Wyatt had been thinking about asking Jennifer to marry him for quite some time now. Going through this ordeal showed him every side of her and he couldn't imagine not being with her. He loved everything about her. He would ask her but not right now. She needed this time to recuperate.

After dinner they went for a walk around the sleepy town. There was not a lot that happened in Cairns but it was relaxing to just stroll up and down the main street. Jennifer hugged Wyatt's arm the entire time they walked and they didn't need to say much. Walking back to the hotel Wyatt told Jennifer he wanted to run something by her.

"There's a topic we both have been avoiding for a long time, ever since we first got those packages from Tim MacCorrmack, and I thought we should start talking about it. At least bring it out into the open and acknowledge or examine their ramifications. I'm fifty-four years old and you're forty-five. I was only twenty-four, married, and just out of the Marines this same time. You were what, nineteen or twenty and in college?"

"Yes. I'm not quite sure where you're going with this."

"I think you know. I'm talking about our disappearances. Both of us have lost about thirty years of a future which we will never see. We have the ability to do something about it. We know exactly when we went back in time unlike that of Elisaio. With him there was a two day window but you and I know exactly where we were and when. Do you know what I'm talking about now?"

"Yes," she acknowledged lowering her head. "You're talking about preventing ourselves from going back in time." There was a long pause. She looked up at Wyatt, "You're right. I have thought about it many times but I didn't know how to bring it up or if I wanted to. I love being here with you and I don't want to lose any of that."

"That's what I wanted to talk to you about."

"If we don't go back Jim, then we are going to lose all of this time we have spent together. We will never meet. I'd lose you and I don't want that even if it means losing those thirty years. We wouldn't be here to help Raj either. No. I won't consider it."

"I have an idea. Just hear me out. Then I want you to think about it for a

143

few days before you say no. We still have eight years to decide before you go back and I have fifteen years. So what do you have to lose?"

Over the next several hours Wyatt discussed his ideas. Jennifer was quick to point out the pros and cons of all of them, which is exactly what Wyatt wanted from her. He knew she would help him fine tune them making their decision a good one no matter which way they decided to go.

After a week had gone by Jennifer suggested they not talk about it anymore, at least not while they were on vacation. They took the next three months to just spend time together not thinking about any of this. They even saw the young version of a famous crocodile wrestler from the 1990's at his father's crocodile farm before leaving Cairns. Jennifer had no idea who he was but Wyatt explained how he would eventually become known as the Crocodile Hunter.

They traveled by car, motorcycle, train, and RV all over Australia. They took the train to the Gold Coast and lay out on the beaches for several weeks. They traveled by car to Sydney and went to several plays and shopped. They rode a motorcycle along the coast on the Princes Highway to Melbourne stopping at every little fisherman port they could find. Then finally they took off across the country in an RV going through Alice Springs and eventually winding up in Perth.

* * * * * * * * * *

The next seven years were long but Wyatt and Jennifer had agreed to take off for at least three months every year to spend time together. They used that time together to travel all over the world. They spent time in the Greek Islands, Spain, France, Egypt, Mexico, Peru, and the Caribbean.

On December 27, 1988 they decided to get married in the Andes Mountains of Peru at the Machu Picchu ruins. They had made all of the necessary arrangements to marry with their original birth names. This would help protect all of their investments in the future.

The altitude was a little hard to get used to at first but after several days and lots of water they acclimated themselves. They traveled all over Peru as husband and wife. They took a boat ride through the Amazon, they walked the streets of Lima, and lived on a small yacht on Lake Titicaca. They were the essence of a perfect traveling team.

Their plan was to see as much of the world as possible in the short time they had before 1992. That year was going to be the pivotal point in their lives. But first and foremost, in 1991, they had to secure Raj's future.

Twenty Nine Palms, California – Detective Dan Buckley
April 3, 2006, 6:00 pm

Dan arrived back at his office after meeting with Tim MacCorrmack. He had been called earlier and asked to come by the Lab. Dan wasn't sure he could give MacCorrmack anymore information this early in the investigation but he agreed to stop by on his way back to his office. After he left the lab he felt there was something definitely suspicious about that entire meeting. He felt like he had just been interrogated by Mr. MacCorrmack. But why? The things they talked about had nothing to do with the case but still he felt something was up.

Being naturally suspicious about everything Dan began doing a little background check on Mr. Tim MacCorrmack. While he was waiting for the data to come up on his screen he looked at the file on the case so far. "What connection do you have with the good doctor here, Ravin," he voiced out loud as if questioning himself.

The telephone rang and he picked it up.

"Detective Buckley."

"Ah yes! Detective Castillo. Thank you for getting back to me."

"Yes. I did receive it. I'm looking at it right now. Mr. Munoz has been a very lucky man from what I can see from the file. He obviously knows how to cover his tracks."

"Well, that's why I wanted to talk to you. I believe he may have slipped up this time. I am working on a murder case that has his name all over it and I wanted to talk to someone who is very familiar with him."

"Well good. I'm sure you can help fill in the gaps. It seems our perp has had some interaction with our victim, Dr. Rajiv Ramakrishnan, but we don't know to what extent. I was hoping you could shed some light on this for me."

Dan listened to the detective tell him how the FBI had arranged a meeting between the two of them but didn't know what the meeting was about. Apparently the doctor had called in a favor from someone at the bureau to set up the meeting and that is as far as the information goes on the reason why. This threw up a red flag on their end and they increased surveillance on Munoz to try to see what, if anything, was up. There had been increased activity at his home. One of his hired guns, Manuel Gutierrez (street name Asesino) showed up a couple of days later then left the L.A. area shortly thereafter. They lost track of him. They didn't suspect a link to the doctor's murder until Dan called them.

"Well, I appreciate all the help you've given me so far."

"So where are you on Munoz? With what I have and what you have on him can we tie him to Gutierrez and hopefully to this murder?"

"When?"

"Well, where is he now? Do you think he is here or on his way here?"

"Why would he risk coming here?"

"MacCorrmack is just an associate. I've talked to him and he claims he doesn't know much about the meeting they had. Do you think Munoz might be going after him?"

"I will. I'll get someone out to his house and keep an eye on him."

"Let's hope not. I'd like to catch him before he does anything."

"Thank you. I'll keep you posted too. Good bye."

Dan hung up the phone then immediately picked it up again and dialed Tim's number at TC Labs. The voice mail picked up and Dan left a message for Tim to call him. He hung up and called Tim's home phone. He had written both numbers on the inside of the folder for the case. It rang several times. There was no answer. They probably went out to dinner. He would try again later.

He called down to dispatch and requested a unit be sent to the MacCorrmack's house just as a precaution and to remain until further notice. If Elisaio was in the area he wanted to pick him up and nail him for the murder of Dr. Ramakrishnan.

Twenty Nine Palms, California – Elisaio Munoz
April 3, 2006, 8:00 pm

Elisaio had finished the last of his Coke. It was flat from sitting for the last hour. At 6:00 pm he had gotten hungry so he went into town to get a quick bite to eat from the closest fast food place. He was gone for about fifteen minutes and when he returned there was another car in the parking lot next to Tim's. He decided to park further away out of sight and watch from a different vantage point.

He saw an older man leave one of the buildings and get into the other car then drive off. He was wearing a cheap suit and looked like a cop. It would stand to reason the cops would be talking to Tim since he worked closely with the Doc so he stayed where he was. Tim would come to him soon enough. He didn't want this little shit continuing with the experiments on lightning where the Doc left off and fuck up his life. So eliminate him and the potential problem would be solved.

Yuma, Arizona—Wyatt and Jennifer
November 11, 1991

Most of the ground work had been done before in 1983. Therefore, Wyatt and Jennifer didn't need as much preparation time for this second attempt to stop Mr. Munoz from traveling back in time. They weren't going to need as many people this time either.

The plan was straightforward. Several vehicles would be strategically placed around the prison and when Elisaio was released one of the vehicles would offer him a ride. The goal was to get Elisaio out of Arizona as fast as possible avoiding the storm all together. If one vehicle failed to pick him up another would be close by to do the same thing. Mr. Munoz would eventually accept one of the offers.

The records of his release indicated he was not picked up at the prison by family or friends and that he apparently started hitch-hiking outside the front gate. So the plan seemed, at face value, to be perfect. Traffic was not usually heavy on Highway 95. Therefore, Mr. Munoz would most likely accept the first offer.

Once in the vehicle all of the other vehicles would follow. If Elisaio began to suspect anything or wanted to be dropped off the driver would indicate he was going to stop by tapping on his brakes lightly several times signaling the driver behind him. Everyone would be radioed they were planning to stop and get into position for the change over. The driver who dropped Elisaio off would then go in a different direction then follow up in the rear.

If all was going smoothly but it looked as though they would get caught up in or near an electrical storm they were prepared to cause a major traffic jam stopping all traffic from going forward into the area of the storm. There, they could either wait it out or turn around and take cover. Everything was hinged on Elisaio's choices.

"Are we forgetting anything," Jennifer asked Wyatt.

"It's almost a no brainer Hun. I doubt Elisaio will want to stay out in the cold weather for any length of time so he will more than likely accept the first ride that comes along. I really feel good about this and I think its going to go very smoothly this time. We have a lot more information than we did in 1983. We don't have to worry about being double crossed by corrupt officials because we don't have any to deal with this time. All we have are the ten drivers and we know we can trust them."

"I'm just so worried. So much more this time than last, probably because this is our last chance."

147

"We still have one last option if for some reason this doesn't work. We tell Raj everything and let him fend for himself."

"I know. Maybe we should tell him anyway."

"I don't think we can, at least not now. If we do it may alter what he does in the future and then he wouldn't have been able to make it possible for Tim MacCorrmack to contact us. It could all change and we can't take that chance. Not right now. We'll do that as a last resort."

"God! I can't wait for all of this to be over," she blurted out very frustrated.

"It will be in six more days. I promise."

Yuma, Arizona—Elisaio Munoz
November 12, 1991

"Hey short-timer. What you got planned when you get out," an inmate asked Elisaio.

"I've had a lot of time to think about this man. I just want to go home, get a job, and straighten my life out. I'm tired of this shit ese. I don't want to end up here again."

"Yeah right. When I get out I'm going to become a priest" mocked the inmate laughing.

"Fuck you asshole! I haven't heard from Arturo or anyone since I got popped in 83. There's no fucking loyalty with these people. Why would I want to take another chance helping those pendejos get rich when they couldn't give a shit about me or anyone else for that matter?"

"I'd bet if you went to them they'd take you in without any question. They know you man."

"That's what I'm talking about you stupid fuck. I'm in here because of them. I didn't rat them out. I protected them. I shouldn't have to go to them. I took the whole thing and they completely abandoned me here. I've had a lot of time to think about it and I'm almost sure they set me up but I don't know why. If I was somehow able to do anything I'd start my own business, if I could, and take those fucks out but I can't. I don't have the money or the time. So, I'm going in a different direction. I'm going legit. Fuck'em all."

"After a few weeks I bet you go crawling to them begging for a job."

"It ain't going to happen bro. I'm out of this. I'm telling you. I don't think they want me around. They left me here to rot and I'm not going to give them another chance to fuck me over. I'm going to go home and they won't even know I'm back."

"They'll know."

"Then as soon as I can I'll move somewhere else. I'll do what I have to in order to survive but after that I'm gone. It would take an act from God to get me in that business again or anywhere near them."

"Lights out in ten," a guard yelled as he walked down the corridor.

"In five days it all changes," Elisaio declared as he lay back in his bunk.

Yuma, Arizona—Wyatt and Jennifer
November 15, 1991

"What can I do," Jennifer asked.

"Nothing. Everyone is here. All we can do is wait," Wyatt replied.

"What about…"

"Honey! There's nothing left for us to do except wait," he asserted grabbing hold of and hugging her.

"I need to get out of here. Can we go to Phoenix tonight? I can't take another minute here."

"I think that's a good idea. We need to get some air, if you will, and get a new change of atmosphere. I'll call the team and let them know we are going in to Phoenix. They can reach us on the car phone if anything should come up."

"Thank you Jim. I know I've turned into a real wimp over this whole ordeal. It just hasn't let up since we started this and I'm tired and beat both emotionally and physically."

"I know. I'm tired too. The day after tomorrow it will all be over. I don't know what I can do to convince you but it will be."

Wyatt phoned the team and told them to relax and enjoy the night on him. He would meet up with them for dinner tomorrow evening and go over the final arrangements. There was no way he was going to let this fail this time.

* * * * * * * * * *

They arrived in Phoenix late in the afternoon. It was a pleasant day, not too warm or cold. There were some late afternoon clouds forming toward the west but this was normal for Arizona. They spent the rest of the afternoon at a park sitting by a manmade lake and enjoyed the quiet. They fed the ducks and watched some squirrels at play. It was a beautiful end to a not so nice time.

They went back to their hotel and cleaned up for dinner. They walked around town and eventually ended up at a little café by the highway. It reminded Jennifer of the little truck stop she worked at in Blythe almost twenty five years ago. She smiled reflecting back to those first days when she struggled with her unusual situation.

Wyatt was also reflecting back to when it all began for him. He remembered the physical and emotional pain he had endured, the fear, the excitement of a new life, all of it. Young Elisaio would never experience any of this if all went according to plan.

The quality of their dinner was less than expected but the atmosphere was a breath of fresh air. The hustle and bustle of the waitresses running in and out of the kitchen, the busboy clanking dishes as he cleared away the tables and the ringing of the cash drawer as customers paid their bills. It was music to their ears.

They ordered apple pie for dessert because pies were always good at these little cafés and it was indeed. Jennifer ordered hers ala mode and savored every bite. When they had gotten their fill of the cafés ambiance they walked around town for a while longer. They thought it would help alleviate the full feeling in their stomachs.

At the end of a long section of shops on Main Street there was a small out of the way jazz bar. The music was inviting so they went inside. They sat in a small booth off to the side of the stage, ordered drinks, and were captivate by the music. It evoked every feeling and emotion they had bottled up inside. They held each other close with their eyes closed and just listened. They stayed in the little bar until it closed. Wyatt asked the bartender to call them a cab to take them back to their hotel. They both had had too much to drink but it was invigorating to feel this way again after so many years, to feel free of stress and worry, to have their minds clear.

On the ride to the hotel they began kissing and pawing at each other like high school kids. By the time they got to their room they were pulling at each others clothes wanting to feel their naked bodies entwined in each other. The passion and the intensity of their lovemaking were unlike anything they had ever experienced before. The years of built up stress, tension, frustration, and anger were released with each orgasm. It went on all night until they were completely exhausted and unable to think about anything but each other. The world around them did not exist for that night. They fell asleep holding their sweat drenched bodies close to each other.

The next morning they awoke to a bright sunny Phoenix morning. They were starving. The calories from dinner were definitely burned off and they had tapped into some reserves as well. They jumped out of bed, showered, and went to the hotel restaurant for breakfast. Their waiter was somewhat surprised at the amount of food they ordered but brought it anyway. Wyatt and Jennifer ate it all and were giggling as they forced the last few bits of it down.

Back in their room the exhilaration was beginning to wear off. They packed their bags, checked out of the hotel, then got in their SUV and headed back to Yuma. Jennifer was more talkative than she had been in the past several years and that made the drive back seem quicker. Her confidence was high and she was ready to send Mr. Elisaio Munoz on his way to his new future.

Twenty Nine Palms, California – Detective Dan Buckley
April 3, 2006, 9:00 pm

Dan had been notified by the police officer outside of the MacCorrmack's house that they had just arrived home. He called them. The telephone was on its third ring and he began to get concerned. Half way through the fourth ring he was relieved to hear a hurried female voice answer.

"Hello, Mrs. MacCorrmack," he greeted.

"Hi. This is Detective Dan Buckley with the Twenty Nine Palms police. Is your husband free to talk?"

"He's not. Do you know when he'll be home?"

"Does he normally work late like this?"

"I see. Do you… Yes I have it here. I'll call there after I hang up with you. Do you know what he's working on at the lab?"

"Yes, I guess it would be top secret. Can I ask you one more thing?"

"Have either of you received any strange telephone calls or been visited by anyone in the last few days?"

"You did. Did he show you his business card or press pass?"

"Can you describe him to me?"

"No. Everything's fine. I'm just following up on a few things. If you could just tell me what he looked like and perhaps what he was wearing?"

"Yes."

"Uh huh."

"How much?"

"Yes, about two hundred pounds. I got it. Well thank you Mrs. MacCorrmack."

"No. Everything's fine. As I said it's just a routine follow up."

"Yes, it was nice talking to you too."

"I will. I'll tell him as soon as I talk to him."

"Good bye."

The description she gave him was pretty close to Munoz's general description. Dan called dispatch and requested the unit at the MacCorrmack's house be given a picture of Munoz. He explained to the dispatcher Munoz had possibly been passing himself off as a news reporter. He wanted the unit to step up the level of surveillance. The dispatcher confirmed she had relayed the new info to the unit on sight.

Dan tried to call Tim at TC Labs. The line was busy. He tried several more times over the next ten minutes then finally it rang. Tim picked up.

"Mr. MacCorrmack. Dan Buckley here. I was beginning to get worried about you. I called your…"

"You did. Good. I hope I didn't alarm her but there is some new information I needed to make you aware of. Elisaio Munoz is in the area and we think he may be looking for you. To what purpose we don't know."

"No. They're fine. I have a unit at your house and they will stay there until we find Munoz. If you are going to be much longer at work I could send a unit over there to make sure everything's is OK."

"Good. I told your wife I would tell you to go home."

"Alright. Call me or 911 if anything happens. There's a police unit right across the street from your home. I'll call you tomorrow."

"You're welcome. Good night."

Dan was relieved to hear MacCorrmack's voice and that he was OK. He would feel a lot better once they got Munoz into custody. It was almost 10:00 pm and he wanted to finish up a couple of things before he called it a night. "Oh hell with it," he said as he threw his pen onto the desk. "I'll get an early start tomorrow." He closed up his office and left for the night.

TC laboratories – Tim MacCorrmack
April 3, 2006, 10:00 pm

"Good night Detective and thank you." Tim hung up the phone. He was tired. He knew he should have gone home before this but he wanted to make sure he tried everything before giving up. He started to straighten up his desk and put all of the files back into a neat stack. He walked over to Raj's desk and began to straighten it up too when it hit him.

"You dumb ass Tim," he yelled to himself. He sat down at Raj's desk and began typing rapidly on the computer. He threw papers everywhere trying to find the information and items he needed. He ran back and forth to the copier and scanner. He printed out several files from the computer. He scanned frantically through his notes tearing out pages then entering coordinates into the STR8 BOLT generator console. For the next few hours he compiled all of the documents he needed. He had everything he needed and was just about ready. It was his last chance.

Twenty Nine Palms, California – Elisaio Munoz
April 4, 2006, 12:00 am

"Ok. This mother fucker is starting to get on my nerves. What the fuck can he be doing in there all this time? I'll bet that little cock sucker stays in there all fucking night. Well, if he doesn't get his ass out here by 5:00 I'll have to go in after him I guess." Elisaio was getting tired and started talking to himself. He was getting hungry again too but he knew the minute he left to get something that little shit would leave. So, he was going to stick it out.

Elisaio wasn't sure how he was going to kill MacCorrmack. He usually used a gun when he killed his enemies but Tim was going to be an easy kill. He toyed with the idea of using a knife. It was a slower death and he was curious as to what it would be like to watch one of his victims die slowly. No one was going to be around at five in the morning. He decided he would go with what ever his gut told him at that moment. He was starting to get excited. He hadn't killed anyone in a long time and he was enjoying the rush.

Yuma, Arizona—Wyatt, Jennifer, and the Team
November 16, 1991

"I know most of you are wondering what is so important about this man Elisaio Munoz. The life of a very good friend of ours is at stake and his safety depends on the success of us getting Mr. Munoz to California as soon as possible. Our mission is simple. Make it easy for him without him knowing we are involved. I've met with all of you separately and we have gone over several scenarios but use your discretion to improvise on the situation at hand. Munoz cannot know we are all connected and working together. It's that simple gentleman. Tomorrow is the real thing and there's no turning back. Do any of you have any questions before we end this meeting," Wyatt asked then sat back in his chair at the head of the long table and waited for questions.

Wyatt arranged for them to have dinner in a small banquet room so they could discuss tomorrow's event as a group in private. Everyone was relaxed and confident the mission would go off without any problems. Wyatt and Jennifer were both very relaxed as well.

"What if someone should pick him up before we get a chance," asked one of the team members.

"We follow close and make sure we are the next ones to pick him up when that person drops him off at what ever their destination may be. The most important thing, gentlemen, is to keep Munoz moving. We don't care if someone else picks him up but we do care that they keep him going toward California."

"What is the significance of avoiding the electrical storm? Why don't we just drive through it," asked another team member.

"I apologize to all of you gentlemen but I can't really explain why this is so important but stick to the plan and we may not have to worry about the storm." Wyatt looked around the room for a moment then asked, "Who's going to be running point when we head west on I-10?"

One of the team members raised his hand and shouted out, "I'm going to take us through Blythe."

Wyatt ordered, "Stay about ten miles ahead of us and make sure you are in constant radio contact. Keep me posted on the storm situation and if I give you the word I need you to block both westbound lanes on an overpass so no traffic can get around you."

"That won't be a problem," the man replied.

"I'll be driving the other rig and I'll be leading the pack. I may have to jack knife my rig too if it looks like traffic starts getting around you. Let me know right away if you see any one slipping by."

"You got it," again the man replied.

"Jennifer will be staying close enough to Munoz in the SUV to keep us posted on his location."

"What happens if we lose him," someone else asked.

"If we lose him, to put it bluntly, my friend is fucked. I don't think we will though. There are enough of us and we will be pretty mobile so we can move around pretty quickly if we have to in order to find him again. But, we are not going to lose Munoz. Am I clear on this," Wyatt ordered while standing. "Anyone else have any questions or concerns?"

Jennifer leaned in toward the table. "I know all of you will do the best you can. I wish we could explain everything but it's not possible at this time. If you men get this done for us I assure you your bonuses will make your retirement a lot more comfortable. Be careful and I look forward to seeing all of you in California tomorrow evening."

Wyatt closed by saying, "OK. If there's nothing else I will see you at 8:00 am. Let's take Mr. Munoz home. Thank you again gentlemen."

Most of the men stayed in the banquet room for another hour talking about tomorrow's activities, trading stories, and just staying loose. Wyatt and Jennifer went back to their room to go over the entire plan one more time just to make sure there were no detectable surprises. Nothing apparent was revealed.

Both of them were anxious but very tired. They got into bed and lay holding each other. "Are you ready for this Hun," Wyatt whispered to Jennifer.

"I'm as ready as I'll ever be," she replied.

Wyatt gave her a long kiss on her forehead and they drifted off to sleep.

Yuma, Arizona—Elisaio Munoz
November 17, 1991

"Munoz! Get your shit together. I'll be back at 11:00 to take you to out processing," called out a prison guard

"You got it boss. I'm ready now," Elisaio replied.

"I'm just giving you a heads up Munoz. I'll be back at eleven." The guard walked away from Elisaio's cell.

"You still think you are going to be able to get away from Arturo and the business," asked his cell mate.

"I said I was and I meant it."

"I'm sorry man, but I just don't see how you are going to make it. You got no money, no job, and nowhere to go," goaded the cell mate.

"I'm not going back to Arturo. I'll find something else."

"What, a dishwasher job at some hole in the wall or a garbage collector? Nobody's going to hire an ex-con. You know that man," the cell mate argued.

"I'm telling you ese, I'm going to make it. Sure, it's going to be tough. I have no doubt about that but it can be done. I know it can."

"Well, I hope you do man. But I won't be surprised to see you back here or on the streets in the near future," the cell mate declared dismissing Elisaio's sincerity in a cynical tone laying on his cot and smiling.

"If you do see me again amigo you'd better be ready for some serious shit to go down because I'll be one pissed off Mexican," Elisaio spouted off half joking. He really did not want to end up back in prison again. It wasn't that his stretch was a hard one or that prison life scared him. As a matter of fact prison life was easy. It's like a private country club except all of the back stabbing and fucking are literal. If you hook up with the right people it's an easy time.

155

Elisaio simply realized he was better than this and felt if he really tried he could turn his life around. He just needed a chance. Sure, if it got so bad on the outside he could go back to his old ways. He knew that. He just wanted to try to see if he had the stamina and will power to turn his life around. This was the major crossroad in his life and he was trying to choose the right direction to go.

At 11:00 am sharp the prison guard showed up at Elisaio's cell. "Are you ready convict," he called out.

"I won't be a convict for long boss," Elisaio replied.

"You'll always be a convict Munoz."

"So you say." He picked up his bag and followed the guard to the out processing wing of the prison. There they gave him his personal affects, took his picture, read the terms of his parole, and gave him fifty dollars and the name and address of his parole officer in El Monte. The out processing officer wished him good luck. Another guard escorted him to the main gate and invited Elisaio to come back and that he would be welcome. Elisaio gave him the finger and walked out toward the front gate.

Yuma, Arizona—Wyatt and Jennifer
November 17, 1991, 11:10 am

"OK. We are getting close. Everyone stand by. As soon as someone sees him yell out," Wyatt instructed over the radio. There were four vehicles positioned within eyesight of the prison gate. There were three more approximately one mile north waiting to move, two south waiting to bring up the rear, and one about ten miles ahead running point. Everyone was ready to go.

There was a little traffic traveling in both directions but not enough to cause concern. Inside the front gate there were several parked vehicle with an occasional car coming in or out. Jennifer had the best vantage point being able to see the gate and the front door. She would probably catch first sight of Elisaio.

"Jen, you set," Wyatt asked her over the radio.

"Yep. I have a clear view and will let you know as soon as I see him," she replied. Her heart was pounding hard, her hands were sweating, and she was breathing faster than normal. She was so ready for this day to end once and for always.

Wyatt was in position and waiting inside his eighteen wheeler about a quarter of a mile south of the main gate. He was going to be one of the first vehicles to pass by Elisaio when he started hitchhiking and hopefully pick him up. That would be his preference but as long as Elisaio got picked up by anyone that was first and foremost.

"I got him," yelled Jennifer. "He just walked out the front door. He's talking to the guard. Everyone hold on a second." It looked to Jennifer like Elisaio gave the guard the finger then started heading for the gate. It was about a hundred yard walk to the gate so everyone was holding until he was over half way there. She said in an excited voice, "OK. Let's move. He's just about… HOLD ON! SHIT! He stopped. He's talking to some one in the parking lot. Hold your position." She watched intently. She couldn't see who the person was because they were blocked by a palm tree. Elisaio stood at the back end of a parked vehicle in the parking lot talking for several minutes. This was driving Jennifer insane. "Come on," she yelled. She started to talk into the radio then stopped. She dropped it on the floor and screamed, "No! No!" She leaned down and frantically searched for the radio but could not find it. "Shit! Shit! Shit! Shit!" she repeated. She saw it on the floor against the passenger side door. She laid across the center console and stretched her arms out barely touching it with her finger tips. "Damn it!" She sat up, unbuckled her seat belt, and tried again to reach it.

"Talk to me Hun. What's going on," she heard Wyatt say to her on the radio.

"Got it," she groaned as she sat back upright. She pressed the button on the radio while looking in the direction of where Elisaio was. She didn't see him anywhere. "Uhhh, I don't see him. Shit! I lost him. I'm sorry guys, I can't see him anymore. Anybody else have a visual on him?" No one answered. She started her SUV and pulled forward to get a better view. "He's not in the parking lot. I don't see him," she relayed into the radio. "There's a car driving out the gate. Can some one follow it. I'm going in the parking lot to have a look."

"Where is he," Wyatt radioed back.

"I don't know," Jennifer shouted in the radio obviously upset.

"OK. Everyone stay calm. Everyone north of the prison start moving. Who has a description of the vehicle leaving the prison," Wyatt asked of everyone taking charge.

"It's a gray Chevy Astro Van with tinted side and back windows," one of the team members radioed back. "I'm right behind it. I'm going to pass it and see if our man is inside. Hold on."

"Hun, what do you have? Is he in the parking lot," Wyatt asked.

"No. I don't see him anywhere. He must be in the van."

"OK everyone. You're looking for a gray Chevy Astro Van with tinted windows. JW, you have a visual on the occupants yet," Wyatt asked the team member passing the gray van.

"Our guy is in the passenger seat. I'll stay in front of them until you guys catch up," he answered back.

"Alright! Everyone move. Let's get in place and keep Mr. Munoz headed in the right direction," Wyatt ordered.

Within ten minutes the team was back in position and the excitement died down. For the next hour and a half the ride north was quiet. They made their way toward Quartzsite at a constant 60 MPH. It gave them all a chance to catch their breath and get mentally prepared for the next step what ever and where ever that would be. Jennifer felt like she had let everybody down and didn't say anything the entire time. In fact the only radio conversation was when some one had repositioned them self.

Twenty Nine Palms, California – Elisaio Munoz
April 4, 2006, 4:30 am

The kink in his neck and his loud snoring woke Elisaio up. He was a little disoriented but quickly snapped out of it and remembered where he was. He looked at his watch and saw it was 4:30. He slapped himself a couple of times trying to get his wits back. "OK," he yelled as if convincing himself he was back on track. He started looking around for something to drink but there was nothing. "God damn it," he shouted in frustration.

After composing himself he looked at the buildings and noticed some activity through one of the windows. There was a pulsating dimming of the lights as if power were being drawn from them. He could hear a whining sound building up and getting louder. He rolled his window down all the way and leaned out. It was beginning to get so loud that he started to cover his ears then a flash of light. Every crack, orifice, and window of the building was engorged with the bright light. It was unbelievable, almost like lightning.

"What the fuck," he exclaimed. He grabbed his gun and fumbled around trying to open the car door. He jumped out of the car then ran toward the building. "I gotta stop that fucker before…," he panted as he tried to run and make his way through the darkness. He stumbled and fell. He was having a hard time seeing because the flash from the light was still affecting his vision.

He reached the building. The whining sound was almost gone now and he checked the door to see if he could get in. It was unlocked. He slipped inside and took a quick look around. "Now, where is that little fucker," he whispered.

Quartzsite, Arizona – The Team
November 17, 1991, 1:05 pm

Jennifer picked up the radio and spoke for the first time since they had left Yuma. "It looks like they are going to exit." She received back several 10-4's from the other team members confirming her message. They had already anticipated Elisaio and his driver might exit in Quartzsite so the team members leading the group pulled off ahead of them and waited at all four corners of the intersection in order to follow which ever direction the two of them went.

After exiting the highway they pulled into a fast food drive thru. The team regrouped in a parking lot at another fast food place diagonally across the street. It took Elisaio and his driver fifteen minutes to go through the drive thru. The team prepared to get back on the road or move in quickly to pick up Elisaio if he exited the mini van. The van started to head back toward the highway but pulled into a parking spot and stopped.

"Heads up," Wyatt told everyone. "I think he's going to get out here. JW, you and Oscar circle around and get ready to pick him up in front of the parking lot." The two vehicles drove past the lot where Elisaio was parked and made a u-turn then pulled to the side of the road waiting for him to walk out toward the street.

The back of the mini van was facing the group and they could not see what was going on inside. There was no visible movement for over an hour. Wyatt was getting antsy and guessing they were going to have to jack knife the truck on I-10 if they didn't get moving again in the next several minutes. He could see the storm starting to build up to the west and according to the weather man the electrical storm was going to hit the Blythe area around 4:00 this afternoon. It was a little after two now. They were an hour and ten minutes away from Blythe. It would be cutting it close.

The brake lights from the mini van came on then a minute later it out of the parking lot. It headed toward the I-10 freeway and turned on to the westbound on-ramp. There was a huge sigh of relief from everyone. The concern now was the time. Should they stop them or let them go on through. Wyatt would make that call as they got closer to Blythe.

A hundred thoughts were rushing through Wyatt's head as they drove down the freeway. He felt pretty confident that as long as the group kept moving and Elisaio didn't get out of the vehicle they might narrowly avoid the lightning but then again when Wyatt was sent back in time he was in his truck driving at about 50 MPH. What if he forced Elisaio to stop? What were the chances of the storm passing by them? If only they had Elisaio under their direct control he could manage the situation better. The "What If's" were driving him crazy. They were too close now for him to start questioning himself. He needed a break. He needed Jennifer.

"How are you holding up Hun," he asked over the radio. One of the other team members radioed back before Jennifer. "Well thank you for asking sweetheart. I'm doing just fine." Everyone got a good laugh and it helped ease Wyatt's tension.

Jennifer answered back on the radio, "I'm OK. I'm sorry I almost blew it back in Yuma."

"We had you covered Honey," one of the other guys radioed back. "That's what we were all supposed to do. Cover each others back."

Wyatt got on the radio. "Everything is going well. You didn't blow anything."

"Thanks guys for making me feel better. You too Jim," she responded. Nothing more was said for the next twenty minutes.

The clouds were getting darker by the minute. They could see the occasional lightning further south and the storm was definitely moving in their direction.

"What do you want to do Jim," JW asked.

Wyatt didn't answer. Jennifer got on the radio. "Hun, it's after 3:00. Traffic is starting to slow down. Should we have the point man start looking for a place to jack knife?"

"We're only about 30 minutes away from Blythe. If we keep up this pace we should be OK," Wyatt finally replied back

"We may have a problem," the point man radioed in.

"What's up," Wyatt asked.

"I just heard over the CB that the Highway Patrol is calling a wind and flash flood advisory. They are stopping all large vehicles from going forward. Yep. I'm coming up on it now. Chippy is redirecting all of the big rigs off the freeway. Looks like I'm out of it Jim."

"Shit," Wyatt yelled. "OK. We have no choice now. We need to keep Elisaio moving so let's get ahead of him and try to keep the left lane as clear as possible. Jen, I'm going to ditch the rig. Pick me up."

All of the team members who had been trailing behind pulled away from Jennifer. She slowed down to wait for Wyatt to catch up. He jumped into her SUV after parking the big rig on the shoulder. She put her foot to the floor and weaving in and out of the increasing traffic she caught up to the group.

Twenty Nine Palms, California – Tim MacCorrmack
April 4, 2006, 4:30 am

Tim finished putting the last few items into the small package. The main computers were set to do their weekly backups from midnight to three so he had to wait for it to finish before he was able to get the last few printouts he needed to complete this final package.

As the large STR8 BOLT generator started whining and building up power Tim did a final check to make sure he had everything he could think of to put in this package. He sealed it up and wrote an address on it then put the appropriate amount of stamps on it and placed it in the chamber.

He stepped behind the large shield and yelled, but could not hear himself over the noise, "This is for you Raj." He pressed the large button labeled ENGAGE.

The power and brightness of the bolt still impressed Tim no matter how many times he fired it off. It pushed him backward one step. He stepped forward and looked at the chamber. The package was gone. He stayed behind the shield while the generator wound down. When it had finished he slowly began turning off all of the switches. With each click the finality of his efforts sunk in. He had failed. His friend Raj was gone. He had done everything possible and there was nothing left for him to do except go home.

He started to walk out from behind the shield then saw someone standing by the front door. He thought to himself, *"Who could that be?"* Then he saw the gun in the intruders hand. He realized right away it was Munoz. He looked around and realized that the phones hadn't been hooked up in the new lab yet. They were supposed to do that today. He looked around for something he could use to defend himself with but there was nothing.

"Excuse me. Anyone here," Tim heard Munoz call out.

Elisaio walked around the lab cautiously looking everywhere for any sign of Tim. "Mr. MacCorrmack? I need to speak to you," Elisaio called out in a luring tone..

Tim was terrified. If only he could find some way to get to the phone in his office before Munoz found him. He waited silently looking for a chance to run.

"I know you're here Tim," Elisaio called out again. "Come out come out where ever you are." He laughed.

Twenty Nine Palms, California – Detective Dan Buckley
April 4, 2006, 4:30 am

Dan was having a hard time sleeping. He couldn't get comfortable and didn't want to wake Paula so he got up. Having been married for over thirty years Dan a police officer and detective, and Paula being a doctor they were used to one or the other getting up at odd hours rarely stirring when the other crawled out of bed. It was the same this morning. Paula's gentle snore didn't falter a bit.

Dan and Doctor Paula Levanthal got married in the spring of 1976 at the top of the Gondola in Vail. They dated for several years wanting to be financially secure before making a commitment to one another. Dan hoped to be a detective and Paula wanted to have her own practice established which they did. They both had a mutual respect for each others careers and it never wavered throughout their marriage. They loved each other very much, worked hard, raised a family, and now they were ready to retire in a few more years and enjoy the fruits of their labor. For now though, he just wanted to serve out his last couple of years in this quiet town and be as safe as possible.

He got dressed and decided to go into work to get caught up on his paperwork. He left the house at 4:20 and grabbed a cup of coffee at the 24 hour donut shop by his house.

With donut and coffee in hand he got into his car and headed toward the office. Driving slowly he took a bite from his donut and a sip of his coffee. He pulled out his cell phone and called the dispatcher.

"This is Detective Buckley. Anything I should know about the MacCorrmack's?"

"Good. What time did Mr. MacCorrmack get home?"

"He didn't! Why the hell didn't someone call me?"

"I... You... Shit!" He threw his phone down on the seat, tossed his donut to the side, and poured his coffee out the window. "Damn it!" He sped up then headed down the street toward TC laboratories.

Twenty Nine Palms, California – Rajiv Ramakrishnan
June 1988

It was his first year at TC Laboratories and Raj was working on a prototype symmetry generator. He had his head buried deep inside one of the panels when someone from the mail room came into his small lab.

"Dr. Ramakrishnan?"

"Yes. How can I help you?"

"I don't know how this could have happened but we were moving some shelving around in the mail room and found this package underneath one of them addressed to you. I'm sorry but we have no idea how long it had been there. There was no post mark on it. I'm sorry Doctor. I don't know what to say. I hope it wasn't anything important," he apologized then handed the package to Raj.

"It is fine. I obviously did not miss it and I was not expecting anything so I do not think there was any harm done. Thank you for bringing it to me."

"You're welcome Doctor. Again I apologize."

"It is OK," Raj reiterated studying the package while the young man left.

Raj was curious. He went to his desk to open it up. It was from someone here at the company by the name of Tim MacCorrmack. Raj did not recognize the name and there weren't that many people working here. He opened the package and was completely taken aback with what he found inside. He fell into his seat and looked through all of the photos and documents. There was a several page letter included and he read through it. Several times he had to go back a page or two and reread it again. He looked through the photos and documents again and again. An hour or so had past. He tossed them on to his desk then leaned back in his chair mentally exhausted. He was dazed and astonished at the same time. As he gazed at the compilation of photos and documents a slight smile began to form on his face.

Interstate 10, Arizona—Wyatt and Jennifer
November 17, 1991, 3:50 pm

Traffic had slowed and the rain was pouring down making it difficult to see. They had almost lost Elisaio a couple of times but the team managed to pick him right back up each time.

They were less than ten mile from Blythe. Lightning was flashing frequently just a couple of miles ahead. They had just passed a bad accident and the traffic flow was beginning to pick up and thin out. Elisaio's driver was not picking up speed though. The team managed to get the left lane pretty clear but he would not pull out and pass. The lead cars slowed to a crawl trying to force him to pass but he was staying put in his lane. They ran out of ideas.

With just a couple of miles left they were right in the heart of the storm. Lightning bolts were flashing all around them now, several getting a little to close for comfort. Wyatt was beginning to think he had made a mistake in not blocking them earlier before the Highway Patrol forced all of the bigger vehicles off the highway. It was too late now. He told the team to box Elisaio in and stay tight until they got to Blythe. Wyatt was hoping by surrounding him that would be enough to possibly shield him from any potential time traveling bolt. The group could see the driver was beginning to get nervous. Several times he swerved trying to make a hole in their tight circle but they had him in there tight.

The electrical storm was intense. Lightning bolts were striking all around them and very frequently. Some of them were so close they actually moved the car Wyatt and Jennifer were in. Every muscle in Wyatt's body was tense and he could feel his heart pounding in his chest. *"We're not going to make it,"* he thought. The storm was relentless.

They were approaching the bridge that crosses over the Colorado River into California. Blythe was just on the other side. Wyatt told the team as soon as they reached the other side to force the driver to exit at the first off ramp. Hopefully he'd be scared enough to stay put until the storm blew by. He told the team once they all got off the freeway they should break off and give the driver some room then regroup somewhere close by.

The plan worked. The driver got off of the freeway and pulled into the gas station on the corner. The team drove on by. They could see the driver was noticeably shaken. Wyatt and Jennifer, who were hanging back, pulled into the same gas station. They wanted to see if the driver was going to stop or try to go again. It didn't really matter much. The storm was passing by and they had completed what they set out to do and that was to get Elisaio into California.

Wyatt and Jennifer saw the van doors open and Elisaio stepped out looking in the direction of the team members as they drove off. Jennifer was smiling like she had not smiled in a long time. Wyatt was happy too. Sixteen years of their life spent on trying to keep Elisaio...

BOOM!

Wyatt and Jennifer could not see. The flash of the lightning bolt was so bright it temporarily blinded them. All they knew was it struck just on the other side of the parked van where Elisaio and the driver were standing. They tried desperately to locate Elisaio but all they could see was white light in their eyes from the flash. Jennifer was holding on to Wyatt and crying.

"Noooooooo!"

Twenty Nine Palms, California – Detective Dan Buckley
April 4, 2006, 4:45 am

Dan was very upset with himself for not following up last night to make sure Tim had arrived home. Tim said he was going to leave and Dan had no doubt he would not. But that was no excuse. Dan should have radioed the patrol car outside of Tim's home to let them know he was on his way. A red flag could have then gone up when Tim didn't arrive home in a timely manner. But now, it had been several hours since Dan talked to Tim. If Munoz had been in the area who knows what Dan was going to find at the TC Lab.

He hit the driveway to the parking lot at a fairly fast speed and bounced to a stop close to the laboratory. He pulled his gun from his shoulder holster and took the safety off. He tried to stay close to the edge of the walkway. He moved cautiously toward the lab door. He could see there were lights on and the door was ajar. He looked around not wanting to be surprised then pushed the door slightly. It started to squeak and he stopped. He peered through the half open door and could hear the faint sounds of voices. Again he carefully looked around before he squeezed through the small opening.

Once inside the door he froze trying to make out what was being said but he was too far away. He looked around the lab and could not see anyone. It sounded like the voices were coming from the larger lab next door. Dan made his way toward the adjoining door. He moved slowly across the lab floor being careful not to bump anything alerting the occupants of his presence. The voices were getting louder but he still could not understand them.

Dan leaned against the wall with his head close to the open door listening. The voices were coming from his extreme right. He moved to the left side of the open door to get a better view of the men talking. It also made it easier for him to hear what they were saying.

Tim was sitting on the floor with his legs crossed and his hands folded in his lap. He was looking up at Munoz. Munoz had a gun pointed at Tim and was waving it around each time he spoke. Tim had blood dripping down from his forehead and lip. He seemed calm. Munoz squatted down to one knee in front of Tim and hit him.

"Fuck! He's going to kill him," Dan realized. He aimed his gun at Munoz.

STR8-BOLT Lab – Elisaio Munoz
April 4, 2006, 4:55 am

"I said tell me what you and the good doctor were doing with this machine? I know it has something to do with lightning," Elisaio spoke calmly to Tim while kneeling down in front of him.

Tim didn't answer and Elisaio hit him in the face with his gun. He fell to his side then sat himself back up and looked at Elisaio with an angry expression. "We burn balls," he replied with contempt then spit the blood from his mouth on to the floor.

"Oh that's funny. You burn balls." He grabbed Tim by the throat. "Don't you understand you stupid fuck? I'm going to kill you either way. So just tell me what I want to know. Tell me how you are planning to use this machine against me. After you tell me I promise to kill you quickly. Otherwise, we still have at least another ninety minutes before anyone shows up and finds you here. And believe me my friend you will not enjoy our time together. So what's it going to be?" He pressed the gun hard against Tim's chin pushing him back.

"Hotdogs."

"What," Elisaio questioned disbelieving his ears.

"Hotdogs. We cook hotdogs with it too." Tim gave Elisaio a big smile and was proud of himself.

Elisaio smiled back then stood and looked around the lab frustrated with this little shit. He turned and hit Tim on the top of his head with the butt of the gun. Blood began pouring out of the open wound and down Tim's face. Tim lay on the cement floor almost unconscious. Elisaio picked him up obviously pissed off now. "Listen to me you mother fucker. I'm going to give you three seconds to tell me what you, the Doc, me, and that fucking machine have in common. If you don't you're going to end up dead just like the Doc but this time I'm going to pull the fucking trigger myself instead of having one of my hired assassins do it. Then, when I'm done with you, I'm going to leave here and have some fun with that cute little wife of yours before I kill her too. I'm going to do things to her that you have never imagined. She's going to beg me for more before I slit her fucking throat. Now tell me what I want to know," he screamed in Tim's face.

Tim tried to kick Elisaio and stand up but was knocked down. "Fuck you," he yelled back.

Elisaio smacked him then leaned down and grabbed Tim's bottom lip squeezing it hard to force Tim's mouth open. "Fuck me? Fuck you!" He angrily cocked the hammer back on his gun and shoved it hard against Tim's teeth. "Tell me," he shouted sternly.

Tim knew this was it. Elisaio was shaking and screaming at him. He had managed to really piss him off. In a second he'd be laying in a pool of blood. Thoughts of his wife being tortured by this animal infuriated him. He could do nothing about it. He tried to fight but Elisaio squeezed and pulled his lip harder pushing the barrel of the gun against his teeth almost breaking them. He visualized Raj flying over the ravine. Everything good that they had tried to accomplish here at the lab turned bad. He was sorry their work had produced nothing but death and sorrow. He closed his eyes and prayed.

BANG!

Tim felt an incredible sensation rush through his body. His entire life flashed before him, visions flooding into his mind. He felt his heart racing and at the same time felt as though he was spinning. He was getting very light headed and nauseous. He fell to the floor. He rolled to his back then, everything went dark.

SIX

"Excuse me sir. Do you know where Blythe is and can you tell me how far it is from here," a man asked stepping out of his mini van.

Elisaio walked toward the man after he had passed through the front gate of the Yuma prison. "What," he replied not really hearing the man because he was angry at the guard for giving him a hard time.

"I am trying to get to Blythe and I am trying to determine if I can drive there with a half a tank of gas. Do you know how far away it is," the man asked again.

"Oh yeah, sure. If I remember it's about 150 miles, maybe less. You should be OK on a half a tank if you take it easy."

"Thank you. I will do that."

Not really paying attention to the man he mumbled, "Do what?" He was still a little agitated by the guards comment.

"Take it easy as you just said."

Elisaio half laughed, "Oh yeah. I'm sorry man. That guard was a real assho… Never mind. Where are you coming from?"

"Oh, I was on vacation in San Felipe with a friend. But I just came from Mexicali this morning. How about you? Are you visiting someone?"

Elisaio laughed loudly this time forgetting about the guard now. "Me! I just got my walking papers today. I'm a free man again."

"Congratulations. I would imagine this is not a nice place to be. You must be happy."

"It wasn't that bad but if I have anything to do with it I won't be coming back."

"That is a good attitude to have," the man encouraged him then smiled.

"Thanks. Listen, since you're heading toward Blythe, can I catch a…?" Elisaio put his thumb up in a hitchhiking motion.

"Are you going to Blythe?"

"I'm going to El Monte California but getting to Blythe would be a good start and it would get me a lot closer than standing out on that highway with my thumb in the air."

"Yes, of course. I would enjoy the company." They both climbed into the mini van then pulled out of the prison parking lot and headed north on Highway 95.

They were both silent for the next fifteen minutes. The drive quickly settled into an even steady pace just under the speed limit. Elisaio rested his head back then stared out the window enjoying his new freedom and the desert scenery.

He felt happy for the first time in his life. He truly wanted to make a new life for himself and all he needed was a chance. He knew being a convict, it wasn't going to be easy but he was going to try. So far it was starting off good. He had gotten this ride without even trying.

A few days earlier he tried to make arrangements to have family or friends pick him up but realized after several unanswered phone calls no one wanted to help him. He was pretty certain Arturo didn't want anything to do with him either and he hoped to keep it that way.

"You said you were going as far as El Monte," the man asked breaking the silence.

"Yes. That's my home town."

"I guess this is lucky for you then that I am going as far as Covina. If you like, I think this would just about get you there. Yes?"

"No shit! That would be great man. Yes. You don't know how much I appreciate this man" Elisaio replied as the concern about getting home faded.

"I hope you do not mind but the drive will be long and I am sure we will get to know each other well during this time. So may I ask, what were you in prison for?"

"Shit no, I… Oh, sorry. No, I don't mind. Drug smuggling. I was in the dope selling business and I was helping a friend, or so I thought, and I got caught bringing a shipment in just after I crossed the border. I got fifteen years and now I'm out."

"You do not look that old."

Elisaio laughed, "Nah, I only did half of it. If you keep your shi… stuff clean you usually get out in half the time for good behavior."

"I see. So what will you do when you get back to El Monte? Are you going to go back into the business as you called it?"

"Not if I can help it. I want to try to get away from all of that crap but it's going to be tuff. I took some classes while I was in the joint and got my GED. I also took a few business classes. I know most people won't hire cons but I'm going to give it my best shot. If all else fails then I'll go back into the old business."

"What kind of work are you going to look for?"

"I have no idea. I'll do just about anything and see where it goes from there."

The conversation continued all the way to Quartzsite. Elisaio talked about his wants and desires for his new life. He was excited and it showed. It was obvious to the man this was a major turning point in Elisaio's life. He was at a fork and he could easily go either way.

When they arrived at Quartzsite they decided to stop and get something to eat. After passing through the drive thru window they pulled into a parking spot so they could eat their fast food feast. Elisaio enjoyed his lunch. Anything was better than prison food.

"So, what were you doing in San Felipe," Elisaio asked with a full mouth realizing he had been talking about himself most of the way here.

"As I said I met a friend there for vacation. For the past few years we have tried to get together at least once per year. He likes to SCUBA dive and fish and he usually talks me into going with him."

"I've never tried to do either of those. Sounds like it could be fun but what about the sharks. Don't they eat you?"

The driver laughed.

An hour had past quickly. They shared different stories about their trips to Mexico. Elisaio's always dealt with some kind of drug deal and this really made him realize just how messed up his life had been after hearing the different things the man did when he went to Mexico.

"I am sorry. We have been talking so much and I never asked for your name," the man asked.

"I'm Elisaio. Elisaio Munoz. My friends back home call me Ravin."

They shook hands. "I like Elisaio. It is a nice name. My name is Rajiv Ramakrishnan."

Elisaio laughed, "Goddamn. That's a mouthful."

"Yes it is. If you like you can call me Raj. That is what my friends call me."

"Well Raj. It is very nice to meet you."

Highway 10, Arizona – Rajiv Ramakrishnan
November 17, 1991, 2:10 pm

Raj had gotten so involved in his conversation with Elisaio he forgot why he was here to begin with and lost track of the time. He was surprised at how interesting the young mans life was and being a researcher he probed and asked lots of questions. He saw the storm clouds to the west were building up and realized he had to get moving. He cut his conversation short and hoped he didn't come across as rude.

As he got on the freeway he noticed several of the vehicles were the same ones that had been rotating around him on the drive up from the prison. It seemed odd to him that after sitting an hour or so at the fast food place that he should see them again. He looked at the drivers as he passed them and they didn't acknowledge him one way or another. He passed it off as coincidence.

Elisaio asked Raj about his job and Raj explained what he did for a living. Elisaio was like a kid, full of questions and Raj was happy to answer. Raj was beginning to really like this man even though this man was going to kill him fifteen years from now. He also realized too that that man in the future was not the same man he was talking to at this moment. That man had not been created yet. Raj knew he had to get this man out of Arizona and stop him from going back in time thereby stopping the chain of events that would result from it.

"Time travel," Raj still smiled every time he contemplated the idea he was going to play a major role in developing time travel capabilities. After receiving the package from his future assistant he had had plenty of time to get used to the idea. Now, he just wanted to make sure he was going to be around to participate.

The storm was moving in fast now. Traffic was getting tight. He decided to slow down. He did not want to get in an accident and get caught right in the middle of this thing. The traffic around him was beginning to squeeze him in tight. *"Why don't they pass me,"* he wondered. *"The left lane is wide open."* But they kept crowding him in tighter. He could see lightning flashing just south of the freeway. Getting across the state line before the storm was going to be close.

The high profile vehicles were being directed off of the freeway. Raj thought about exiting with them and turning around but he wasn't sure Elisaio would stay with him. So he decided to keep going. He would feel a lot better once he reached Blythe. According to the weather data Tim had sent him he knew approximately the time and location the center of the storm would hit. It was in Ehrenberg at 4:00 pm. If he could get through there before 4:00 he would be in the clear. But with the traffic slowing down he was not leaving much room for mistakes.

"These people are getting aggressive," Raj mentioned.

Elisaio had noticed it too. "Why don't you pass," he asked.

"I probably should have when I had the chance but now they have me completely boxed in here."

The lightning was flashing all around them. It was almost 3:45. He had about a fifteen minute window to get across the state line. The traffic had thinned out a little and they were moving at a pretty good pace. He was starting to feel confident they were going to get through just in time but was still nervous. The other vehicles backed off slightly and were not being as aggressive. They helped keep the flow of traffic going so Raj settled in and picked up the pace when ever he could. He decided as soon as they arrived in Blythe he would get off the freeway to try to break away from this pack.

It was a spectacular show. The lightning bolts were flashing in every direction, shape, and size possible. The sky was dark and windy from the cloud cover and that only enhanced the show as they approached the bridge into California. It was hard to keep his eyes open during some of the flashes because they were so bright and loud.

He wanted to slow down when he got half way across the bridge but could not. It seemed to Raj the bunched up vehicles were rushing him now but he didn't care anymore as he came to the end of the bridge into California. He saw the exit just up ahead and turned his signal indicator on. The other vehicles signaled they were getting off too. He saw a gas station to his right and decided he would pull in there and survey the situation. The second he turned into the station the other vehicles continued on past and went in several directions at the traffic signal.

Raj and Elisaio stepped out of the mini van and looked at the other vehicles going away. Raj asked, now relieved it was over, "What was that all about?"

"I don't know," Elisaio answered as he walked around to Raj's side of the van.

They both exhaled in a sign of relief. The storm was headed away from them on the Arizona side and Raj was silently rejoicing realizing he had done it. He knew he had accomplished the unthinkable. He altered the future. Elisaio could not go back in time now. The thought of lightning and time travel opened up a door of immense possibilities for him. His mind was racing. He could not wait to get back to his office to start writing down all of the ideas that were forming. He looked around again and could not see any of the other vehicles then he looked back at the storm as it moved away. It was over. He really did it.

He leaned over the front of the mini van and smiled for a moment. There were so many things that needed to be done. He was ready to go and wanted to get back on the freeway but they needed to gas up before they got on their way. He started to turn toward Elisaio when, BOOM!

The power of the lightning bolt lifted him off of his feet. He felt a numb tingling sensation over his entire body. He also felt like he was falling for a long time. Everything was dark. He wondered what had happened. Everything seemed to have stood still. Then, after what seemed like a long passage of time, he suddenly felt himself hit the ground hard on his back. The jolt yanked his senses back to actuality. His head fell back into some bushes and he could feel the sharp branches cut at his face. The pain was startling. He was having a hard time seeing. The flash from the light temporarily blinded him. He sat up and tried to focus but could not. He heard a muffled voice say over the ringing in his ears, "Are you OK?" Raj was dazed and confused. He couldn't form the words in his mouth to answer. He rubbed his eyes and ears.

"Goddamn, that was one big fucking lightning bolt."

Raj recognized the voice now. It was Elisaio's. He looked in the direction of his voice and groaned, "Yes, yes. I think I am fine. How about you? Are you OK?" He was not sure where or when he was.

"Yeah! I'm good. Damn! That thing knocked us right on our asses. I'm still shaking."

Raj started to stand. He was able to make out Elisaio's form helping him to his feet. He tried to look around but was having difficulty. The white flash in his eyes was making it hard to see. Elisaio helped him over to the van and leaned him against it.

Feeling the van with his hands Raj asked, "Is this our car? I can't see it."

"Yeah man. You were looking right at that fucking thing. No wonder you can't see anything yet."

Hoping it was true Raj asked, "Is the storm still moving east?"

"Yeah man. We must have just gotten the tail end of it."

Raj smiled. They were OK. It was still 1991. He broke out into hysterical laughter. Elisaio looked at him like he was crazy then got caught up in the infectious laugh and joined in.

Fullerton, California—Wyatt Coleman
January 3, 1989

She was just a few years younger than when he first met her almost twenty years ago in 1970. She was beautiful but in a tomboyish sort of way at this age. There was definitely a wild side about her as well and Wyatt just watched her from afar for a couple of hours. She had no idea who he was which felt strange to him.

They were at one of her favorite nightclubs, which Jennifer had told him about. She was doing tequila shooters and dancing with several different people. Wyatt couldn't help but laugh as he watched her. She was having a blast from what he could see.

It was around 11:30 pm when he approached her and asked if she would like to dance with him. She gave him a strange look, made a couple of smart ass remarks then accepted. He felt like a lecherous old man but he knew this twenty five year old lady in ways she hadn't even imagined yet. After a few dances and some conversation she seemed to enjoy their time together but made it very clear she was not interested in him in a sexual way. She said she liked him and wanted to talk and dance more with him but that was it. Wyatt was relieved to hear her tell him that. He was there for a whole other reason.

At the end of the night Jennifer asked Wyatt to walk her to her car. There she told him she had a nice time and was going to be at a different place tomorrow night. She suggested that if he was interested he might drop by and they could talk and dance some more. Wyatt told her he would be there.

Ontario, California – Jennifer Tomas
January 3, 1989

Jennifer almost choked on her drink when she broke out into laughter as he entered the bar. She was flabbergasted at how young he looked at twenty-nine. Wyatt was forty when they first met and she could not stop laughing at how cute his younger version was. He walked over to the end of the bar and sat alone. The place was called the Rusty Horn Saloon and he was just getting over his first marriage. He liked to listen to country western music and drink beer whether or not he was happy or sad. He usually sat at the bar when he first arrived and enjoyed looking at people and listening to the music. Country bars always made him feel good.

She sat down at a table not far from him so she could watch him for a while. It was still early. There had been several ladies that already asked him to dance but he politely declined each one of them. She knew he needed a few more beers before he got up the courage to get out on the dance floor. Even in his late fifties he was still like that. After he finished his third beer she walked over to him and offered to buy him a beer. He was very courteous and said no thanks but asked if he could buy her one. She accepted.

For the next few hours they talked. The conversation was stimulating. Jennifer already knew his interests so it was easy to steer the conversation in the direction she wanted it to go. The nice thing about country bars back in those days was by the end of the evening you could still hear each other talking because the music volume did not increase as the evening progressed unlike other night clubs where by 11:00 conversations were pretty much non-existent because the volume of the music would drown out all other sounds.

Young Wyatt seemed to be attracted to her and he warmed up to her quickly. There was something about her that made him feel comfortable. He wasn't sure what it was but it made him want to spend more time with her. He didn't care that she was older than him. He just liked talking to her. It came easy and he wanted it to continue.

The evening had come to an end almost as soon as it started. Both of them could not believe the time flew by. Wyatt asked if she would be here tomorrow evening and Jennifer said she would be. So they agreed to meet at the same spot and continue their conversation where they left off.

As they exited the saloon young Wyatt insisted on walking Jennifer to her car. He didn't want the evening to end. He tried to engage Jennifer in more conversation but he could see she was tired. He bid her good night and started to give her a good night peck but she quickly jumped into her car and told him she would see him tomorrow night.

Diamond Bar, California – Wyatt and Jennifer Coleman
January 4, 1989

"Good morning. I didn't hear you come in last night," Wyatt moaned rubbing the sleep from his eyes.

"I didn't want to wake you. If I remember what I was like in my twenties, I probably ran you ragged dancing and hitting on you all night," Jennifer teased with a sheepish smile.

"On the contrary. You made it very clear you liked me but not in a sexual way."

"Oh my God! I actually said that to you," she asked holding her hands over her face embarrassed.

175

"I was so relieved when you did because I didn't know how I was going to tell you I just wanted to talk and get to know you." They both chuckled at the idea of a sexual encounter with their younger selves. Wyatt asked, "So, how did it go with my younger version? Did I bore you with my sorrow and self pity over my divorce?"

"Not at all. You were very talkative once I got a few beers into you. If I hadn't put the brakes on though I think you would have jumped me in the parking lot. I'll tell you what though, I was tempted. You were so damn cute you little stud."

Wyatt wrestled with Jennifer in the bed and jokingly accused her of cradle robbing. They played around for a while longer and got in the mood for some love making that went on the rest of the morning.

They finally crawled out of bed at noon and went out for breakfast. At the restaurant they started talking more about their plan.

"So, what do you think," she asked.

"I think they are both going to be shocked as hell when they find out who we are."

"I know. I'll probably think you're crazy but when we all meet I'm pretty sure I'll be all ears," Jennifer supposed.

"I don't know how I will take it. So you shouldn't say anything until we meet. Then let me do the talking. Once he sees me I'm pretty sure I can make him come around quickly."

"You think next week will be OK? You don't think that's too soon," Jennifer asked a little concerned.

"I think the sooner we do it the sooner they'll have time to adjust."

Jennifer shook her head not really believing what they were attempting, "OK. Let's plan on Saturday then. That will give us a few more nights to work on them."

Vail, Colorado – Dan Buckley
May 1995

"Hi honey. How was your day," Paula asked her husband Dan as he walked into the house.

He took his jacket off and sat down on the couch by the stove. "Slow. I really hate this time of year. The Mud Season has got to be the worst time of year. I didn't leave the station all day. Jacobs had a parking lot hit and run and that was it."

"I'm sorry Dan. It's slow at the hospital too. We watched a video in the break room after lunch."

176

"Several of the older guys have been talking about getting out of here and maybe, going somewhere hot to serve out their last few years before retiring. They're tired of the tourists and snow and want to go any place other than here. I'm starting to see the attraction too."

"Yeah, I was thinking we should start looking for another place to go before we get ready to retire too. The kids are gone now, except Terri, and she'll be graduating in a few weeks. She's going to Florida State in the fall so maybe we should think about moving there or we could go in a different direction all together. Either way, I think it's time we find a new place to call home."

"Someone was saying there were some openings for detectives in California out in the desert area by Palm Springs. They just opened a new station. I could easily apply and be ready to start in a few months or at least by the end of the year. What do you think," he asked looking at her.

"I'm sure there's a hospital there too. I could find a practice somewhere close by. Why don't you do me a favor and see what you can find on the Internet and I'll make some phone calls."

"So, you're serious then. You're ready to leave Vail," Dan asked.

"I think it's time. We both moved here from other states and we didn't plan to be here forever. So, why not? It's a good time for both of us. You're still young enough and like you said if you put in ten or fifteen years at this new job you can retire with a nice pension from both jobs. And I could leave the medical profession with a nice retirement too. Yes. I say let's do it."

"OK then. But, what about the house? I think we should keep it. It'll be paid for in two years. We can spend vacations here with the kids and they can use it too. I'm guessing with the growth rate of Vail and the other ski communities around here it could be worth something when we actually do retire. It will be our nest egg if you will."

"Oh yes. Definitely keep the house. Who knows, we might even want to come back here for retirement. I'm excited Dan. I think this is going to be good for us."

"Me too Sweetheart. Me too."

The next several weeks Dan and Paula contacted hospitals and law enforcement agencies in the Palm Springs area. They discovered there were many employment opportunities available for each of them. It was just a matter of deciding which ones best suited them. They were moving to California.

Diamond Bar, California – Wyatt and Jennifer
January 11, 1989

The name of the Restaurant and bar was McArthurs. Jennifer and Wyatt had arranged to be seated in two booths next to each other. They were waiting for their younger selves to arrive. As they waited Wyatt and Jennifer didn't talk much to each other mostly because they didn't want to surprise and possibly scare their younger selves away to quickly.

Young Wyatt was the first to arrive. Jennifer greeted him and they sat down. They were having a pleasant conversation when their waiter returned with their drinks. The waiter asked if they were ready to order. Jennifer told him she wanted to wait a while before ordering. She asked young Wyatt if that was all right with him. He nodded his agreement.

It was about fifteen minutes later when young Jennifer showed up, late as usual. She sat down and gave Wyatt a quick hug. She explained why she was late and Wyatt listened and smiled. She ordered a beer along with his and they drank them quickly. She said she was hungry but Wyatt asked if they could talk about something before they eat. She agreed but with some concern. He assured her it was nothing bad but what he had to say would definitely have an affect on their future.

Both Jennifer and Wyatt talked to their younger selves for an hour and as expected there were some statements regarding sanity but the younger versions continued to listen somewhat close minded. As time continued to pass more and more was revealed about them. They had lots of questions and concerns about how so much was known about them but Wyatt and Jennifer kept trying to explain with little progress.

Still with the younger versions disbelieving and Wyatt and Jennifer feeling the frustration of not being able to convince their younger selves of the situation the final moment of truth had come. Wyatt grabbed young Jennifer's hand and stated, "I'd like you to meet someone. Will you sit here for just a minute and wait, please?" She folded her arms and agreed she would not leave. Wyatt stood up and walked to the restroom area and waited.

Jennifer saw Wyatt get up and she knew that was the signal he was ready. She told young Wyatt to please give her five more minutes. He fidgeted in his seat then agreed. When she stood up she asked him once again to please wait for her to come back. He said he would. She walked to the restroom and met with Wyatt.

"Well, that went well," he declared sarcastically.

"Let's give them a few minutes to calm down then let's just spring it on them. What have we got to lose at this point," she suggested.

Wyatt agreed then gave Jennifer a big hug and kiss. A couple of minutes later they took deep breaths then Wyatt walked back toward the booths. Jennifer followed a moment later. Wyatt walked up to where his younger self was sitting and sat down across from him.

"Excuse me. That seat is taken," young Wyatt asserted

"Hi Wyatt," Wyatt greeted his younger self and offered his hand.

"Who are you," the young man asked looking over his shoulder for Jennifer.

"Look at me," Wyatt asked the young man.

Young Wyatt looked at him then suddenly realized the man across from him looked like an older version of his father. It disturbed him but he replied in a smart ass tone, "You look like my father but he's been dead for a long time." He started to get up.

"Sit down. I'm not your father smart ass. I think you know exactly who I am," he retorted somewhat irritated with the inference of age. He saw Jennifer walk by him and wink as she went to the booth next door. Young Wyatt saw her walk by too and tried to say something to her but Wyatt interrupted, "Do you remember what Jennifer was talking to you about?"

"How do you know Jennifer," he asked perturbed.

"We'll get to Jennifer in a few minutes. Did you hear what she was telling you," he asked again.

"Yes. She was trying to tell me something about how she had an accident that sent her to this time and how she knew me before we actually met. Frankly this whole thing is starting to piss me off."

"Well, she's not crazy and you're not pissed off. You're scared. You are afraid she might be telling you the truth. Look at me," he insisted.

Young Wyatt looked up at his older self. He mumbled, "This is impossible. It can't be happening."

"My name is James Wyatt Coleman. I am fifty-nine years old but I was born in 1960."

"You're crazy old man. You can't possibly be me," he declared starting to get up again.

"Oh, I'm you alright! Sit down." Wyatt produced several documents and gave them to his younger self.

The young man sat back down and looked at them in total disbelief. "I don't know how you got these but this can't be. How can it be?"

Wyatt took a deep breath and started from the beginning, explaining

179

everything. He gave him names, dates, and places of things that only the two of them could know. Young Wyatt just sat and listened shaking his head not wanting to believe what was being said.

Meanwhile, Jennifer was having much better luck than Wyatt. Young Jennifer was so excited to see her older self and was convinced almost immediately about the truth in all of this. She became a chatterbox. She went on and on about how good she still looked, what all of this meant, how her life was going to change, etc. Jennifer slowly tuned her out and could hear the difficulty Wyatt was having. She asked young Jennifer to sit tight while she helped Wyatt out. She got up and moved to the next booth and pushed young Wyatt into the middle.

The two of them worked on him for several more minutes. Young Wyatt was still shaking his head and trying to make some sense of this entire conversation. Finally, after ten minutes Jennifer called around the booth and asked Young Jennifer to join them. She sat down next to Wyatt and saw the younger version of him sitting in between the two of them.

"Far fucking out," she shouted.

"How can this be happening," young Wyatt asked.

Wyatt started to speak again to his younger self when young Jennifer interrupted. She took over the rest of the conversation and was instrumental in convincing young Wyatt that all of this was indeed real. Once he became receptive to it the four of them discussed how all of this could possibly effect their past, present, and future. Older Wyatt introduced a proposal he and Jennifer wanted to offer them.

It was after 10:30 when the manager of the restaurant came over to them and asked them to move their conversation to the bar area because the restaurant had closed. They found a secluded booth in the back away from the music and continued their conversation until the bar closed at 1:30 am. They never did order dinner.

TC Laboratories, Twenty Nine Palms
April 5, 2006

He could hear voices all around him but could not make out what they were saying. Everything was muffled. He wanted to open his eyes and tried to force it but as his eyelids fluttered he only manage to form tiny slits. He could see faint images of shadows moving about. He tried to move but was unable. He became aware of his breathing. He could hear each breath going in then out and with each breath he became more aware of his senses. He started to feel pain in his head. It was a muted throbbing. He took a deep breath then the pain took over and pulsated down his back and to his face. He took another deep breath in an attempt to make the pain subside but it caused him to wince and woke him up. He opened his eye and began to focus on his surroundings. The muffled voices suddenly became audible.

"Tim, can you hear me?" That was the first thing he heard clearly. He started to move and someone said, "I think he's coming around. Tim. Wake up Tim. Can you hear me?"

Tim managed to croak out, "Yes." He could hear the two people leaning over him let out a sigh.

"Go see if the paramedics are here yet," one of the voices ordered. "Tim, just lie still. We have help coming."

The voice sounded familiar to him. He tried to remember where he knew it from. He tried to sit up but was held back and told to lie down and not move. He definitely knew that voice but the name that went with it escaped him. He wanted to sit up and tried again to lift his head. He asked, "What happened?"

"Just lay still Tim. We can talk about that later."

"I'm OK. Let me sit up," Tim demanded and pushed the hand away from the man that was holding him down. He struggled to sit up as the pain in his head increased and started to throb even more. He grabbed his head.

"That's one hell of a lump you have on your head. I bet you're really feeling it now."

"You got that right," Tim managed to groan out.

"You sure you don't want to lie back down?"

"No. I'll be fine. Just let me sit here a minute." Tim rubbed his head trying to make the pain decrease.

Nothing was said for a couple of minutes then the voice asked, "Do you know what happened to you Tim?"

"I'm not sure. I know I'm at the lab because I recognize everything in it but I don't know why I'm here. I think I was working late on something. I just can't...," he stopped and continued rubbing his aching head.

"Boy, I'll tell you what. You scared the hell out of me. This is my first day on the job here as head of security. I was walking the early morning rounds with my second in command and I saw you lying on the floor. We thought you were dead. I thought to myself, what a way to start out my new job but thankfully you're still with us."

"How did you know my name was Tim?"

"I make it my business to know everyone if I'm going to be responsible for their security. My name is Dan Buckley. I'm very happy to meet you."

"Dan Buckley! Why do I know that name? You look familiar too," Tim inquired staring at him trying to collect his thoughts but was having a difficult time. His mind was being flooded with conflicting images.

"Perhaps you saw my picture on the announcement memo that went around last week telling everyone I would be starting as head of security today."

"Maybe. But I have a very strong feeling we have met before. Give me a minute to think of where."

Someone came running in and when Tim saw the man's face his heart nearly exploded in his chest. Fear ripped through his mind and he started to push backward on the floor and crawled away from the man coming toward him. He felt very nauseous and almost fainted.

"Whoa Tim! Relax. Calm down buddy," Dan shouted as he reached for Tim.

"Stay away from me," Tim demanded obviously very frightened.

"It's Okay Tim. He's here with me. We're trying to help you."

"Why is he here? What's he doing? No, wait a minute. I think I know him. Who is he," Tim asked apparently very confused.

"This is my senior security officer Elisaio Munoz. I believe you know him. He's worked here many years."

Tim settled down and realized he did know Munoz but not as a security officer or did he. His head was hurting even more now. He tried to recall how he knew Munoz but it made him light headed to think about it. He laid back down on the floor.

"Paramedics are just pulling into the lot," Munoz relayed to Dan.

"Just relax Tim. The paramedics are going to be here in a second and they'll have a look at you."

Tim was feeling very baffled and disoriented. When he closed his eyes he could see contradictory images of Munoz both as a fellow employee but also as a criminal of some sort. But he knew Munoz. He'd had many conversations with him over the past few years.

He had different images of Buckley too as a policeman. He knew he didn't know the man but he could remember glimpses of conversations he thought he'd had with him. His head was pounding now. He groaned.

The paramedics arrived and began to work on him. They had him wired up and were monitoring him in a matter of minutes. They examined him from head to toe and were in constant contact with the hospital. After thirty minutes they concluded he was going to be all right. He had suffered a pretty hard blow to the back of the head and had a concussion. They wanted him to go to the hospital for x-rays but Tim insisted he would come down later.

After the paramedics finished working on him Tim heard someone say it was 8:00 am. He got up, walked over to his desk, and sat down. Dan asked him some questions while the paramedics unhooked their equipment from him. Tim was ignoring all of them because he was trying to figure out what was going on. He still felt very confused. Dan told him there didn't look like fowl play had been going on and that Tim must have slipped and hit his head. Tim just wanted them to leave him alone so he could have a few minutes to figure out what was going on in his mind.

Tim looked up and noticed someone walk in through the doorway of the lab. The glare from the early morning sun shielded the identity. The figure walked toward him and as the door closed the figure manifested itself.

"What has happened here," the man asked.

Tim recognized the voice immediately, "Raj! Oh my God. You're alive. But. I thought. I…"

"Yes of course I am alive. What is going on here Tim," Raj asked very surprised.

Dan Buckley introduced himself and explained what had happened. Tim just sat there completely stunned and mystified. Raj thanked everyone for taking care of Tim and assured all of them he would drive Tim to the hospital immediately to have him checked out. Everyone left the lab and Raj walked back over to where Tim was sitting.

"Are you OK my friend?"

"Yes, I think so. I'm so confused though. For some reason I thought you were dead."

"Well my friend, I am very much alive and so are you. Let us get you to the hospital and have the doctor's look at you. We can talk about all of this later."

"But, I know you were…"

"Come my friend. Let us walk to my car," Raj interrupted him.

Raj helped Tim to his feet and they walked to his car then drove to the hospital. It was a short drive and nothing was said. Raj pulled into the parking lot and helped Tim out of the car then walked him into the emergency room. The doctors took Tim in immediately and Raj waited in the waiting room.

About ninety minutes later Tim and a doctor came out to Raj. The doctor reported Tim had a slight concussion and should take it easy the rest of the day. He further explained that if Tim decided to go to sleep he should not fall asleep for long periods. He should be woken up about every hour. If he doesn't wake up then get him back here immediately but he doubted there would be any problem.

Back in the car Raj started to take Tim home but Tim asked to go back to the Lab. Raj told him he needed to rest and what ever Tim needed to do at the lab could wait until tomorrow. Tim insisted. He said he wanted to get some things clear in his head before he went home. Raj complied with his request.

They arrived back at the lab and Tim walked slowly inside looking around as if he were expecting it to look different. There were a few minor things he noticed that looked out of place but nothing significant. He walked over to his desk and sat down. Raj went to his own desk and sat down then made a phone call while Tim looked around for some clue to help him figure this out.

A few minutes later Raj pulled his chair close to Tim and asked, "Are you OK my friend?"

"I'm so bewildered right now Raj. I have memories of something that happened but at the same time I have other memories that conflict with them. I'm just trying to sort it out."

"Perhaps I can help." Raj threw a small package onto Tim's desk. "Does this look familiar to you?"

Tim picked it up and recognized it but was having a hard time remembering what was in it.

"Go ahead my friend and open it up," Raj insisted.

Tim fumbled with it a moment then opened it up. When he saw the contents some of the conflicting memories he was having started to make sense as they rushed back into his head. His heart started pounding. "You were dead," he declared feeling the sorrow he had experienced. "But you're here."

"Well, I have no memory of that because to me it did not happen."

"But it did happen. I remember now. I was told Friday that you had been murdered. They thought Munoz… but how could that be. I have known Elisaio for several years. But I also remember him as someone completely different. Oh God," Tim grabbed his head because his mind was spinning.

"Tim. Take a deep breath. I can only imagine what you must be feeling right now. Let me see if I can help you put this into perspective. First, what you remember about my death and the events that lead up to it, for me I have no memories about any of that. I only know what happened after I received this package from you in 1988. You are having these conflicting memories because you are the original source, the catalyst if you will, for everything that has transpired from then up to today."

"But I see it all so clearly. You getting killed in the car crash, Elisaio holding a gun to my head, Buckley investigating the case, all of it but at the same time I can see none of that ever happened. How can both sets of memories be so apparent," Tim pleaded for clarification.

Raj explained how in June 1988 he received the package from Tim dated April 4, 2006 and from that moment on his life had changed from what Tim had known about it prior to today. All of those memories Tim had were now his alone and that other life of Raj's ceased to exist once he opened that package.

Those next eighteen years following that Raj altered his life by making different choices and living his life differently because of the documents Tim had sent him. They revealed what his future might be like if he did not do something to change it. Apparently he made the right decisions by only changing a few things.

Raj described how excited he was in learning he had invented a time machine and how it helped him make the decision to take matters into his own hands regarding Elisaio. He told Tim at the time he had no idea who those other people were that Tim had tried to contact and devised his own plan to alter Elisaio's future actions himself. In the process of executing his plan he discovered Elisaio had already decided to make major changes in his life. It had been the circumstances of going back in time that turned him into the ruthless criminal Tim remembered. He described to Tim how in the short time they were driving from Yuma to Blythe, Raj discovered he really liked Elisaio and decided to help him out. He offered to get him a good job here at TC Enterprises. Raj had enough influence to convince the company to hire a man with a criminal record.

Raj's explanation was interrupted when two people came into the lab. Tim looked their way but Raj continued, "The reason you have conflicting memories of Elisaio Munoz is because you know both versions of him. You know the ruthless criminal version that went back in time and was succumbed with power from knowing the future, but because I was able to stop him from going back in time you also know him as a valued and dedicated employee here at the company. Separating those memories I believe will become clearer in the next few days. You just need some time to let your mind sort it out."

The two people who walked in stepped into the light next to Raj. Tim recognized them immediately. It was JW Weston and his wife, but they looked a lot different than he remembered. They were smiling and greeted Raj then looked at Tim.

"Are you OK Tim," asked Mr. Weston.

"Yes, thank you," Tim replied as memories of them started to rush into his mind. Something was not right. "I don't understand. You're... But how?" Tim suddenly felt very light headed again. "God! I think I'm going to be sick." He sat back in his chair and took several deep breaths.

"Relax my friend," Raj responded to his sudden reaction to the couple.

Tim leaned forward and uttered excitedly, "You're Wyatt Coleman and James Bolaire. How can you be...," he paused when he saw and recognized Jennifer then moaned and almost fainted again.

Jennifer ran to get a wet paper towel from the restroom. She came back and placed it on Tim's forehead. "It's OK Tim," she assured him.

Tim finally caught his breath. The three of them were now standing over him. Tim stuttered, "How can you be Mr. Weston?" His memories of the Weston's were of an older couple in their sixties and seventies but how he wondered. They now looked thirty years younger.

JW Weston pulled up a chair and sat next to Tim. "Tim, let me tell you about my life since you played an integral part in the development of it. I was born James Wyatt Weston. My father, John Weston, died in 1974. My mother had gotten remarried to a wonderful man named Francis Coleman. Because my stepfather had no children of his own he adopted my brother and sister but I chose to legally keep my name of Weston. For simplistic reasons I used my stepfathers last name because the schools, churches, and neighborhood could not grasp the idea that my name was different from that of my parents and siblings. It caused a lot of problems. So I used Wyatt Coleman or J'Dub Coleman with my family. I never thought much about it but for what ever reason I never used my legal name after that."

Tim stared and asked, "J'Dub?"

"J W got shortened down to J'Dub when I was a kid. My father had this thing about nicknames"

Tim slightly opened his mouth and nodded.

"Anyway, you were correct Tim. The name Jim Bolaire was part of my life when I went back to 1970. Wyatt Coleman didn't really exist and I knew the Colorado police were looking for him. So it made sense to make Wyatt Coleman disappear since he didn't legally exist anyway. When I formed TC Enterprises in 1975 I got all of the necessary documents to start it in my real name of James Wyatt Weston but continued to use Bolaire until we moved the company here to Twenty Nine Palms in 1984. Once we had our laboratory completed in 1988 I had the company hire Raj. I have known Raj for a very long time."

"Yes Tim," Raj interjected. "Mr. Weston was my young friend J'Dub when I first came to the United States. I lived with his family my first year here. Several years after his father died we lost contact. I did not recognize him at first from the pictures you sent me because he was thirteen the last time I saw him but after several months of looking at the photos I figured out who he was."

"How did you not recognize him last year when you and I were investigating people who may have traveled back in time," Tim asked.

"As I said Tim I do not have any of those memories. I cannot give you an explanation. Perhaps I was just too busy to study the photos. I do not know. As I said it took me a few months to recognize him from the photos you sent me in 1988. But anyway, after the company hired me it wasn't until several years later that I actually met with him and rediscovered my old friend. It was not until now this day that JW, Jennifer, and I could talk to you about any of this."

"Why couldn't you say something before now," Tim wondered.

JW responded, "Because Tim, we could not take the chance of changing anything you would do. It was because of everything you did over the weekend that led to this day. Now that it has come to pass we can talk about it all we want."

Jennifer placed her hands on Tim's shoulder and added, "And because of you Tim, JW and I got a second chance in life too." She pulled three packages from her purse and handed them to Tim. "Given that Jim and I were sent back in time we were going to lose thirty years of our lives but because you sent these packages to Wyatt and Jennifer we were given a choice. Jim and I were contacted by Wyatt and Jennifer and they gave us the opportunity to decide if we wanted to live our lives without going back in time or to live the life Mother Nature had chosen for us. It was a very difficult decision."

"Yes, I knew there was something different about the two of you but I couldn't quite put my finger on what it was. My mind is so jumbled up with different images." Tim stopped then looked up into Jennifer's eyes and realized what she was telling him. "You didn't go back," he whispered in a low voice as the images of the older couple became clear in his mind.

JW cut in. "Yes, we decided to not go back. It was a very hard choice for all of us to make. Wyatt and Jennifer showed us everything in those packages you sent them and we looked at every possible option for several months. It came down to whether Wyatt and Jennifer or Mrs. Weston and myself would cease to exist. There was no way all four of us could continue on after 1992, at least for Jennifer then 1999 for Wyatt. We all had to agree on our decision. Once the decision was made Wyatt brought Mrs. Weston and I into the company and that's why very few people saw him or me for several years until I took over."

"But how did you and Mrs. Weston, and Wyatt and Jennifer end up together? You just didn't happen to all bump into each other one day, right," Tim asked.

Everyone laughed and JW replied, "No Tim. Wyatt and Jennifer met several years after they went back in time. They fell in love and eventually discovered they had more in common than they realized. After coming to the decision to give us the choice in deciding our fate, in 1989 they arranged a meeting for the four of us and that's when Mrs. Weston and I met for the first time. Wyatt and Jennifer knew we would eventually fall in love just as they did. Mrs. Weston and I got married in 1993 after Jennifer disappeared."

"Jennifer stopped me from going back in time and because I did not go back she ceased to exist on August 2, 1992 and Wyatt on October 27, 1999," Mrs. Weston interjected.

"Did she know she would disappear when you didn't go back in time," Tim asked.

Mrs. Weston answered, "We were fairly certain that would be the case. It wasn't until that day we knew for sure. The four of us spent every possible minute together and shared stories and memories. Even though she was me, we were different people. The only memories I have of hers are from when I met her and what she told me about the twenty-five years she had relived."

"It must have been awful for them waiting for that final day," Tim sensed feeling sad for them.

"Several months before Jennifer's last day Mr. Weston and I took over the company. Wyatt and Jennifer took off together on a sailboat and spent her last days somewhere in the Indian Ocean. We said our goodbyes knowing we would never see her again," Mrs. Weston replied.

"And Wyatt spent his last seven years sailing around the world by himself. We received an occasional letter from him telling us where he was," continued JW.

"I've got to tell you Mr. and Mrs. Weston, this is all so amazing," Tim admitted. "I don't know what's real and what's not."

"Please. Call me Jennifer. In a few days that feeling will pass and you will know the difference," assured Jennifer. "JW and I both went through it when Wyatt and Jennifer revealed themselves to us for the first time. It will pass."

"There's one thing I don't understand," Tim asked looking at JW.

"What's that," he inquired.

"Where does Buckley play into all of this? I knew him before today but not as the head of security."

JW broke out laughing and Jennifer just smiled. JW explained, "Wyatt felt so sorry for Dan when he disappeared on him in Vail back in 1970. Of course, Dan has no memory of it but Wyatt wanted to make it up to him by giving him an easy job with excellent benefits before he retired. It was something Wyatt asked me to do for him. You'll have to tell us one day what Buckley was like."

"Let me get to know him a little better then I'll tell you if he has changed." Tim chuckled relieved it was all over.

JW stood and put his hand on Tim's shoulder and requested, "Now, let's get you home my friend. You've had a busy weekend."

Epilogue

Kempner, Texas
April 5, 2007

Waylan Henderson was sitting in his old recliner chair next to an open window watching television when he was slammed backward from the energy of a lightning bolt that struck just outside of his window. There was an unusually strong thunder storm passing through town and Waylan couldn't be bothered with it. He just wanted to watch his television shows like he had done for the past eight years.

Waylan was sixty nine years old and a bitter man. He worked for the same company for thirty five years. He gave them everything, loyalty, time, his whole life. Then just before he retired the company went belly up. It was a major scandal. The executives of the company had bankrupted it turning all of its employees stocks and retirement funds into worthless paper. He had invested heavily into the company to secure himself and his family.

Just a year prior to the scandal Waylan lost his wife and seventeen year old daughter in an auto accident during a sever thunder storm like the one he was experiencing today. His entire life had turned to shit in a matter of a couple of years. Waylan was angry and miserable. He had no choice but to live out his final years in retirement, broke, alone, in his run down forty year old home, eating cheap microwave food, and watching TV.

The lightning, that morning, had been more active than storms of the past. Waylan hated thunder storms after his family died. He had cursed louder with each thunder bolt. He kept turning up the volume on his television to drown

190

it out. But now he was really pissed off. His heart was racing and he felt tingly all over. The bolt struck so close to his window that it knocked him back against the backrest so hard that he thought the old chair had finally broke.

When he settled down from the excitement he noticed the chair was fully reclined and felt different too. The television must have moved also from the power of the lightning bolt because it was about ten feet from where it normally had been. The power chord must have pulled out too because the screen was dark with no picture unlike it had been just a moment ago. There was another thing that seemed strange. It was now bright and sunny outside. The storm had completely dissipated. That was the weirdest thing he had ever seen.

He leaned his chair back upright and started to stand when he noticed he was buck naked. He looked around and saw no clothes anywhere in the room. "What the fuck is this," he said annoyed.

Waylan stood and began mumbling to himself wondering if senility was beginning to set in. He slowly walked across the living room grumbling and annoyed at having to get up from his chair. He turned down the hall and walked toward his bedroom so he could find some clothes to put on. As he ambled down the hallway he began to notice things missing or out of place. His daughter's bedroom door was open. He had always kept it closed after she died. He looked in and saw it was in complete disarray. It looked like it did when she would come home from school and throw her books and back pack on the bed then toss the clothes she had been wearing that day on the floor in order to change into shorts and a tank top. Waylan got very upset at the sight of this.

"Who would do such a thing," he asked himself. His eyes were beginning to well up and he almost started to cry as visions of his deceased daughter raced through his mind when he heard the bathroom door open up behind him.

"Hi Daddy. How come you're not at work and why are you walking around the house naked in the middle of the day," his seventeen year old daughter asked giving him an odd look. "Where's mom?" She leaned over and kissed him on the cheek. "You look terrible Daddy. Are you sick?"

Printed in the United States
65542LVS00004BA/56